SS

JEFFREY SALANE

SCHOLASTIC PRESS | NEW YORK

**To my den of thieves — let's steal
more time together**

All rights reserved. Published by Scholastic Press, an imprint of Scholastic Inc.,
Publishers since 1920. SCHOLASTIC, SCHOLASTIC PRESS, and associated logos are
trademarks and/or registered trademarks of Scholastic Inc.

Library of Congress Cataloging-in-Publication Data Available

ISBN 978-0-545-45029-4

10 9 8 7 6 5 4 3 2 1   13 14 15 16 17
Printed in the U.S.A.   23
First edition, April 2013

The text type was set in Gotham Narrow Book.
Book design by Phil Falco
Illustrations © 2013 by Jake Parker

It is an instance . . .
of carrying away something that is not yours to carry away.

For example . . .
if I am carried away by an idea, this idea becomes for me a thief.

— Sabrina Orah Marks, "The Definition of a Thief"

CHAPTER 1

AN INTERESTING INTERVIEW

I always knew I had a purpose.

Seven simple words were written in straight, clean lines on the top of M's stack of note cards. They were her introduction, an introduction to a speech that M had slaved over because it needed to be perfect. One by one, she riffled through the cards in her deck, reading and whispering the speech aloud. This was going to be, perhaps, the most important hour of M Freeman's life.

She had agonized over her speech during the entire ride to New York City. It was rare for M to travel to the city, even though she lived only a few hours away. In truth, she never really traveled anywhere. So when the limo had arrived to pick her up, in order to not freak out, M had thrown herself into her preparations, as the empty countryside slowly grew into bridges, traffic, buildings, and crowded sidewalks.

And now, sitting in a waiting room, M repeated those seven simple words to herself and she knew that she was in full interview mode.

The room looked like a blank canvas. The waiting area was a long hallway with chairs lined against the wall, mostly empty.

But M wasn't completely alone. Sitting several chairs down from her was another girl, one who looked slightly older than M. A teenager. M had smiled and said hello when she'd come in, but this girl had her game face on. M didn't take it personally. This was a competition.

Across from M there was the door that led to the interview room. She glanced at her reflection in the door's glass window, a slight girl dressed in her brand-new black interview suit. Even though it was an expensive suit, M knew it didn't fit her as well as she wanted. With her brown hair worn up, her elfish nose looked even smaller and more compact than usual. M never trusted reflections, but seeing herself always got under her skin. Maybe she didn't belong here?

It's weird, she thought, how a door that, once you walk through it, could change your life looks just like any old door. Or maybe every door that you walk through carries the same potential to change your life? But still, she had hoped for something more special, more memorable. This was the Lawless School, after all.

When the door opened, though, M felt something otherworldly. It was as if a passageway to her future had opened and someone was inviting her in.

"Ms. Freeman?" a well-dressed woman called from the doorway. "Please come in."

As M stood, the other girl rose from her chair, too.

"Ah yes, Ms. Smith, I'm glad you could join us as well. Please, both of you, this way."

The interview room looked out over a park. M could see

trees, penned in by buildings on every side. The park was buzzing with activity, children and parents and pets all playing in the lush green fields. August had been so hot, but the first chill of September was finally drifting through the air and everyone was celebrating.

M sat down at a long table and the other girl, Ms. Smith, sat down two chairs away from her. She was wearing a white cardigan with a gray pencil skirt, which would make most people look like a librarian, but on Ms. Smith, it looked smarter, keener, sharper. M could imagine her cutting through a crowd like a hot knife through butter. She could also imagine Ms. Smith disappearing into the same crowd if she needed to, and no one would ever remember that she was there.

"Ms. Freeman, I am Ms. Watts," the interviewer announced. "We will start your interview now, so please make yourself comfortable."

Ms. Watts sat on the other side of the long table, directly across from M. M started to wish she had worn something other than a blazer. Next to Ms. Smith, she felt like a child in a school uniform.

Still, M composed herself and began her speech. "I always knew I had a purpose, Ms. Watts."

"I'm sure you do, Ms. Freeman, but allow me to ask you a few questions first," Ms. Watts interrupted. "Can you tell me which direction is southwest?"

This was weird, thought M, but of course she knew the answer. M pointed behind herself and to the left. "That way."

"And how can you be certain?" asked Ms. Watts.

"The sun," said M, motioning outside the window.

"And if there was no sun?" she asked.

"You mean, if it were nighttime?" asked M.

"If that's what 'no sun' means to you, then yes," said Ms. Watts.

"Then the stars."

"And if there were no stars?"

"Like, if it were cloudy?" asked M.

Ms. Watts wrote something down quickly in her notebook then smiled. "Ms. Freeman, perhaps we are getting ahead of ourselves. Can you tell me how many stories are in this building?"

"Thirteen stories, but the elevator says fourteen because it's supposed to be bad luck to have a thirteenth floor," M answered.

"And the buildings around us, how many stories do they have?"

"The building to the left has seven stories. The building to the right looked to be fifteen stories. There is a parking lot behind us, which is probably four stories plus a roof deck. And there's no building in front of us. Just a park." M smiled.

"Do you always notice how many stories are in a building?" asked Ms. Watts.

"Yes, ma'am," said M. "I'm afraid of heights. My mother always told me that whatever you are most afraid of, then that's usually the first thing you notice wherever you go."

"Your mother, how is your mother?" asked Ms. Watts.

"She's well, thank you," said M. "Do you know her?"

"No, I'm sorry, I meant, please tell me about your mother. What does she do?"

Ms. Watts leaned forward in her seat, scratching even more notes into her book. M took a minute to consider this last question. She looked over at the other girl. When was Ms. Smith going to get her interview? And would M have to sit through that?

M studied Ms. Watts's face carefully. Why did the woman look so familiar to M one minute and like a total stranger the next? And the way she'd asked about M's mother was so casual, not at all like an interviewer and certainly not like someone who had never met her mother before.

"My mother is an art historian," M finally answered. "Excuse me, Ms. Watts, I'm sorry, but have we met before?"

"An art historian can be a demanding job," interjected Ms. Smith, from her side of the room. "Is your mother around much?"

It was true — M's mother was a total workaholic. She constantly flew from museum to college to private art collection all around the world. M wished she could tag along sometimes, but her mother was very strict about her sticking to her home-school studies.

"My mother is very good at her job and sometimes her job keeps her from the house, but that's true of a lot of single parents," M said, though instantly she wished she hadn't.

"Oh yes, I should say that I am sorry to hear about your father. I see that he passed away," said Ms. Watts. "Were you close?"

M had only a shadowy idea of who her father had been. She was not quite six years old when his plane crashed into a remote mountaintop somewhere in the Andes. He was also an art historian and had been on his way home from a collector's house in South America. There was an ice storm in the jet stream that night, and the pilots didn't want to fly, but her father had insisted that he get home as soon as possible. It was M's birthday the next day, and he had wanted to be there to make her breakfast in bed.

After the accident, M's mother had taken over the family business, running whatever artistic empire it was that her mother ran and becoming an unstoppable workhorse in the process. "Business never mixes well with pleasure, dear" was her response whenever M asked her why she had to travel so constantly — and why M could never come along.

M knew only four things about her father for sure. He had been a good man. He was her namesake, M Freeman. He had loved her with all of his heart. And he had attended the Lawless School.

"Yes, we were very close," M spoke a little above a whisper. "I mean no disrespect, but is it important that you know about my family beyond what I've included in my application?"

"No, you are quite right, there's no need to live in the past," said Ms. Watts with a bright smile. "Shall we proceed, then?"

"Yes, ma'am," said M, happy to be away from the subject of her family.

"Wonderful. If you found a wallet on a street near your house, what would you do?"

"Is there anyone around the wallet when I find it?" asked M.

"No, the street is empty," said Ms. Watts.

"Is it a well-traveled street or a side street?" M followed up.

"A side street." She smiled. "It's not on your regular route, if that's what you're hinting at."

"If it's not on my regular route, then why am I there?" asked M.

"Good question," said Ms. Watts. "Let's assume that you are on that particular side street for a similar reason that you're here today. Because it is a path less traveled, which leads to some place unlike anything you can imagine."

M thought for a moment. "I would look to see what was in the wallet. To see if there was a driver's license or a library card or any sort of note that the owner may have left to remind him or herself of anything, anything that may give me a hint as to who the owner may be. Once you have someone's name, you can easily find them. Then I could return the wallet through the mail along with a kind letter that would let them know where I had found their wallet and that I would like to return it, no reward necessary. If I could avoid calling the police, that would be best. I like to handle these types of situations myself. Why spend taxpayers' money on lost wallets?

"Of course," added M, "all this happens only after I rule out that the wallet isn't a trap."

Ms. Watts smiled at this answer. M could feel even the mysterious Ms. Smith lean in closer, too. This was certainly turning into an interesting interview.

"Can you tell me about a time that you have worked with a team to solve a problem?" asked Ms. Watts as she turned her attention back to her notepad.

The question caused M to pause. Instantly she recalled her surprise when her mother had first mentioned the Lawless School. Homeschool was fine. M was thriving in every subject — except for the subject of friends, of course. Her lessons were private and her days were filled from morning till night. On the occasions that she had contact with kids her age, they seemed a little, well, not all there in the social skills department. They were always yelling, being overdramatic, and talking about the most mundane things, like clothes, movies, their friends, or their friends' friends. And judging by the sometimes vicious way these kids talked about their friends, M wasn't sure if she ever wanted to be included in any clique.

"Well, I've been homeschooled up until now, Ms. Watts," said M. "All by myself. My work generally begins and ends with me."

"So you're a loner?" asked Ms. Smith.

"Not on purpose," said M.

"Fascinating," said Ms. Watts. "And thank you, M, for being honest. Now please look at this photograph." She pointed toward Ms. Smith, who was holding up an eight-by-ten black-and-white photograph.

"What do you notice?" asked Ms. Watts.

For one thing, M had noticed that Ms. Watts left very little time between her questions.

"Well," M started, "it's the inside of a restaurant. It looks busy. There are fourteen tables, eleven with patrons seated at them."

"Hmmm. And is that all?" asked Ms. Watts.

"Well," continued M, "the waiter on the left is struggling to hold up his coffeepot, but the waiter on the right isn't, so he must be running low on coffee, but it's likely that the first waiter is serving decaf, which no one wants. The waiter by the bar isn't wearing his flower lapel pin like the others, so he probably just got off his shift. The people at the tables toward the front of the picture seem to be enjoying their food, but the people sitting by the windows and the front door have hardly touched their meals."

When M turned from the picture, Ms. Watts simply looked down and ticked off a single mark in her notebook. Then she looked up and asked, "And if you were in this restaurant and you had to leave, how would you do so?"

M glanced at Ms. Smith, who sat calmly two seats away, holding the photograph. What was she in here for? M wondered.

"Well, I wouldn't go through the front door. That's for sure. The two women at one table by the door are eating their salads with dinner forks, and this is too fancy a place to get a window seat and not know to use your cutlery from the outside in. Then there's the guy at the next table who isn't wearing a tie. . . . Who's he fooling? So that leaves the service entrance or the bathrooms. But the bathrooms are out, because the direction sign says that they're downstairs. I might go talk to the waiter getting off work for a bit, pretend to be an aspiring chef, ask to see the kitchen, then leave through the back door. But then again, I have no idea who or what may be in the kitchen, so if I were forced to leave . . . I'd use the front door."

Ms. Smith laughed out loud, but fell silent as soon as Ms. Watts gave her a glance. M couldn't help but grin. It felt good to have finally figured out the angle of the interview. It was a "shake-up, shakedown." A fairly simple power play, but only if you understand your role in it. Ms. Watts was the interrogator. Her job was the easiest: Ask the subject questions, shake the tree, and see what falls off the branches. Ms. Smith was the second fiddle. She played the harder role: Support the interrogator and keep the subject off balance. While that may seem like the easier part to play, it actually requires the ability to read two people at once . . . to know where the interrogator is leading the subject and to guess how far the subject is willing to be led.

Then there's the subject, who is part of the play, whether they realize it or not. M had picked up on it in time. Ms. Smith had balked with her laugh. Ms. Watts had balked with her reaction to it: a simple look, just a cut of her green eyes. And like that, the interview had taken on a completely different light.

"And if Ms. Smith would hand me the photo, I could tell you how many cooks were in the kitchen, the number of staff working that night, and maybe even what city the restaurant was in," M said with total confidence.

"I have no doubt that you could, Ms. Freeman," said Ms. Watts. "You *are* a delightful subject. Now be a doll, Ms. Smith, and leave the room for the remainder of the interview."

Ms. Smith stood up slowly, keeping her eyes on M as she walked out of the room. M tried to read the girl's look, but it was unlike anything she'd encountered before. There was a sharpness to it, like she was staring daggers at M, but at the same time, there was a hint of satisfaction, and perhaps even respect.

After Ms. Smith had closed the door, Ms. Watts shut her notebook and pulled out an envelope.

"Ms. Freeman, in this envelope is the ticket to your future. Or maybe not. I don't know; that is, I have not been informed as to your acceptance or rejection to the Lawless School. I am only a point person chosen to ask you several questions and hand this to you. I have my own thoughts on the matter of your future, but I have been instructed to keep my thoughts to myself."

Then Ms. Watts clicked her ballpoint pen, and a slight humming sound whirred within the room. Ms. Watts's expression did not change, but her shoulders tensed faintly.

"Ms. Freeman, I'm going to go off record for a moment, which is why I've excused Ms. Smith from this room. If you repeat anything I say from this moment on, I will deny everything. I knew your father. I knew him very well. You are your father's daughter, and I hope you'll understand in time why I'm telling you this. Forget the Lawless School. Forget everything that just happened. Walk out that door, do not talk to Ms. Smith, get in your car, and go home. Do not open that envelope I've handed you. Burn it and scatter the ashes."

Click went the ballpoint pen again, and the humming was gone as quickly as it started.

Ms. Watts continued in her full interview voice, "That said, I'll ask Ms. Smith to see you out. Thank you for coming in to

11

meet with us. I understand that you've traveled a long way, but unfortunately we are not set up to meet anywhere near your home upstate. I trust the limo we sent was a comfortable enough ride?"

"Yes, it was. Thank you," said M, who was confused and alarmed, but knew she should take Ms. Watts's lead.

Ms. Watts rose from her chair and Ms. Smith came back into the room as if the entire thing had been rehearsed a million times.

"Ms. Smith, please escort Ms. Freeman to her car," Ms. Watts said flatly. "Ms. Freeman, there is one more thing. I have to ask that you do not read what's inside the envelope until you get back home. I know it seems mysterious, but you must understand that the Lawless School is known for being just that. Best of luck to you."

With that, Ms. Watts stayed behind the table and gave M a knowing nod, as if the two of them had exchanged a grave secret . . . except that M had no idea what it was. She lifted the envelope from the table, smiled, and left the room, followed closely by Ms. Smith.

The elevator ride was completely silent except for the clicks between floors as they descended. Ms. Smith did not make eye contact with M, and M was busy trying to put the pieces of the interview together.

When the elevator door opened, the limo was already waiting for them. Ms. Smith walked over to the rear door and opened it for M. M slipped inside and turned back to Ms. Smith.

"Um, I'm... I'm not sure what exactly happened back there," M said aloud, more to herself than to anyone else.

"Seriously?" Ms. Smith said. "Dear, you need to clear your head and get with the program. You just got into the Lawless School. Your life will never be the same."

Then she slammed the door, and the limo took off into the darkening light of the late afternoon.

CHAPTER 2

ADMISSIONS POLICY

An average envelope with one slip of paper inside will weigh less than one ounce.

But M knew that it was the contents that counted. What was written in the letter, that's the real weight of the envelope. And as the limo drove through the city's traffic, the envelope in M's lap weighed a million pounds.

Ignore it, she thought. Ignore the elephant-sized envelope in the back of the limo. She'd been given strict instructions not to open the letter until she returned home.

Or had she been given strict instructions to burn the letter and never read it? What's a boarding school applicant to do?

Ms. Watts had been perfectly clear on one point: The school was mysterious, best known for being largely unknown. There was no pamphlet for Lawless that highlighted its dorms, its state-of-the-art study labs, its meal plan package or teacher-to-student ratio. There was no Web site with images of its library, its gyms, its manicured lawns so perfect for student festivals. She had looked. Web searches, message boards, *US News & World Report* rankings, they all said the same thing:

The Lawless School didn't exist. Or, if it did exist, it didn't want to be found.

It wasn't only by chance that the Lawless School had first come to M's attention. After her cartography lesson one day, as M was putting away her things, her teacher Mr. Giles made a very odd statement. He began with, "I know that with all these maps and charts, M, the world can seem overwhelming. After all, if the borders and history of countries are so easily rewritten, what about the borders and histories of individuals like ourselves?" This was not the statement that caught M's attention. In fact, Mr. Giles often made broad, mystifying declarations like this one. He loved to think out loud, and M was used to his grand conjectures. But then he continued. "All in all, though," he said, "I should truly hope that you have made up your mind by now."

"What's that, sir?" M had asked. "Made up my mind about what?"

"The Lawless School, of course," he said with an awkward smile. "Your mother must have discussed this with you by now."

"I'm afraid not, sir," M replied. "What is the Lawless School?"

Mr. Giles paused a moment before continuing. "Forget what I've said, M. I have you confused with another student of mine. Blast these hectic homeschool schedules." He tried to laugh away the moment, but something hung in the air.

It was the first time M had seen fear in an adult's face.

That night M had asked her mother about the Lawless School. She did not tell her mother where she had heard about the school, and her mother did not ask.

"M, I know how strange this will sound," her mother answered, "but it's better if you don't know about that place. This is something you will learn more about in time. For now let's say that the Lawless School is what your father would have wanted for you."

M let a smile sneak up on her now, thinking about her father as the limo floated on through the crisscross traffic. He was a beautiful mystery. And he had been a doting dad, from what she could remember. Every moment they'd shared together, he'd focused solely and completely on her. One time, he left the house on a "special assignment" just before she went to sleep, and he was home when she woke up in the morning. He told her that he'd gone to the moon and brought her back a piece of it. Then he gave her a jewelry box. Inside was a necklace with a small stone centerpiece.

A lot of fathers want to give their children the moon. M's actually had.

It took her hours to get the truth out of him. There was about a thirty-second period when she believed he might have really traveled to the moon. But the truth was simply that he had flown through the night to visit a rare rocks collector in Colorado to settle a dispute over whether a moon rock in the man's collection was the real deal.

M laughed at the memory and traced her finger along the moon-rock necklace, which she still wore.

Her father had given her more than happy memories and trinkets, though. He'd had tons of advice for her, too. *M, I know that most parents tell their children to never talk to strangers, but I think that's a big mistake,* he had told her one time. *You should always talk to strangers. The more you know about the people around you, the more you know about the situation you're in.*

What caused her to think about that? she wondered. Though, come to think of it, with a long road ahead of her and a mysterious white envelope sitting in her lap, M realized that her father's sage advice might just help her learn something — anything — about the Lawless School.

M pushed the call button for the driver. The window clicked and came alive with a mechanical sound as it rolled down to reveal the back of the driver's head.

"Do you have anything to drink back here?" asked M.

"Yes, ma'am," the driver's deep voice boomed. "Right there in the refrigerator. Everything's on the house."

"There's a refrigerator back here?" asked M, surprised, which made the driver laugh. "Can I get you anything?"

"No, ma'am, I'm fine." He was smiling. M could hear it in his tone. She slid closer to the front of the limo and started looking through the fridge.

"Is this a regular drive for you?" asked M.

"Not regular, no," he said.

"What is regular, then?" asked M as she slid forward.

"A tour bus. I actually drive musical acts around," he answered.

"Ever drive anyone megafamous?" she asked.

"Oh, I never drive the VIPs around, just the stage gear. The roadies break everything down after the show's over — the stage, lights, amps, drums, and whatever else those acts dream up — then load it all into my truck. I race to the next town before the band and the roadies get there to build the set all over again."

He wasn't used to driving conversations; M could tell by the way he went on in such detail. But since he was clearly ready to open up, she decided to push things further. "So you don't consider me a VIP?"

"Sorry, ma'am. Of course I do. Whoever I'm driving around, they're the VIP. I mean, unless they're the gear."

M let the comment sink in. Maybe she wasn't the VIP after all. "So," she continued, "how does one go from driving rock-star stages to chauffeuring potential students to and from their interviews?"

"It seems far-fetched, doesn't it?" he said, and his shoulders relaxed a little. He took one hand off the steering wheel and made eye contact with M in the rearview mirror for the first time. "Nah, the truth is that Lawless runs both operations."

"You're telling me that the Lawless School helps run a traveling rigging service?" M asked. What in the world was this school?

"No, no, no. Lawless, the man. Fox Lawless. He owns the trucking company, and I work for him. He has me do these meet-and-greet drives during the big outreach month for the school. Ever notice that the best bands never tour this time of year?"

"Can't say that I have ever seen a concert, Mr. . . ." M angled, hoping to get a name from the driver.

"How rude of me, ma'am. My name's Terry," he said with a slight nod of his head toward her. "You're a real talker. Most kids never put the partition window down, and they never want to talk."

And there it was — Terry the limo driver was no longer a stranger. "Most kids you come in contact with are probably used to riding in the back of a limo," said M. "Hey, Fox Lawless sounds like a cool guy to work for. . . ." But before M could work in her next question, a phone rang in the front of the car.

"Excuse me, ma'am." Terry smiled, flipping the phone open. "Hello. Uh-huh. Yes, I understand, um, one minute, please." He caught M's eyes in the mirror once more. "Ma'am, I hope you don't mind, but I'll need privacy for the rest of this call." And with that, Terry rolled the partition up and M was alone in the backseat again.

After an hour it was clear that Terry's call was going to last for the rest of the drive. M had shifted her attention back to the envelope. How could something so thin, so easily torn to shreds, still be so intimidating?

It was better to put it out of her mind again. When she was home, then she could open it, she could read it and get on with the rest of her life. Sure, Ms. Smith had seemed certain that M as good as had one foot in the door of a spacious new Lawless dorm room, but why should M believe her?

With the envelope silent in her lap and the cold shoulder from Terry, M's options for the ride were dwindling. She kicked herself for not bringing a book along. Sleep looked like the best option. M leaned back into her seat and closed her eyes. She tried to recall what Ms. Watts looked like, but the interviewer's features were already slipping away. She went over every detail of the interview that she could remember.

M's eyes shot open with sudden realization, and she flipped the envelope over in her hands. Ms. Watts had instructed her not to *read* the letter before she arrived home, but that didn't mean she couldn't *open* the letter in the limo. M's heart was pounding in her chest as she opened the envelope with one swift motion.

To her surprise and displeasure, the envelope was completely empty.

Within moments, the entire backseat of the limo was a mess. Seat belts had been untucked, soda and Perrier bottles were rolling up and down the limo floor. M had searched under every floor mat, through the nooks of every seat, and into every possible retractable cup holder, armrest, and headrest. If there had ever been a letter in that envelope, it wasn't in the limo.

Could Ms. Watts have given her the wrong envelope? She checked the front of it again. *Ms. M Freeman* was handwritten there. No, a mistake didn't seem likely. Would Ms. Watts have done something to the letter? She really hadn't been psyched about the idea of M going to the Lawless School.

Perhaps Ms. Smith had something to do with it. But when would she have had an opportunity? Certainly not in the elevator — M and Ms. Smith had stood too far apart from each other, and M had kept a power grip on that envelope until the door to the limo had slammed shut.

Or maybe there never was a letter. That's the answer M kept returning to. She felt it, somewhere deep inside her gut. The lack of a letter, that was the message. But what it meant, M couldn't say.

The scenery of the city had shifted from buildings and traffic to bridges and tunnels, back to a remote highway lined with colorful trees. The fall foliage leaned over the road as if it were spying on M as the limo took the last exit ramp and drove deeper into the heart of the forest.

Home already, M thought to herself as a security gate slowly opened up for the limo. Beyond the driveway was M's house, which wasn't so much a house as a small castle. With its imposing stonework, eighteenth-century turrets, and acres of fenced-in land, a person could be forgiven for expecting to also find a moat, a drawbridge, and a dragon. But M never thought it had been weird growing up here. She never felt like a princess or a prisoner. All of her best memories were set here . . . although most of them had been before her father's accident.

With nothing but an empty envelope with her name on it

and a painstakingly crafted handwritten speech she never got to deliver, M sat as the limo pulled around to her front door. And of all the millions of questions she had about the Lawless School, only one came to mind in that instant:

What am I going to tell Mom?

CHAPTER 3

TRIAL BY FIRE

"Welcome back, Ms. Freeman," Jones said as he opened her car door.

Jones was the family butler. Although, at six feet seven, Jones looked less like a butler and more like a hired goon. M was dwarfed next to him. "Your mother is inside. She's very excited to hear about your meeting. I trust all went well?"

"I've definitely got some news," M said as she walked up the stairs to the house. The front porch was weathered but still sturdy under her feet. As she walked, every creak and crack were in exactly the same places as she remembered. It was comforting, but as she swung open the antique front door, she still had no idea how to explain the events of the last few hours.

"I'm home, Mom," M called out.

"We're in the library, dear," her mother answered from the back of the house.

M first ducked into the bathroom. Pulling out the empty envelope, she flipped it open again as if she could have missed something, but there was still no letter. She quickly reviewed her options. Avoid the subject? Avoid her mother? Or tell her the truth: that she had no idea whether she'd been accepted into the Lawless School?

Or she could do just what Ms. Watts had told her to do. Burn the envelope.

The fall weather had come early this year, and M's mother was already insisting on having a fire going in the drafty house. The main fireplace was in the front living room . . . conveniently on the way to the library. M lifted her head. She smelled smoke. And where there's smoke, there's fire. And where there's a fire, there was an answer to M's dilemma.

Leaving the bathroom, M walked to the living room, which had to be one of the least used rooms in the house. It was full of uncomfortable chairs and sofas that might as well have come from some French king's mansion. The walls were lined with famous paintings by Vermeer and Degas and Basquiat. Well, not the *real* famous paintings, of course. These were copies that her mother had painted. In addition to being a historian, she was a well-known restoration artist. She was often called into museums and private exhibits to clean paintings and sometimes even to retouch them. Her ability to mimic so many different styles always took M's breath away. But here, with so many old images and so few places to sit, M had taken to calling this room the *once* living room.

The fireplace sat beneath a white marble mantel. M casually walked over, grabbed the tongs, and pretended to shift the loose logs around, then tossed the envelope into the crackling fire. She watched as its corners started to curl upward and the paper began to slowly burn. But there was something else happening to the envelope.

Words were appearing on it, out of thin air.

"The heat from the fire!" M whispered to herself. She quickly snatched the envelope with the tongs. Ashes from the burned paper floated through the air as she held the envelope up to read a short, scorched message: *DON'T TRUST ZARA.*

"Who in the world is Zara?" M asked.

"M, honey?" called her mother. "We have company."

"On my way," M said as she stood frozen in front of the mantel. Finally she tossed the envelope back into the fire and made her way down the hallway to the library. As soon as she entered, she recognized the young woman sitting next to her mother. It was Ms. Smith.

"M! Welcome back! How was your interview?" her mother asked.

"Yes, M, please do tell, and don't spare us any details," Ms. Smith joined in.

"Um — I," M stuttered. "The interview, I . . . I actually don't believe you've introduced me to your new friend, Mother." It was like M was looking at a ghost. How could Ms. Smith have made it up here faster than her?

"Oh, you are right, and that's the most exciting news!" exclaimed her mother proudly. "M, I'd like you to meet Zara Smith, your new roommate at the Lawless School!"

With the dull roar of the fireplace echoing in the hallway, M took a moment to breathe. The books in the library gave off the sweet, damp smell of old paper bound in leather. This used to be her favorite room in the house. It was quiet, serene, and lined with stories, any of which she would prefer over the one she was in the middle of right now.

In one chair was her mother, a small woman who always became the center of attention as soon as she entered a room. Her hair swept into an immaculate bun, her nails perfectly manicured, her clothes tailored to fit. M's mother was the very picture of an impeccably stylish artist mogul. And this bothered M to no end, because even sitting there, beaming with excitement about M's great news, her mother still silently claimed all the bragging rights.

In the other chair, sipping tea, was Ms. Smith, a mysterious stranger who hours ago ushered M into a limo in New York City, who minutes ago was the subject of a hidden, burning warning, and who now turned out to be M's new roommate at the Lawless School.

How else could M react to this situation?

"Zara!" M shouted. "Get over here and give your new roommate a hug!" M ran over to her new friend before she could get up and smothered her with a bear hug. *Always keep your enemies close*, she reasoned. "And, Mom! The Lawless School! I got in!"

"M, I never doubted for one minute that you would get in," her mother said. "The Lawless School would be foolish not to accept such a talented young woman."

With one final squeeze, M finally let go of Zara. The older girl shrugged her shoulders and gave M a slow smile, as if she were trying to figure out M's game.

"So, Zara," asked M, "where are you from?"

"Originally, California, but my parents moved to Boston a few years ago."

"Oh, Boston," chimed in M's mother. "And what brought your family out East?"

"Work, of course. My parents are psychologists."

"What kind of psychology?" asked M's mother.

"Criminal psychology." Zara smiled.

"Well, it would be *criminal* of me not to ask you more important questions!" sang M. "Are you bringing a TV for the room? What type of music do you like? And what's your stance on the minifridge?"

"The dorms all have fridges," said Zara primly, addressing M's mother instead of M. "And there's hardly any time for television. Too much watching and not enough doing leads the Lawless student down a dead end. That's one of our mottoes."

Zara's visit was a definite act, thought M, but why? M had never witnessed anything so sickeningly rehearsed and pandering at the same time. Everything Zara said was scripted, effortless, and crawled right under her skin.

"Ah yes, M, I should have told you. Zara is a second year at the Lawless School," said M's mom. "And she's been assigned to you for your first year. What's the term you used, Zara?"

"I'll be M's guardian," Zara said, with a certain delight.

"Dead ends and guardians, eh?" asked M. "Sounds a little dangerous. Do you think I have what it takes to make it at Lawless?"

"Someone thinks you do," answered Zara. "I always say you never know until you try. People are full of surprises."

"Yes, they are, aren't they," said M. "So what's the next step?"

"The next step is we leave for Lawless tonight," replied Zara.

"Tonight feels kind of sudden, don't you think?" said M. She tried to sound nonchalant, but she felt as if any control she had over the situation was slipping away fast.

"You know what I always say," began M's mom.

"There's no time like the present," M finished her mother's favorite saying.

M's mother stood up and guided M to the front of the house. As they walked down the hallway, M felt like she was being forced onto a roller coaster that she wasn't completely ready to ride. But that didn't matter to her mother. It really never had. Her mother had a history of forcing the future on her. When she was afraid to swim, her mother was more than happy to push her into the swimming pool. When M could not stay awake to study for a test, her mother had the wonderful idea of giving a cup of coffee to a ten-year-old. Yes, her mother had two mantras: There's no time like the present and . . .

"You'll thank me for this later, dear," her mother said.

Jones was outside, loading M's suitcase into the same limo, which still idled in the driveway. "Now, dear, I know this seems rushed, but when opportunity knocks, we must open the door. I had everything packed while you were away in New York!"

"But my homeschool classes, my teachers . . ." started M.

"All handled, all dealt with, and they are all extremely proud of your accomplishment," her mother said, without missing a beat. She was beginning to sound rehearsed, too.

"But what about you? When will I see you? Do they have, like, a parent's weekend or whatever?" asked M.

"We'll figure this all out in time, I'm sure," said her mom. "For now you have Zara, and you have a limo waiting. I know this might be hard for you to understand, but we, your father and I . . ." She paused for a moment and looked like she was fighting back tears. She composed herself and continued. "We've worked so hard to achieve this for you. Every parent wants something like this for their child. The Lawless School is your future. It's where you were always meant to be. Not here with me, I'm afraid."

The questions were forming too fast for M to ask them all. Why was her mother rushing her into this new life and away from her old one? For all of her mother's shortcomings, she was, after all, still her mom . . . and the only family M had left.

"We should get out of here if we're going to make our flight," interrupted Zara, placing her hands on M's shoulders and pulling her backward toward the limo.

"Wait, flight, like in an airplane?" started M, but her mother hugged her before she could finish her thought. And just as quickly as M had opened the empty envelope earlier, she was steered back into the limousine.

"Be safe, dear. Be smart, be well, and remember that you are special," M's mother said, with a look M had never before seen from her. She looked proud of M. "You are a Freeman," she said with a confident smile. "And you *will* thank me for this later, I promise."

"Wow," said Zara, as soon as the door had closed, "what a truly sentimental good-bye."

M's eyes stayed on her mother through the tinted window as she answered Zara. "So the show's over already, huh?"

Zara flashed a fake smile that would have made a shark blush as she rapped the window partition to give the go-ahead sign to Terry. The limo rolled down the long driveway and M watched her mother, Jones, her home, and her old life grow smaller and smaller through the tinted glass.

CHAPTER 4

MOVING TARGETS

"Mom's gone," said Zara, with a certain glee.

There are days that feel off, and there are days that make you want to crawl back into your bed, and there are days in which you feel like a baby bird forced from the nest. *And then there are days like today*, thought M. She turned to face the front of the limo. The last thing she wanted was for Zara to think that leaving her mother was something that she couldn't handle.

After her father's death, M had assumed everything else in life would be easy to deal with, but it wasn't. It wasn't the death that was hard to deal with . . . it was the absence of the person who'd passed that clouded everything else. M's mother changed after the accident. She chose longer art assignments. She stayed away from home, traveled constantly, and distanced herself physically and emotionally from M.

Actually, the conversation they'd just had was maybe the most they had said to each other in years. Their typical conversations were more like a well-rehearsed dance consisting of steps one, two, three:

Step 1. How are you?

Step 2. How are classes?

Step 3. Study hard and good-bye.

No, M wasn't going to miss her mother as much as she was going to miss knowing what to expect.

"Where to now, Guardian Zara?" asked M.

"Keep up with me, M," said Zara. "We're going to the Lawless School."

"Okay, but why right now?" M was squirming in her seat. Her hand went to her necklace out of habit. "And why does it involve a flight? Aren't we just going back to the city?"

"Who said anything about the city?" Zara replied. "You don't think we'd let applicants anywhere near the actual campus, do you? M, there's a lot going on here and I'm not sure how much you know, but this was a nice thing we did for you."

"I know that you are getting on my nerves," M snapped.

Zara scooted closer to her. "Look, we needed to meet you to evaluate you. You handled all of the questions perfectly, which isn't normal."

"Ah, well, everything seemed *really* normal to me," said M.

"Listen, M," Zara continued, "these next few days are going to go by really fast, and the sooner you realize that your old life is over, the better. Hold on to your puppy, dear, and kiss Kansas good-bye. We let you go back home to see your mother for the last time."

"The last time?" M repeated.

"You're a Lawless student now. And that's a good thing." Zara looked around as the limo drove on. "We're getting close to the site."

"The site?" M repeated.

"Okay, you can't just keep repeating my last words," said Zara. "It's annoying."

"It's annoying, isn't it?" M laughed. She wanted to put off the strange feeling growing in the pit of her stomach, and getting on Zara's nerves might not be a good idea in the long run, but it seemed like good fun in the meantime. Unfortunately, a ringing phone ruined her plan.

Zara answered her cell. "Yes? Already? Where are you now? Okay, five minutes." As the conversation ended, Zara hit the intercom to the front of the car. "We're picking up a package in five minutes, Terry. You'll know it when you see it."

The limo drove along a side road that laced through the pitch-black forest surrounding M's home. The phone call had changed Zara's attitude. Her body language was tense; she kept her back straight. She clenched her jaw, too, and her smile went back to being as forced as it had been at M's house. When the car slowed to a stop, Zara remained still, but her eyes searched the perimeter of the car. She was looking for something. Something that made her nervous, M guessed, if it made her lose her cool this much.

The door opened and two other kids climbed into the limo, both boys.

"Thanks, Zara," said the boy with blond hair. "Figured you might be just getting to the drop." He was a West Coaster, M knew right away. The textured shirt under the velour V-neck sweater with gray jeans screamed surfer chic, and the solid tan that glowed even in the unnatural light of the limo's back-seat left no room for debate. By most girls' standards, thought M, this guy was cute.

The other boy was a total geek. Glasses, acne, and a face only a computer screen could love . . . which was probably where he spent most of his time. His hands tapped continuously against his legs. M figured he shared Zara's nervousness, but he was trying to be brave, especially in front of M and Zara, at whom he kept sneaking glances.

"I knew we'd run late, Foley, but you're always clockwork," said Zara. M committed Blondie's name to memory.

Zara slid down toward Foley, leaned back, and took one deep breath. It was the first moment M had seen Zara drop her guard and look vulnerable. But it passed fast.

"The Fulbrights took our car," said Foley. "My recruit is intact, but if they know about us, they know about Freeman, too."

Without missing a beat, Zara regained her composure, faced M and the other boy, and said, "I figured Freeman would be a hotter ticket than your Crimer here."

"The name's Merlyn," the boy next to M said, smiling at Zara. He tried to look relaxed, slinking back into his seat, but his anxiety was unmistakable to M. "Merlyn Eaves. And you are?"

"Not your guardian and not your business," said Zara sweetly. How could she make something so harsh sound like a compliment? Zara switched her attention back to her phone, texting a lightning-fast message to somebody.

"Okay, then, ummm, maybe I'll have better luck with you." Merlyn turned to M. "I'm Merlyn."

"Yeah, I heard. I'm M."

"M? Is that short for something?"

"Nope, it's just M." M studied Merlyn. *What would anyone want with this scrawny boy?* she wondered. "So what exactly is a Crimer?" M asked.

"Since I can see your guardian is really forthcoming with answers . . ." Merlyn said, with another smile, one that brought attention to the sweat that sat right above his upper lip. "I'm good at computers. That's what a Crimer does. You're a first year, too, then?"

"I am, as of today," said M.

"Yeah, all of us found out today. Good timing, too. My twelfth birthday's coming up," Merlyn said, looking around every window in the car. "I didn't expect the Fulbright situation yet, though."

"And the Fulbrights? What were they like?" asked M, glancing at Zara to make sure the older girl was still giving her full attention to Foley.

"You've heard all the stories about them, right? When we were growing up, they were like the boogeyman. I almost thought my parents had made them up," Merlyn said quickly and quietly. He seemed spooked. "But they're real. And now with the limitation coming up, we're supposed to choose. My parents were all, pick a side, change the world, all that jazz. But . . ." He paused for a moment. "Who are we kidding, right? We know exactly where we're going to end up. It doesn't

matter what we want, really. It's a Lawless future for me ...
and apparently for you, too."

"I can see he's not a happy little Crimer," said Zara, addressing Foley but making sure everyone heard her. "And he'll be a
dysfunctional Crimer if he doesn't zip it around my recruit."
Zara leaned into the center of the limo, leering at Merlyn.
"How much info could a Crimer gather with a broken right
hand, do you think?"

"Your right-handed threats mean nothing to me," answered
Merlyn, mustering some courage. "I'm left-handed and right-
brained."

"All right, you two, let's everyone relax," said Foley. "We'll
hit the site soon enough, and then we'll go somewhere that's
bigger than the back of this luxurious but growing-smaller-by-
the-minute limousine."

"Wow," Merlyn mouthed to himself. Then he whispered to
M, "Good luck with your guardian, man. If you didn't know
already, she's holding back some serious information from you."

"Merlyn, be cool. The conversation's over," said Foley with a
pleading look. M could read that look a mile away. It was similar to the look her mother gave her the night of her father's
accident. A delicate look, a flash, a cut of wet eyes fluttering
back and forth between the bearer of bad news and the recip-
ient. Something bad was on the horizon and, as usual, everyone
assumed it was better for M to not know what it was.

"Okay, that was safe base on the phone," Zara said matter-
of-factly. "The plane's gassed and prepped, two minutes and
closing. Everything looks clear for now. Crimer, your bags ...

apparently we're the only airline that can lose your luggage before you give it to us."

"Yeah, about that," said M. "You were at the interview, right? I seem to remember you being there. And since you were there, you would remember that I am deathly afraid of heights. Ergo, I am also afraid of planes. Especially planes."

"M, there's no need to worry. I've got something that's perfect for your jitters," said Zara.

The limo pulled into a pitch-dark open field, far from the lights of civilization. The tires sounded like they were making a new path in the dry dirt, as the limo finally came to a stop.

"We're now boarding Lawless Airlines, flight number 1768, flying nonstop to . . ." Zara smiled as she let her voice drift off ". . . a nonstated destination of our choice. Now seating rows you and you." She pointed to Merlyn and M, then shoved them out into the night.

As her eyes adjusted to the darkness, M started to make out shapes all around them, and the shapes were not simply the trees in the woods. Limousines, maybe thirteen or fourteen of them, were parked in a semicircle around something larger, much larger.

A jet.

M froze in place. A light breeze lifted a stray hair out of her face. She watched as Foley led Merlyn to the jet's staircase. Now the older boy was nervous, too. With quick glances, his eyes passed back and forth over the edge of the clearing where the field met the forest.

"Time to disco," Zara said from behind M.

But M was finally ready to stand up for herself. The plane was the last straw.

"As big as that thing is," said M, "and as great as whatever you have for my 'jitters' is going to be, you'll never get me on that plane."

Zara chuckled and patted M on both cheeks. "You're cute when you're brave. Listen, M —"

But before she could continue, Foley screamed a warning into the night.

"They're here!"

Immediately, Zara pushed M to the ground and crouched low over her. At the same time, the edge of the open field came alive with slow-moving shadows, shadows of humanoid figures creeping closer and closer to the airplane. They were surrounded.

"What is that?" M gasped in a loud whisper.

"It's not what, it's who. Those are the Fulbrights," Zara whispered. There was fear in her voice. Zara's hard shell was showing some cracks.

As M watched, a sickly, glowing green erupted from the eyes of each shadow. Their heads moved slowly back and forth as they patiently scoured the field. They were looking for something. The figures floated soundlessly like wraiths, crossing the meadow at an alarming pace to descend upon the rows of parked limousines.

Only then did M notice that all the night noises had disappeared. Cricket chirps, the wind in the trees, and the howl of distant trains had all fallen to silence — a silence that was absolute until a low rumbling voice boomed through the night. "The limitation is up, guardians. The children come with us." The voice was almost gentle, but threatening, too. Though it was unsaid, there was an "or else" that was still clearly stated.

As the Fulbrights moved into the moonlight, M saw something that made her heart skip a beat. The figures shimmered, their contours changing with each step, like they were made of crystal clear water. It was as if their bodies were mirroring the landscape, blending in with the terrain until all M could make out were the green glowing eyes. The rest of the Fulbrights' bodies had become nearly invisible.

M and Zara hunkered down in the shadows, crouching out of view beside the limo, but they would be found soon. M had little doubt of that. She could barely hear anything over her own breathing in and out. Did she always breathe so loudly? Luckily, Zara kept M's mind from wandering too far from the moment. "M, change of plans. On three, we're out of here — make for the plane," she whispered, pointing around the open limo door. "One, two, three."

Zara kicked the door shut, setting off the limo's alarm. She pulled M up onto all fours and screamed, "Crawl!" over the bleating. The shadows suddenly cupped their ears and heaved back in agony. Their camouflage disappeared, and M saw the figures for what they truly were — masked men in black jumpsuits. M guessed their glowing green eyes had been night vision lenses of some kind. But how could a car alarm cause them so much pain?

M didn't stop for an answer. She crawled across the wet

grass, weaving among the parked limousines, swiftly kicking each one to add to the cacophonous blaring. Maybe someone would hear the racket and call the police?

Zara had been in front of her, but now she was gone. M was alone, with voices all around her — masked voices addressing one another, recovered, calm, and comfortable now over the blasting alarms. At first, they sounded like idle chatter in a crowded restaurant. M couldn't focus on what they were saying, hopefully because none of them was too close to her. Then she finally centered in on a conversation.

"All are on the jet but one," said one voice.

"Will someone kill those alarms?" asked another.

"Find her and keep chatter to a minimum," answered the next. "And ditch the camo-shine, there's no need to hide now."

The men have radios in their masks, thought M. *Radios and a volume booster to help them hear everything around them.* That explained their sensitivity to the alarms. She could see their shuffling feet from under the cars and she did her best to avoid them, while still moving toward the plane. One by one the car alarms stopped until the night was silent again.

M froze in place and tried not to panic. She risked a look at the stairway to the jet, and it was completely unguarded. Which meant it was too good to be true. These men were professionals. Professional whats, she had no idea, but they knew what they were doing and they knew who they were after: her.

So what was the best way to avoid a trap? Build a better trap. M knew that the stairway to the jet wasn't safe, and she hoped Zara knew the same thing, too. She took her next step very deliberately. A stick snapped under her foot. Then, before she could blink, M was lifted off the ground and slammed against the side of a limo.

She was face-to-face with a Fulbright. The mask had wires laced all around and through it, like it was a cloth circuit board. The eyes were glowing green embers. The effect was inhuman. The Fulbright did not say a word, merely held M against the car in a death grip. M twisted and squirmed to no avail. But she knew now that the Fulbright was only human under that mask. Quickly, she gave him a strong kick to the knee, and the Fulbright finally buckled. M snatched the mask right off his head as he fell to the ground. But to her surprise, the Fulbright was not a man or a monster, but a girl who looked barely older than M. The girl gripped her leg where M had kicked her. She had tears in her eyes. M wasn't sure what to do next.

"Sorry," she said, and she darted toward the plane.

Behind her, she could hear the wounded girl screaming, "It's M Freeman! Close in on the jet!"

Four bigger Fulbrights lifted out of the shadows around the stairs to block M. Her plan had worked, sort of. She'd lured them out into the open. But there were too many to avoid them all. *I'm done for*, thought M.

But then Zara came rushing from behind the Fulbrights. She tackled the first and threw him into the second. Where did those muscles come from? wondered M. Then Zara raised an air horn and let out a crippling blare that sent the other Fulbrights to their knees.

"On the plane," she commanded, and M didn't think twice.

As she climbed the steps, M turned to glance down the thoroughfare in the distance . . . the same road that M had ridden up and down all of her life. And that's when she saw the flood of car lights. She wasn't going to wait to see who was coming.

Once on board, M found the last empty seat near the front of the plane. Zara should have been right behind her, but she wasn't — and the door slammed shut.

"Zara!" screamed M. The cabin was dark. The windows had been blacked out. She looked behind her at the rows of students. How could they just sit there? They all looked as if they were sleeping.

"Hello?" yelled M. "Anyone? Foley? Merlyn?" She was grasping at names, but no one answered.

The jet rocked back and forth and before M knew it, she fell back into the empty seat as the plane flew into the night. They were airborne. Next stop . . . who knew.

When the jet balanced out, M finally noticed the Fulbright mask she had been clutching since stripping it off that girl. She had gripped it like it was a lifeline all through the jet's rapid ascent.

The jet bounced once more, and that's all it took. M slipped out of her seat and rushed back to the bathroom. And then she did something she hadn't done for years. She threw up.

After cleaning herself up, M looked in the mirror. She looked terrifying. Her hair was drenched with sweat. Her interview suit was muddied and torn. There were rings under the rings under her eyes. She ran water, cleaned her face, pulled her hair back, and the suit, well, the suit could not be brought back from the dead.

As she stepped out of the bathroom, M saw something she wasn't prepared to see. The rows of slumbering students, not a surprise. The plane ride to no-one-knows-where, no problem. No idea when she would ever see her mother again, why worry. But seeing a hulking, shadowy figure step out from the cockpit and into the aisle was not a welcome sight.

"So what now?" asked M.

And the last thing M saw was yellow gas spilling from every air vent in the plane, as the figure reached out to grab hold of her.

CHAPTER 5
WELCOME TO LAWLESS

M was shaking. Not too-cold shaking, not scared shaking, but shaking with an insistent turbulence that can only happen during air travel. The bumps bobbled her head forward, then backward. Her knees knocked against a hard table surface. M tried to open her eyes, but they were wired shut. She could not wake up.

Waves of hissing static reached out to her in her dreams. *Shhhhhh. Shhhhhh. Copy? Shhhhhh. Shhhhhh.* She heard a quiet voice, barely audible among the white noise around her. *Shhhhhh. Shhhhhh. Do you copy? Your nose is too low. Over. Shhhhhh. Shhhhhh.* Then she began to feel something other than turbulence, a buzzing in her hands. She tightened her knuckles and stinging fire shot up her arms. Her arms, they were sore, tired, and rubbery. She felt like she had been rock climbing all day. *Shhhhhh. Shhhhhh. Copy? Shhhhhh. Shhhhhh. Nose too low. Over. Shhhhhh. Shhhhhh. Do you copy? Shhhhhh. Shhhhhh.*

As if waking from a nightmare, M gasped and pulled her body back out of the deep sleep she had settled into. Before she could remember the last thing that had happened to her, she immediately wished she had never opened her eyes.

"I'M IN THE COCKPIT!" M screamed. She looked around and was equally surprised to find that she was *alone* in the cockpit. "I'M FLYING THE STUPID PLANE!"

"Copy! Do you copy!" a voice called out through the static coming from a small headset that dangled in front of her. It was the voice from her dreams.

Quickly M put the headset on and called out, "Mayday! Thursday! Whatever! Someone help!"

Out of the front window, M could see only clouds, but the whiteness was whipping by at an incredible speed. Directly in front of M was a panel full of flashing lights, dials, and signals that were swirling out of control. M's hands were clutching the steering wheel. It was like her entire body had betrayed her and walked her willfully into this death-defying situation.

"Do you copy? Please, do you copy?" The familiar voice came through the headset.

"Ms. Watts?" asked M. "Um, Ms. Watts, it's M." She glanced around the cockpit again. "I'm . . . I'm in a plane and there's no pilot."

"M, you're the pilot," answered Ms. Watts.

"No, no, you see, I'm in the cockpit, but I'm not the pilot," said M. "I can't be the pilot. I just woke up!"

"M, I need you to listen to me," Ms. Watts said calmly. "You . . . are . . . the . . . pilot. And whatever happens, you need to land that plane."

"What do you mean, 'whatever happens'?" asked M just as the clouds rolled away. M finally saw something worse than herself alone in the cockpit. The ground.

It was not a welcome sight.

A lush mountainside, filled with thick green trees, was coming up to meet her. The cloud cover she had flown through must have been a descending morning fog. She could see the sun beginning to peek over the eastern range.

"M, can you see the sun?" asked Ms. Watts.

"Yes, yes, I see it, on the right," M shouted.

"Good. Now pull back on the wheel and feel the jet lift upward," Ms. Watts directed. "Try to get the jet even with the horizon."

"Not working," grunted M. "The wheel is pulling me down."

"Then pull back as hard as you can," said Ms. Watts. "Pull back or you're going to crash."

Crash? The threat worked like a magic word, unlocking superstrength in M, the kind of superstrength that mothers with their children trapped under massive objects must feel. M clenched her jaw and pulled back with every last bit of energy she could muster. Her feet strained against the floor, lifting her slight body out of her seat. As her back started to burn, the wheel slowly rose closer and closer to M, inch by inch, until she had pulled the plane out of its nosedive. When the plane felt level and the control board's instruments seemed to quiet down, M turned her attention back to her headset.

"Level. I think — I think I'm level now," she whispered.

"Good, M," said Ms. Watts. "Now steer away from the sun until you find a river. Do you see it?"

"I see a dark line, but in the mountain's shadow, it's hard to make out," said M, scanning over the forest, while still gripping the wheel.

"Yes, you'll follow that line until you see a waterfall," Ms. Watts said.

"And then?" asked M.

"Let's prepare for then now," said Ms. Watts. "Do you see the throttles next to you on your right?"

She looked down quickly. There was a control of some sort next to her. "Does it look like something you would find on a boat?"

"Yes, that's it," answered Ms. Watts. "When the time is right, you will have to slowly pull that lever from front to back. But remember, the key word is *slowly*."

M squinted. The sun was almost blinding as it rose over the mountaintops. "What about the wheels? Like, the landing gear or whatever they're called. How do I get those down?"

"M, you've got a good head on your shoulders," said Ms. Watts. "I knew that from one minute into the interview. The landing gear controls are located on your left. You can activate them now to make sure everything is still in working order."

M set off the landing gear and felt a small bump from beneath her seat, followed by the slow mechanical exhale of the pumps lowering down the wheels.

"It worked," said M. "I almost for . . ." But before she could finish, her stomach lurched. She broke into a cold sweat and began to take quick, shallow breaths. "I . . . forgot . . . my . . . fear . . . of . . . heights."

"Stay with me. Don't lose focus just because you're up higher than you're used to," coached Ms. Watts. "You are carrying precious cargo. Yourself included, you've got fourteen first years onboard. And I won't be able to face the next Lawless PTA meeting if you crash."

"I . . ." M paused, as if she were still making up her mind as to whether she was scared or not. "I see the waterfall. It's dead ahead."

"Not the best choice of words, M, but that's good," said Ms. Watts. "Try to find the ledge halfway down the waterfall."

"Okay, got it," said M. "Now what?"

"Just fly directly into the waterfall, aligning so that you're even with that ledge," said Ms. Watts.

"Just fly directly into the waterfall. Check. That doesn't sound totally crazy or anything!" screamed M. "Don't you people do anything the normal way?"

"This is the normal way," said Ms. Watts calmly. "We've done it this way for a long time now, long enough that it's normal to everyone involved with the Lawless School."

"Not normal enough for me, though. Remember, I'm only a first year!" yelled M. She was so frustrated! Waking up from a Fulbright attack to find herself at the helm of a jet plane in a nosedive and then being asked to fly straight into a waterfall!

"We have a visual and it looks like you are in range," said Ms. Watts, ignoring M's outburst. "If you keep the plane level with the ledge, then we can guide you in remotely. We are taking over the plane now."

M felt a shift in the plane as the controls stopped yelling at her and, for a moment, everything seemed okay. Her piloting days were over; Ms. Watts was flying the plane from somewhere else. M loosened her grip on the wheel as the plane headed closer and closer to the ledge jutting out of the waterfall until —

CRASH! A thunderous jolt hammered the plane down hard against the ledge as the waterfall pounded against the roof. The broad and mountainous horizon was violently replaced with a long cave, dimly lit with lights striping the ground like a runway. The wheel began to fight against M again, pushing and pulling in every direction. That didn't seem right. M tried to hold the wheel in place, but the plane fishtailed, drifting left, then right. The wings smashed against the cave walls, heaving out the harsh sound of metal smashing in on itself. Then, up ahead, M saw the end of the runway — an open port where the air traffic control must be located. They were running out of runway, fast.

"M, we've lost control! You're coming in too hot," said Ms. Watts. "Throw the throttle all the way back in reverse!"

M let go of the steering wheel and slammed down the throttle. Instantly she was hurled forward against her seat belt as the engines shifted into reverse. Then, just as suddenly, the plane's power cut off and they drifted quietly and slowly to a stop against the wall of the cavernous terminal.

M's rib cage felt like it had been cracked open. Her arms

were as heavy and damp as the ropes on a sailboat after a long voyage. But she was alive.

"Welcome to the Lawless School, Ms. Freeman," said Ms. Watts over the headset.

M sat back in her seat, but her hands stayed tightly wound around the throttle. Her heart pounded. She stared at her own shattered reflection in the windshield, with splintering that spread like a spiderweb of cracks from the crash. Her brown hair was tangled and loose all at once. This was not the glorious entrance into the chic, mysterious boarding school that she had expected.

Slowly M unlaced her pale white fingers from the controls. She stiffly unbuckled the seat belt and stumbled out of the captain's chair. From the cabin behind her, she could hear the plane's door unlock. The tap of footsteps climbing the stairs was followed by a knock on the cockpit door.

"I'd like to complain about the service!" Zara said.

M swung open the pilot's door and slumped in the doorway like a rag doll. "This is your captain speaking. What seems to be the problem?"

"Yeah, um, the landing was a little bumpy, don't you think?" Zara said, with a smile that might have meant she was actually proud of M or may have just been mocking. M honestly couldn't tell the difference.

"You get what you pay for, roomie," said M.

"Oh yeah, good reminder," Zara chirped, and she handed M a lone silver key. "I forgot to give this to you during all the preboarding ruckus. It's your room key. And in case you were wondering, I call top bunk." And with that she stepped back off the plane and down to the tarmac.

M moved forward into the cabin, which was a complete mess. Emergency masks hung from every overhead compartment, suitcases cluttered the aisles. There were fourteen seats on the plane, and thirteen of them were occupied by girls and boys with totally calm, relaxed looks on their faces. They'd slept through the entire ordeal. And they made no move to get up now.

"Um, hello, everybody. We're here," said M, adding, "wherever that is."

She noticed Merlyn sitting in the second row, right behind the empty fourteenth seat. Her seat. Obviously the guardians had taken a different flight. *Why* was yet another question to add to her list.

Then M saw the discarded Fulbright mask in her seat and a shiver shot through her body.

"All right," M said to herself, "that mask is a creep factor nine." She turned away from it, grabbing Merlyn by the shoulders and shaking him. "Hey, hey, hey — Earth to Merlyn Eaves. Get up, Merlyn!"

"He can't hear you." A voice surprised M. It was Foley, Merlyn's guardian. "He's in a state, you know? They all are. Their guardians are on the way over to gather them and take them to their rooms."

"My guardian seems to have left me behind," said M.

"Zara's going to be the best guardian in our class," said Foley. "She's great because she knows exactly how much her cadet can handle."

"Yeah, she seems totally sold on my abilities so far." M laughed. "Especially if she thinks I can find my own dorm room in this madness."

"Well, you did survive a Fulbright attack, then fly a plane without any prior training," said Foley. "I'd imagine that finding a room in a dorm shouldn't be too hard for someone like you."

M watched as Foley guided Merlyn from his seat and off the plane. The Crimer was in some sort of trance. One by one, the other guardians boarded the plane and took their unresponsive first years away. Once the last of them had left, M sat back down in her original seat and studied the black mask.

"Most people would take that as a sign of victory." It was Ms. Watts. "An empty black mask is something we don't often see. Usually it comes attached to a Fulbright, and that means trouble.

"At least you made it here safely," Ms. Watts continued. "May I ask what happened once you were on board the plane?"

"Ms. Watts, it's been a long . . ." M paused, "night? I'm guessing because the sun was rising as I landed, but from all I can remember, we could have circumnavigated the entire globe before landing here."

"We'll call it a long night," said Ms. Watts.

"Well, we got to the plane and were, I don't know" — M searched for the right word — "ambushed? Basically a ton of creeps in masks tried to grab us before we got on the plane. Only the attack, I think it was a red herring. There was someone waiting for us on the plane. We were gassed — it came pouring out of the vents. Then I woke up in the pilot's seat."

"It sounds like someone had a plan for you, doesn't it?" said Ms. Watts. "Allow me to tell you what I know on the walk to your room."

M followed Ms. Watts off the plane. The tarmac smelled of burning metal, gasoline, and damp cave. There were huge industrial lights along the tunnel. They walked toward the silver doors of an elevator that were built right into the wall of rock. A line of glass windows extended up from the doors — an elevator shaft. M lifted her head toward the carved roof of the cave.

"Going up?" said M. The doors opened, and she stepped into the elevator.

"Not really," said Ms. Watts. As soon as the doors closed, the elevator began to move — sideways. Another line of glass panels appeared and M could see the entire airport operation from the windows as they traveled around the exterior of the tarmac.

"The most we can tell, as you know," started Ms. Watts, "is that your plane was boarded successfully. All the necessary precautions had been taken. The other first years were seated and their guardians had left the rendezvous."

"Why wouldn't they fly with us?" asked M.

"To confuse anyone who might be following you," said Ms. Watts.

"Like the Fulbrights?" M asked.

"Ms. Freeman, I know this will come as a shock to you, but not everyone thinks so highly of the Lawless School. Some people will stop at nothing to shut us down. We go to great lengths to protect this school, its students, and its traditions."

"Who are they, anyway? At first I thought they were monsters, but when we were fighting them, I pulled that mask off one. She was just a girl, like my age," said M.

"In a manner of speaking, they are students," said Ms. Watts. "Students from a rival school, if you will. Now, Zara and Foley did report the ambush, but noted that the plane took off according to plan. But you claim that someone else was on board. This unknown assailant approached you. And from there, it gets fuzzy?"

"Afraid so," said M. "The next thing I know, I'm landing the plane."

"Let's be clear, you didn't land the plane, we did," said Ms. Watts, in a matter-of-fact tone. "*You* weren't even flying the plane, not really. The gas that filled the cabin, it's a special Lawless School sedative. We administer the gas to all incoming first years."

"The gas was *you*?" asked M.

"It's better for first years not to know where they are being taken," answered Ms. Watts. "Given the circumstances, you can understand why we take such precautions. What you will learn is that the gas has two separate effects, which make it very useful. The first is, as I said, a sedative. The second is a suggestive agent."

"A suggestive what?" asked M as the moving room left the view of the tarmac and entered a tunnel.

"When the sedative takes over, the human mind is open to suggestion. It believes whatever it's told," explained Ms. Watts. "So when I told you over the headset that you could fly a plane, then you could simply fly a plane."

"I think, therefore I am," said M to herself. It was one of her father's favorite sayings. "Wait, you told me? Where was the pilot in all of this?"

"There never was a pilot, M," Ms. Watts said. "Everything was handled by remote computers."

"If there wasn't a pilot, then who came out of the cockpit?" asked M.

"The gas can have unpredictable effects on some people," answered Ms. Watts. "My guess is that you imagined this mysterious man as a side effect."

"I saw someone on that plane," insisted M.

"Perhaps you did *see* something," said Ms. Watts, "but there was no one else on that aircraft. I am sure of it."

"So, if the plane was remote controlled, then why even put me in the driver's seat?" asked M.

"To help you conquer your fear of heights, of course." She smiled. "You'll find there's little room for weakness at this school, M, and this seemed the best way to help you overcome yours. You shouldn't have woken up from the gas until after you had landed, though. Which is why we were very surprised to hear your voice over the radio."

"My voice? But I was in dream land until I heard *your* voice on the radio," said M. "What was I saying?"

"Oh, it was a very clear message, though I'm not sure you would understand it now," said Ms. Watts.

"Try me," she replied.

"Six, seven, nineteen, fourteen, thirteen, three, twenty-eight, twenty-nine, twenty-nine, twenty-eight, thirty-one, thirty-six," Ms. Watts said flatly.

"Hmm, you're right. That doesn't sound like the usual string of numbers I like to recite," said M. "What's it supposed to mean?"

"It simply means: Abort mission," said Ms. Watts. "The numbers are a cipher. A very famous and precise code that is almost impossible to crack."

"Can't be too tough," said M. "You said it was a very clear message."

"That's the most interesting part, Ms. Freeman," said Ms. Watts. "The only reason we can read that cipher is because it was scripted at the Lawless School, by your father."

Finally, the room eased to a stop and the doors behind M opened. The bright sunlight took her by surprise, almost as much as hearing Ms. Watts talk about her father again.

"This way," said Ms. Watts, taking a step outside.

When M's eyes adjusted, she was still not sure what to make of her surroundings. The buildings, the campus, the library, everything looked so ... normal. Just like an average boarding school campus. Except for the scene beyond the buildings: a dense thickness of pine trees that reached all the way up the steep mountains surrounding the school on all sides.

"Ms. Watts," said M, as she took everything in. "Can you help me with one simple question?"

"I can try," she answered.

"What is this place?" asked M.

"This is your future, M," she answered. "And you've shown a great willingness, above and beyond, to — how can I put this best — go with the flow, but your future can wait for you to get some real sleep first. Before you learn anything else about the Lawless School, I'd say you've earned yourself some rest."

"After the night I've had, I don't think I can wait for my future to explain itself," M said as she stopped by a bench in the courtyard.

"Very well. You've certainly earned the truth," Ms. Watts said. She took a deep breath before continuing. "The Lawless School is a special school for the children of master criminals. Your father, M Freeman, was an accomplished art thief, famous in the underworld for many of the most successful and spectacular art heists of all time. You are here to train in his footsteps."

M was stunned. Her father, a thief? "And — and my mother?" she stammered.

"Only a low-level con artist, I'm afraid," Ms. Watts continued. There was something she clearly did not like about M's mom. "But she won your father's heart. He introduced her to the Lawless world and, after he passed, she took over the family business."

"Stealing art?" asked M.

Ms. Watts nodded, looking into her eyes. "M, this is a lot for one day. More than the average Lawless student has to deal with."

"The other kids all know, don't they? They know who their parents are, what this school is," said M. "They know what they're meant to be."

"Yes, most first years already know the history of the Lawless School. Most are excited and honored to attend this program," said Ms. Watts. "You are a rare case. One of the rules of the Lawless School is that only a graduate of the school can discuss the details. Your mother could never tell you any truth about the school other than that it exists and that your father was a graduate. I'm sure he himself would have told you in time."

And with that, M followed Ms. Watts into a dormitory without another word, as dazed as if she had been exposed to a sedative for a second time. At the end of a hallway they found room 103. And sure enough, Zara was there, sleeping soundly in the top bunk.

CHAPTER 6

MARK

"Rise and shine, sleeping beauty" were the words that pulled M out of the murkiest sleep of her life. The voice, of course, belonged to Zara. "Class starts at nine, and it's eight thirty now."

"Eight thirty P.M.?" asked M.

"A.M., my friend. As in, long sleep, aye, M?"

Had she slept for more than twenty-four hours? Was it the next morning already? From the taste in her mouth and the amount of drool on her pillow, M figured that Zara must be telling the truth.

M rubbed her eyes and saw the room for the first time clearly. The furniture was all made from old, solid wood. The bunk bed, the deep desks, the floor-to-ceiling bookshelves, and the ornate dressers with carved claws for legs — it all must have been built during a time when furniture was made to last forever.

"Wakey wakey and pay attention," snapped Zara as she placed several objects on the empty desk beside the beds. "I know you've had 'the talk' with Ms. Watts, so I'm going to dive right in. On your desk is a map of the campus. Your classes are all highlighted on this map. Until you've learned the school layout, keep this with you at all times."

M saw that the map showed the entire grounds of the school up to the edge of the forest. The campus was laid out with the library at the heart of the school, the cafeteria, the dorms, and the classrooms all spilling out around it.

"This is your school ID," said Zara.

"It's got a picture of me already?" asked M.

"Yes, a recent photo was mandatory to the interview process, remember? Now stay with me, 'cause we each have only a few minutes. Your ID goes with you everywhere. So does your key, which most students keep around their neck, so I suggest you do, too. Next is your meal plan card. If you want to eat, you'll want to hold on to this. There's no getting in or out of the cafeteria without it. Library card. Dorm card. You can tell the difference because the library card has a picture of the library on it, while the dorm card has a picture of your dorm. Genius, right?

"Now, this," she said, holding up a thin black metallic card, "is your most precious ticket. It's called the club card. Think of it like your *everything else* card. It's a credit card, for one thing, so you'll definitely need it on any future field trips. Do not lose this card. I cannot stress that enough."

With that, Zara put everything back on the desk. M got up and walked to the dresser to find that all of her clothes were unpacked and neatly folded.

"The rest, you'll figure out. Fast learner, right? I'll see you right before commencement." With that, Zara turned and left the room before M had a chance to clear her throat.

"But where's my first class?" M asked aloud, to the empty room.

Quickly she looked at the campus map. The buildings were all color coded according to days of the week. The map, she realized, must function as her class schedule, too. Monday was blue. M traced her finger across the map to find the first blue building, marked *Professor Bandit, 9:00* A.M.

"For once in my life, I sure hope it's Monday," M said as she hauled tail out of the room.

It was nine o'clock on the dot when M raced through the back doors of the auditorium. The head of every student turned to look at her, and then they all turned back around. The professor must not have been there yet.

"Freeman, over here," called Merlyn. "I saved you a seat."

"I'm not late, am I?" asked M, as she sat down.

"No, you're just in time," said Merlyn. He turned his open laptop toward M and pointed at his screen. "You see this dot here? That's Professor Bandit. He's walking up the steps now."

"Wow. Where do I get one of those?"

"You already have one, I suspect," said Merlyn. "Did your guardian give you a campus map? I digitized mine and modified it to fit my needs."

"You *need* to know where your professors are at all times?" asked M.

"Keeps me from running circles around campus trying to beat them here if I can tell that they're running late themselves," he answered with a smile.

The doors at the back of the room swung open again. This time M was in the audience, but when she turned around to see Professor Bandit, she wished she had slept late and missed the class. Dressed in a sharp suit creased and fitted in all the right places, the professor moved with all the grace of a ghost floating down the stairs toward the front of the class. Then, with one green eye and one blue eye, Professor Bandit stared back at his class and let loose a toothsome smile. It was an intoxicating smile, full of confidence, and it fell full force onto M.

"You, my dear first year, were almost late to my class," the professor said. "Do not make a habit of it. And to the rest of you, students, abandon all of your expectations for this classroom. The extent of what you will learn here does not begin or end at those doors behind you. However, those doors will remain locked whenever we meet."

At that, a doomsday locking sound from the back doors echoed throughout the room.

"And now we can begin," said Professor Bandit, as he sat down behind his desk. He flipped open the single folder there and pulled out one sheet of paper. "Roll call. When you hear your name, stand up.

"Blank, Miriam. Dodge, Kristofer. Draw, Richard. Eaves, Merlyn."

As the students stood up, M recognized a lot of them from the plane. They looked more lively now. For better and worse. They were no longer vegetables and the calm serenity was long gone, but in its place was pure fear. Not just first-day jitters, either. There was something about this Professor Bandit that freaked the entire class out. Good, thought M, at least she wasn't the only one. As soon as Bandit called a student's name, the student stood up as if they were being asked to stand in front of a firing squad or walk the plank.

"Fence, Calvin. Hollows, Derrick," Professor Bandit continued.

M flashed a questioning look at Merlyn. The professor had skipped her name completely and kept going with his roll call. Merlyn shrugged as if to say, *Who knows what's going on?* M decided not to say anything just yet. In her brief, yet very eventful experience with the Lawless School, it seemed there was always a method to their madness. Now she expected the madness, but their methods kept catching her by surprise.

"Zoso, Devon." A tiny Asian girl stood up behind M, kneeing M in the back and calling, "Present," in a thick French accent. As she sat back down, M thought she saw Professor Bandit giving Devon the evil eye . . . but it was hard to say for sure, because it looked a little like the professor gave *all* the students an evil eye.

"Thank you, all," Professor Bandit concluded.

Hmm, thought M. Could Zara have given her the wrong map? She studied it again, shuffling papers around in her lap, trying to unravel one of the smaller mysteries that she probably should have already figured out — what class she was supposed to be in. A great start to her first day. Zara wasn't trying to show M the ropes, she was trying to tie her up with them.

Then the classroom became too quiet. She looked up from her map and was face-to-face with Professor Bandit.

"Sir, Professor Bandit," she whispered. "I can explain everything."

"Class," Professor Bandit said, with an eerie certainty. "We are graced with one more student for this term. Please stand up, Freeman."

M lifted herself out of her seat and the papers fell from her lap. She held Professor Bandit's gaze and made no move to pick them up.

"Freeman," he said, while writing her name onto the student list. "Mark."

"Wait, what?" said M. "Professor, I'm sorry, but there's been some mistake. My name is M Freeman, not Mark Freeman."

"Class, please note that for future reference," the professor stated. "You may sit back down, Freeman. Pick up your papers and try to not disrupt my classroom again."

M sat back down and gathered her things.

"Way to make a first impression, Ms. Right Place at the Wrong Time," whispered Merlyn with a crooked smile.

"I have that effect on people around here," mumbled M.

Professor Bandit turned from the class and approached a giant blackboard at the front of the room. He wrote one single phrase on the board, slowly, taking great pleasure in his perfect and exacting handwriting. The swirls and swoops of each letter poured out of him through the chalk and onto the chalkboard.

Activated and dismissed for duty.

A few students scribbled the words down into their journals, while others, like Merlyn, tapped them into their computers.

After admiring his work on the blackboard, Professor Bandit turned back around to face the students and simply stated, "Class activated and dismissed for duty." And then, as gracefully as he had entered the classroom, Professor Bandit exited from a second pair of doors beside the blackboard.

"I guess we've got the rest of the morning off," said Merlyn as he packed away his computer.

M turned to face Devon, but the small girl had already left her seat. It was obvious that clipping M's back with her knee was a sign, but what kind of sign was it? It definitely wasn't a simple hello.

"So, Professor Bandit, huh?" said M, following Merlyn out into the hallway. "What do you think his story is? Even his name sounds ominous."

"Actually, he's one of the better teachers at Lawless," answered Foley. The guardian was outside, apparently waiting for Merlyn. In fact, all of the first years were greeted by their second-year counterparts. All of them except for M, of course. Zara was nowhere to be found.

"We've got to go," said Foley to Merlyn. "The big introduction is happening today. The commencement."

"Commencement? What's that?" asked M.

"According to my parents, it's when Fox Lawless officially welcomes us all to his school," said Merlyn. "He'll thank us for choosing Lawless, like we had a choice, and then he'll probably brag for, like, an hour about how awesome he is and therefore how awesome we'll all be by the end of the program."

"Merlyn, that's for her guardian to explain," Foley cut in. "Come on, I'll show you around campus. M, I'm sure Zara will be with you soon."

As the two boys left, a lithe voice with a French accent sprang from behind M. "Missing a guardian, are we?"

M knew who it was before she turned around. Devon Zoso.

"Must be that kind of morning," said M. "I see you're alone, too." She wasn't sure how to act around Devon. Merlyn and Foley were both easy to talk to, but Devon had an intense look in her eyes. She was studying M the same way someone stares at a puzzle.

"Not really," echoed another two voices in unison, from behind M. Startled, M wheeled around to see a twin on either side of her. Devon slipped around M to join the other two girls. "Oh, I'm not alone. Meet Lucy and Kitty Flynn, my guardians."

"Two guardians, eh?" said M, looking back and forth between the three girls.

"Two's better than one," Devon said with a smile. "I'll see you at commencement . . . or not."

Devon sauntered off with her guardians. The girls didn't speak to one another, but M noticed that the twins were following Devon. Why would a first year ever lead a second year . . . much less lead two second years?

"Watch out for Devon. She's got a giant chip on her shoulder." It was one of the boys from her class approaching while his guardian hung back. "Hi. I'm Calvin. My friends call me Cal." He held out his hand. His green eyes pierced through his blond hair that had slipped down into his face.

"I'm M," she said, shaking his hand. "Did I put that chip on her shoulder?"

"No, rumor has it that Professor Bandit did," said Cal. "The word is that Devon isn't really a first year. She was held back last year by the prof. Now she has to take his class again, and I don't think she's thrilled about it."

"No, I guess I wouldn't be, either," said M. She watched Cal flip his hair back, then try to tuck it behind his ears. It made him look nervous, but with his broad shoulders and kind smile, he seemed more like a giant teddy bear than a master criminal in the making. M wondered what crimes his parents had committed.

"If you can help it, though, I wouldn't get in her way," he said, still watching Devon. "She strikes me as the type that gets what she wants."

"And if she doesn't, then I bet she takes the whole ship down with her," said M.

"Ha, that's funny!" Cal said as he patted M on the back. Unfortunately, what he must have considered a gentle tap almost forced M to the ground. It was a totally clumsy move, and it caught her by surprise. She wasn't used to friendly physical contact. That wasn't part of her past life.

"Okay, I'm off to the commencement," continued Cal, as he trotted away toward his waiting guardian. "See you there?"

"I'll be there," said M. "Hey, what building is it in?"

"Student center. It's on your map," said Cal. "You can't miss it."

M pulled off her backpack and paused for a moment to

make sure there were no more fellow students waiting to surprise her. The coast was clear. She opened up her bag and searched for her map, but it wasn't there. She must have left it in the classroom when she'd dropped her papers.

M went back through the auditorium doors, but the room was completely dark. She felt around the walls by the doorway for a light switch, but could not find one. But the dark didn't bother M too much.

She made her way down the steps toward her row. As she walked, she recounted her steps from when she had first come into the room. It was an old trick of hers, one she had learned from her geometry teacher.

The easiest way to understand a space is to envision yourself in that space. You are the most familiar form of measurement to yourself, her teacher used to say.

So, at a young age, M had started to count her steps into and out of every room. At first it seemed kind of crazy, especially because she tended to count out loud to herself. Jones, the family butler, never blinked an eye when she entered a room, but the other staff always stared at her and shook their heads. She must have looked like a loon to them. Over time, M learned to count her steps in her head. Then it became second nature. M often walked around her house, in and out of rooms, without ever turning the lights on. She figured it would be a cool party trick one day, but now she found herself in a situation where recounting steps actually came in handy.

When M reached her row, she dropped to her knees and started feeling the floor for her lost map. Nothing there. It was pitch-dark inside the room. M moved forward, shuffling her hands back and forth along the aisle until they found something . . . and it wasn't a piece of paper. It was a shoe . . . a shoe with a foot in it. A foot that belonged to a person who was standing there in the dark. M had no sooner pulled back her hand than she felt a swift wind shift over her and heard the soft tapping of footsteps bouncing down the aisle until the person had reached the front doorway. The doors flew open and slammed closed, just as the lights turned on at last.

"Freeman?" called Zara from the back of the room. "You down there?"

M stood up with what must have been a totally startled look on her face. She turned from Zara to look at the front of the room again. The curtains over the doors were settling back into place, but it was clear that someone had been in this room in the exact spot that M had been sitting. They must have been able to see, somehow, and that meant they'd watched M come all the way down the stairs and then watched her crawl into the exact same row where they were standing. She physically shuddered at the thought.

"Don't look so shocked. Hide-and-seek is over," said Zara. "We need to get you to commencement."

"I know, I was about to walk over, but then realized I forgot something in here," said M.

"And you opted to find it in the dark?" asked Zara.

She climbed back up the stairs. "Couldn't find the light switch. You were late, you know."

"I wasn't so much late as I was held up," said Zara. "Your

personal champion, Ms. Watts, caught me on my way over here." She was looking back down into the room, surveying the scene. "Did you find what you lost?"

"Sure did," M lied. She wasn't certain why she lied to Zara, but she thought it better to keep this unexpected truth to herself.

The duo headed over to the commencement. It was held in the student center, a large complex that lifted out of the center of campus, next to the library.

"This place looks like that art museum in Paris. The Centre Pompidou," remarked M. "Like it's been built inside out."

Zara snickered. "Of course you would notice the similarity. There's a good reason it looks like Centre Pompidou. It was the prototype for the museum. I have to say, M, people here have high expectations for you and so far you haven't disappointed."

"Well, I haven't passed a test yet," said M. "And Professor Bandit thinks my name is Mark."

"Say it ain't so!" Zara laughed as she put her arm around M. It was the most they had touched since Zara had thrown her to the ground to hide from the Fulbrights. "Well, old Professor Bandit can be a little wacky. Plus he's got that one bad eye . . . he probably just made a mistake. Now, are you ready to meet the rest of the Lawless School? Walk this way."

CHAPTER 7

TRICKS OF THE TRADE

"IDs, please."

The security guards all wore gray uniforms that barely contained their muscles. Each one looked bigger and sharper than the next. M's hand dove into her pocket where she had placed her ID that morning. But her pocket was empty.

"Here you go, sirs," Zara said coolly as she flashed her own ID almost out of thin air.

"You're good, Ms. Smith. Ma'am, ID."

"Sorry, it's my first day," M said as she flipped her backpack upside down and shook out the contents. Notebooks and pens, but no ID.

"Ma'am, we cannot let you into the center without your ID," said a guard.

"Yeah, M, I explained that to you this morning," Zara said as she walked through security. "Remember, you need that ID to get anywhere on campus. Don't you have any of your other cards?"

Of course, her other cards — where were they? M turned out her pockets again, she flipped through her notebooks, but nothing turned up. How could all of her personal information have disappeared already?

"Zara, *all* my IDs are gone. You can help, right? Tell them who I am, that you're my guardian," M hollered from around the guards. But Zara kept walking into the building without her.

"Time to improvise, I guess," said Zara. "She's not with me, sirs. I have no idea who she is. Though she should remember that this meeting is mandatory for all students."

With that, the security guards turned their full attention back to M. "Ma'am, please step away from the building."

M bent down to repack her backpack and shot a quick glance at Zara, who backed into the front doors of the student center, holding up M's ID in her left hand and waving good-bye with her right.

As the guards closed in to block the entryway, M threw her backpack over her shoulder and casually strolled around the building.

There's a good reason it looks like Centre Pompidou. It was the prototype for the museum. That's what Zara had said, and if that was true, then M knew exactly how she could get in.

Centre Pompidou is a famous museum in Paris, but it's perhaps most famous for the building itself. It was designed to look like it had been turned inside out, so that the air vents, the electric wires, the stairways were all put on the outside of the building to make more room for the art inside. The building was like a giant jungle gym.

As soon as she was out of the guards' view, M shimmied up the metal scaffolding that formed the building's frame. She moved carefully from level to level until she found what she was looking for: an air-duct hatch. With her fingers, M unscrewed the hatch. She knew this was almost always the weakest part of a building's design, which is how birds and other little critters can sometimes work their way into airways to escape the outside elements. The hatch popped off with little work and she slid inside the duct.

The air was blasting and surprisingly hot, sucking her deeper into the ductwork's maze, but M didn't mind. If this meeting was mandatory, she was going to attend it no matter what. M hadn't realized until now, slipping through the tiny crawl space, that she was at Lawless for a bigger reason than following the family plan. She was here to put together the missing pieces of her father, to fill in the blank spaces of her own past. And she was tired of being on the wrong side of a locked door.

M moved slowly forward. The light from the outside faded behind her as she was swallowed by darkness, and though the air vent had been clean at the entryway, farther in it was covered with built-up dust and cobwebs. Her mom used to complain all the time about paintings and statues that she had to clean because so much filth and grime flowed through the air-conditioning at museums and blew directly onto the artwork. Though now M wondered if her mother was actually complaining because she had to climb through the filth to break in.

M flashed back into the moment as she slid her hands through fistfuls of dirt and debris. Finally she reached the end of the first vent and was met with a powerful blast of freezing air. It was the main air canal that connected the entire building.

With her eyes closed, M listened for a sign of something over the whirring air. A room full of murmurs, a microphone feeding back for a moment, the shifting and knee bouncing of an auditorium filled with students — any of that would do. But the echo that came to her was much more obvious.

"Welcome to the Lawless School commencement!" The announcement bounced off the walls of the shaft and the feverish cheering and excitement of the student body rocked the small space that M occupied. Keeping in mind that sound travels in waves, M pinpointed the uptake of the echo. This gave her the direction she needed to follow. Another trick she picked up from her science teacher back home. Most of the time, when people hear loud sounds, like helicopters overhead, it's hard to know where the sound originated. That's because people tend to listen only to the crest of the sound wave, when the sound is at its loudest. A trained ear can hear the movement of the sound and instantly find its location. M crawled forward and the cheering became louder and louder.

The ductwork was swaying significantly as M shifted along. Her forearms started to sting from bracing against the cold metal and her back ached like it was on fire. At first, she thought the movement of the vent was due to the cheering and stomping in the auditorium, but when everything quieted down, she realized why ductwork was best suited for small animals. It was not supposed to handle too much weight. The thin metal beneath her started to dent around her knees. But M saw a light at the end of the tunnel . . . an air vent just ahead that led to the auditorium. Perhaps she could slip in unnoticed, though probably covered in dirt and crawling with spiders, but at least she wouldn't make a big scene for once. She wasn't someone who ever made a big scene. Not until she came to this school.

Unfortunately, as M pulled up to the vent, she knew she was due for her next big scene. The auditorium was at least a fifty-foot drop below her.

Why couldn't the vent just lead to an AV room in the back of the auditorium? Instead the path she'd chosen put her directly above and between the front row and the stage. The room had gone completely silent, save for the clicking dress shoes of someone walking up to the podium beneath her. From her bird's-eye view, M could see the man was dressed all in black, with a shock of red hair that fell in locks around his face. His teeth gleamed in the spotlight as he stepped confidently to the microphone. And then, in a deep voice, the stranger introduced himself.

"Students, friends, castaways, and deviants, I, Dr. Fox Lawless Jr., would like to be among the first to welcome you to your new home."

He held up a finger to warn off any applause. "But," he said sharply, "you have chosen more than a home here. You have chosen a dark future, an unexplained life, an experience that most people could never imagine and would never understand. We will not prepare you for Harvard, Yale, Cambridge, or Oxford. You will not go on to be CEOs or doctors or librarians. In fact, you will have no future that the light of day will ever look upon. You belong to Lawless now."

Wild applause erupted from the audience, as M crouched frozen atop the gaping maw of a life that surrounded her with bitter chills. Of course, maybe it was just the air-conditioning coursing past her that made her feel so cold. But maybe not. What had she gotten herself into?

"While you are here, you will obey the rules set forth at this school," Lawless said, in a vaguely threatening tone. "And let me be totally honest with you, since we all share the same heritage, the rules of this school will become your rules for life. We are thieves, ladies and gentlemen. And we have honor for each other and for no one else in this world."

As M listened to his speech, she realized that Lawless spoke like the fox from the gingerbread man story. Calmly beckoning his prey closer by pretending to be something he's not: safe.

"As many of you may have no doubt heard," Lawless continued, "we had quite an exciting time gathering our East Coast first years from the United States. I must admit that we did not expect or prepare for such circumstances. These bon voyages are usually mundane affairs, but it seems we have a special class this year, one that has already dipped their toes into the criminal life. Make no mistake, the Fulbrights are out there, training for the day they meet every one of you. Training in different ways to trap you, steal you, and break you down until you are willing to give up your own parents, much less this extremely private and exclusive school. So this is why we must train you twice as hard to never surrender, to never succumb, and to never let the self-proclaimed 'good guys' win. You will become shadows. You will become bumps in the night. You will become fictions of imagination. You will become what you came here to become. Nothing and everything all at once."

"Wow, he *does* like to talk a lot," M whispered to herself. With the vent buckling slightly under her weight and Lawless going on and on, M realized that she needed to find another way out of this air vent. She scanned the room from her bird's-eye view. Oversized spotlights, with heavy electrical wiring strung through the ceiling, dangled around her. Between the lights were wide, flat sound panels that hung from sturdy-looking wires, but considering how easily the panels swayed in the air-conditioned breeze, walking across them wasn't going to be a viable option. Where was the catwalk? Every auditorium this size should have a catwalk so the crew could run the show from high above the audience. M's view was too limited with the hood of the vent in place, so she shifted forward and twisted and pulled at it.

The hood popped open easily. M stuck her head out and found the catwalk only a few feet away. Her best bet was to swing from a bundle of electrical wires that looped down from the ceiling and connected to an overhead light. But as she worked up the courage to enact her plan, the familiar, and unwelcome, sound of metal snapping rang out all around her.

The air duct gave way and tossed M headfirst out of its mouth.

M grasped at the electrical wires as the auditorium below erupted with gasps. She held tight to the cables as her legs swished in the air in an attempt to reach the sound panels. She caught a toehold on one panel and shimmied along the ropes. But the catwalk was no longer an option — it had instantly filled with security guards pouring in from every possible exit.

"We have a visual, Dr. Lawless," came a buzz of radio transmissions. "Should we capture or wipe out?"

M wasn't going to stick around to find out how Lawless would handle the situation. Looking at the wires, she could see that they weren't going to hold her weight much longer, so she swung her body and tugged down with all of her might. The cables snapped loose from the ceiling and M dropped down ten feet until the cables caught again, and snapped again, sending her and several spotlights plummeting toward the floor below. During the fall, M wrapped her hands and legs through the loops of cables, hoping that they would catch one more time before she hit the ground. And they did.

As the spotlights exploded in the front row, M's arms were jerked backward. Her body stopped short, too, but her legs whipped forward and flailed only a few feet from the stage floor. There she hung, in front of the entire student body, like a life-sized puppet on a string.

"Excellent!" cheered Lawless as he applauded over the silence of the auditorium. "What a dangerous but daring and memorable entrance. This is what the Lawless School is all about! Oh, it is going to be a good year indeed."

M lifted her head. She was face-to-face with Fox Lawless. His eyes were wide with excitement. He actually looked impressed with her feat.

Her whole body started to shake uncontrollably. She tried to steady herself in Lawless's gaze, but she realized it wasn't nerves making her tremble. The security guards above her were severing the wires that held her suspended in the air. With one last snap from above, M dropped onto the stage, the cables looping on top of her like strands of dead snakes.

M freed herself from the pile of wires as the student body, in the enveloped darkness of the auditorium, erupted in a mixture of laughter and applause. She felt her whole body flare up with heat. It might have been the embarrassment, but it was more likely the sense of feeling coming back to her arms and legs after traveling through the frigid air-conditioning vents. Then she felt someone taking her hand and guiding her away from the wreckage. It was Lawless.

"What's your name, dear?" he asked.

"M, sir," she answered. "M Freeman."

"Students, may I introduce one of this year's high hopes: M Freeman," announced Lawless, to his roomful of new recruits. M nodded as the group clapped politely.

"Thank you, sir," said M. "I'll take my seat now."

With that, she turned to find Zara waiting for her by the side of the stage, waving M's ID card carelessly in the air.

"Now that's improvising," Zara said, with a smile. "Color me impressed."

M took her ID without a word and walked into the audience

at last. The commencement recommenced, and Merlyn had been right. Lawless talked until he was blue in the face about how great everything was going to be. But M's attention faded. She focused on her ears, still burning, maybe because of the air-conditioning, or maybe because she knew everyone at school was going to be talking about her. No doubt she had just made a few more enemies. So much for lying low.

CHAPTER 8

JUST MISSED

Like all things, the commencement finally came to an end. M slid deep in her seat, hiding as best she could as the other students cleared out of the room. Once they'd left, a cleaning crew of security guards appeared from behind her and started straightening up the mess she'd made. The spotlights and shards of glass were swept up. The cables were wrapped and bundled. M wondered if she should offer to help.

"Get used to it," said Zara, peeking over M's shoulder. "The crew always gets the tough follow-up jobs. Our focus is on making chaos and walking away."

"That doesn't seem fair," said M.

"Who said anything about being fair?" asked Zara. "This is the Lawless School. There is no fair. Now look," she continued, "you can choose to hide in here and pretend that none of this ever happened, or you can come with me to the cafeteria and get some food. Because I know you must be hungry after your high-wire act."

"Can't," said M. "No meal card, remember?"

"If you can sneak into the student center, how hard can it be to get past a few lunch ladies?" asked Zara.

M *was* hungry. Was the last time she ate just after the interview two days ago? She looked at the red marks on her bare arms and suddenly felt the tremor pains of hunger in her stomach. Zara was right. She needed food in her system.

"Okay," M relented. "But is there, like, a private place that I can eat alone?"

"Sure thing," Zara agreed, but M had a feeling that she was heading right back into the throng.

Zara boldly led M into a massive cafeteria within the same building. As they approached the security desk, Zara pulled her through a group of older students who were leaving the room. Using the confusion of bodies as cover, they were able to sneak into the cafeteria unseen and unchecked.

The room was filled with what must have been every teacher and student at Lawless. Keeping her head down to avoid eye contact, M still canvassed the cavernous room. The floor-to-ceiling windows let in every ounce of light possible. The tables were long rectangles of heavy oak, crowded with people craning their necks to sneak glances at M.

"This hardly seems private," said M.

"Oh yeah, sorry about that, I wasn't telling the truth on that one," answered Zara. She dragged M through the rows of tables toward the back of the room, where the food was being served. "You shouldn't feel weird, you know," said Zara.

"About what?" asked M.

"Well, about all the lookee-loos," said Zara. "They're just jealous."

"Jealous? Of me, the dangling idiot?" She laughed. It seemed absurd that anyone would want to switch places with her.

"Oh yeah, totally," Zara said while scooping up some mashed potatoes. "I mean, you're basically like a star on the criminal walk of fame now. You survived a Fulbright ambush, flew a plane, crashed the commencement, and you've got Lawless's attention. If anything, I'd be worried that you may have too many friends begging for your attention after today's fireworks."

"I guess I don't see it that way," M said as she cruised behind Zara with an empty tray. "You didn't really help me fit in, you know, by stealing my ID."

"That one's on you. You made me do that," said Zara.

"I what?" demanded M.

"Yeah," said Zara as she took a bite of an apple. "Bandit named you the mark. That's what you said, right? So it was my duty to lift whatever was left on you."

"No. What? He just made a mistake with my name," said M.

"Um, no, *mark* as in the target of a con," answered Zara. "It's the entry game into the Lawless School. Boy, you sure don't know much about this place."

M put the pieces together. Devon kneeing her in the back. Cal falling on her. Did Merlyn steal something from her, too? Suddenly the familiar weight of her necklace was gone from around her neck. Her hand went straight for her collar, but nothing was there. Someone had stolen the one thing she had left from her father: the moon rock.

"Is the next step to find what's been stolen?" asked M.

"Ha, now there's a good idea!" said Zara. "No, the next step is that after lunch you go back to Bandit's class and everyone returns everything they took. Honor among thieves, you know." She paused while M sat down across from her. The row of students at the table shifted in their seats to give them room. "All right, clueless, let me ask you some questions. How did you know the game that Watts and I were angling in the interview?"

"You had an awkward moment in the back-and-forth of questions," said M, looking down at her food for the first time. An apple, mashed potatoes, and cereal. She didn't even remember grabbing anything while in line.

"No, I got that," said Zara, "but how did you know to notice that sort of thing?"

"One of my teachers," M said absently, picking at her cereal. "Linguistics — like, the study of language and communication. It's important to pick up on conversational quirks like that."

"Important for what kind of job?" asked Zara.

"I don't know," replied M, "like a lawyer, maybe?"

"Or a cop . . . or a criminal," said Zara.

"Anyway," she continued, "I noticed it and used it to my advantage."

"So you were homeschooled?" asked Zara.

"Yes, my whole life," answered M.

"And in all that time, you never had any friends . . . and you never learned about the Lawless School?" asked Zara.

M shook her head and looked around at the room again. The students had stopped staring and gone back to their individual groups. She saw that the students were definitely broken into different collections of kids.

"Are you looking for anyone in particular?" asked Zara.

"Why is everyone separated like this?" M answered with another question.

"Perceptive you are," Zara gave her best Yoda impression. "It's the school cliques. Your first year is all about finding out who you are as a criminal. What are your strengths? What are your weaknesses? We call it foundation. But starting next year, you'll choose a focus for your studies. And the cliques grow pretty naturally from the specializations. So you've got the Crimers, the tech nerds and hackers." She pointed toward a group of kids wordlessly clicking away on various tech gadgets. "Then there are the Gossips, who keep dirt on everyone. The Muscle, who are a lot less subtle. Shadows are the master trackers, whereas Idents can become anyone they want, total masters of disguise. The Cops are sitting on the other side of the Crimers there."

"There's a group of criminals called Cops?" M asked.

"They're counterfeiters. Good to know in case you get into academic trouble. Need a good report card? Look for the Cops. Who am I forgetting? Right, last but not least, there's the Smooth Criminals."

She motioned toward a table full of the most normal-looking, well-adjusted kids M could imagine. They looked like extras from TV commercials — attractive, but not movie-star attractive.

"What are the Smooth Criminals?" asked M.

"They're the first in and the first out of a con," said Zara. "They inspire trust from their victims, usually by pretending to be dumb but likable, but they are always three steps ahead of the mark."

"What group is Devon Zoso with?" asked M.

Zara ignored her question. "So you really didn't know that your parents were, like, big-time thieves?"

"No — I mean, I thought I was a pretty normal, boring kid," said M.

"Oh, you just missed normal by a mile." She laughed. "But you hit boring right on the nose."

"You don't know anything about me or my family," M said, a little too loudly.

Zara gave a quick smile before speaking. "M Freeman, female, only child born to namesake M Freeman and Beatrice Freeman (maiden name Bonart), two parents with a penchant for pilfering fine artwork and various other knickknacks (diamonds, jewels, precious stones), known in the real world as art historians and restorers, but used this cover as an entry into the very world they wished to steal from. M Freeman, graduate of Lawless, meets Beatrice Bonart while on an art heist in Hamburg, Germany, and falls in love. Beatrice is a bottom-feeder sleight-of-hand artist, little more than a street performer, but she performs the greatest feat of her career when she steals M Freeman's heart. M Freeman dies years later in a tragic plane wreck; his person is never retrieved, presumed dead on impact. M Freeman, daughter, lives her life locked behind her parents' front gates. Subject mostly unknown, presumed dreadfully dull and possibly too much of her mother's daughter to hack it at the Lawless School."

"You got the part about my parents' meeting each other all wrong," snapped M. "They met in France while working at the Louvre." M had been told the story of how her parents met so many times. It was probably the most tender story her mother had ever shared with her.

"Is that what you think?" said Zara. "No, they met in Germany."

"According to whom?" demanded M.

"According to whoever keeps all of that information that I had to learn about you and your family for your guardianship," Zara stated casually. Then with a sigh, she continued, "Listen, I don't know, M. It was on a sheet of paper and I memorized it."

It was the first time she had used M's name without any attitude. And also for the first time, Zara sounded like she felt sympathy for M. A total stranger, she still knew more about M's own family, and more about M, than M did herself. Totally abandoned by the reality she once knew, M got up and bused her tray.

"Where are you going?" asked Zara.

"To class. To get back what's mine," answered M, as she made her way through the oversized carved doors with a crowd of other students.

The student center was a garish blemish on the Lawless campus, thought M as she walked the path back to Bandit's classroom. Every other building looked to have been built a long time ago. Brick masonry mixed classically with limestone foundations that made M think of the Ivy League colleges she always assumed she would apply to one day. But Lawless students didn't go to college. This was a terminal degree.

Her mind reeled at the revelations of the day. When M reached the building for her class, she realized that she finally had a moment to herself. She sat down on a bench in front of the entrance, closed her eyes, and tried to remember her life from only a few days ago. Actually, not too much had changed on the surface. Her father was still gone. Her mother was still absent. She still had weird teachers and odd studies. But now the curtain was drawn fully open, the stage was revealed, and the other actors were waiting to play their roles. So what was her role in all of this?

She took a deep breath and stood, walking back into Professor Bandit's auditorium and making her way down to the same seat she sat in earlier. Before she folded down the seat, she saw a piece of paper in the aisle. It was her map. "How come I couldn't find you earlier?" M whispered as she picked it up. She remembered the mysterious shoe from the dark room. Could it have been another student doing their due diligence to make their mark? Why not return the map to her personally, then?

She felt a hand on her shoulder and turned to see Merlyn.

"I'm sorry, M," he said. "I should have warned you about the mark thing."

"So *you* took my map," she said as the seats around them filled with their classmates.

"No, but I did take your meal card," admitted Merlyn. "I did it as soon as Bandit named you the mark. Here you go." He handed the meal card back to her, and she accepted it with a smile.

"It's okay," said M. "Can't blame a shark for biting a surfer."

"Or for biting a bigger shark," said Merlyn.

Before she could respond, Professor Bandit burst through the doors at the back of the room, which closed solidly and locked behind him. As he took his place at the front of the class, he announced, "Your first operation is over. Please return Ms. Freeman's belongings."

Calvin Fence stood up from his seat and clumsily returned M's dorm card. "Don't worry, I didn't go into your room or anything," he said, with an awkward smile.

Devon Zoso stood up next and handed M her library card and her club card. "These are from the Flynn sisters. They lifted the cards when we were talking outside," she explained. Devon spoke to M like a dismissive parent handing a child a toy to play with. "And here's your key back." She held out a single finger, from which M's necklace hung. "I lifted it during roll call."

M snatched the necklace back and shot a furious look at Devon. She clutched the moon rock and was about to sit down when she remembered something.

"Hold on, you stole my necklace *before* Professor Bandit named me the mark," she said.

"Lucky guess," said Devon, as she turned her gaze back to the front of the room.

Professor Bandit regained the class's attention with several loud snaps of his cane against the blackboard, where he had written a new phrase: *Criminals and victims.*

"There are two kinds of people in this world, class," said Professor Bandit. "It is up to you to decide which you will be in life, but rest assured, you will fall into only one of these categories. Remember this, as it is your first lesson at Lawless.

"For your next lesson," he continued, "you need to learn how to hunt. Before you can see the crime, you must be able to see everything *around* the crime. This is known as surveillance."

The lights in the room dimmed as a projector flashed and clicked at the back of the room, casting a photo of Foley in front of the class.

"Here is your next mark," said Professor Bandit. "Freeman, Fence, Eaves, it is your job to track him, observe him, and place this item on his person before the end of the day."

The professor held a delicate, small wire between his fingers. He strode gracefully to Cal and placed it in his hand. Then, with a wicked smile, Professor Bandit snarled, "And as for the rest of you, class, do your best to stop them from completing their mission. Activated and dismissed."

CHAPTER 9

FENCED IN

M, Merlyn, and Cal walked out of the classroom and onto a campus that was filled with chirping birds and prying eyes. Cal and Merlyn craned their necks, looking for the perfect place to discuss the assignment. But M had other ideas. She stopped short and said, "So let's talk strategy."

Cal balked. "Um, like, don't you think we're kind of out in the open here?"

"He's right," agreed Merlyn. "The hounds are loose and they all look starved."

It was true. Every student from their class hovered maliciously a few steps away from the trio. They were targets hunting a target.

"Look, we're at a school full of criminals," said M. "Why bother with a suspicious private conversation? They know what we're talking about and if we hunker down in some hushed corner, I'm sure they'll already have it bugged. We're probably bugged right now."

"Okay, now I think *she's* right," said Merlyn. "So what's your plan?"

"Can you keep tabs on Foley with your computer?" M asked him.

"No way," he said. "That Devon Zoso is a Crimer genius. She'd crack any code I write like it was an Easter egg."

"Well, he's your guardian, right?" asked Cal. "He's got to be around you."

M nodded. "Cal's got a point. Foley is responsible for you. Maybe we can use that to our advantage?"

"How?" asked Merlyn. "Should I pick up the phone and call him? 'Hey, Foley, it's me, Merlyn. Can you come by so I can plant this wire on you for a school project?'"

"I don't know," admitted Cal in a frustrated huff. "It was just an idea. And can somebody please tell these birds to shut up!"

"Birds . . ." M trailed off, listening to the rising cacophony of birds calling from all around her. The heavy forest must be home to hundreds of species, she thought. She began to catalog the birdcalls that stood out. In her free time, she had taken to recognizing birds by their songs. She found it lovely that each species spoke a different way, had its own language to share only with one another. And then it hit her.

"I know how to keep an eye on Foley without him knowing," she announced triumphantly. "Triangulation!"

"Whoa, I don't want to hurt anybody!" said Cal.

"Hurt him? No," continued M. "Triangulation, like the points on a triangle. You guys don't know anything about bird-watching?"

"Bird-watching?" echoed Merlyn. "Why would we know anything about bird-watching?"

"They didn't teach you this stuff in school?" M asked. "Triangulation is a bird-watching trick. You can track birds without disturbing them by setting up a three-person team around the bird's tree. Without a single danger to hone in on, the bird will continue its routine. And if the bird flies away, the team is in position to track it easily."

"We're dead," said Cal, looking completely mystified. "Merlyn, she's talking about birds."

Merlyn ignored him. "The difference between nesting birds and humans like Foley is the ground they cover. Birds tend to stay near the nest most of the time, but humans go wherever they like. How can we accommodate for that?"

M smiled. "Then we move the triangle around him. Plus, we have the element of surprise. Foley doesn't know he's a mark."

"I hate to break up this meeting of the minds," said Foley, as he appeared seemingly out of thin air. "I just needed to tell Merlyn one thing: You're never going to catch me. But I'll give you a sporting chance. My next class is on the east side of campus."

With that, he broke into a run, splitting through a group of first years. Instantly the group of students swarmed shut and blocked M, Merlyn, and Cal from giving chase.

"To the east side," Merlyn said with a grin. The hunt was on.

M burst through the tight pack of students, followed by Merlyn and Cal. With the sun behind them, the trio headed east. It was the only clue they had to go on. Foley's tracks were completely covered, stamped out by a sea of other footprints heading in every direction. But then Cal stopped suddenly by the window of a building and motioned for the group to be quiet. They moved closer to the open window, through a tall hedge that swallowed them up in its branches.

"Mr. Foley, please do join us," came Ms. Watts's voice through the window. "We're so happy you could make it to class today, albeit a little late."

"Sorry, Ms. Watts," answered Foley.

"We've got him," whispered Cal. "Now what?"

"Here's what we do," said M, pulling out her campus map. "We set up our perimeters apart from one another. Merlyn, you stay here under the window and keep an eye on the front door. Cal, you move over there, by the" — M paused to look at the map — "boys' dorm, just beside the entrance. You'll have a clear view of Merlyn, as well as any windows on the far side of the building. I'll go over here, to the forest's edge behind that tree. This will give me a direct sight line to both of you, and I'll also be able to see the windows on this side. We have Foley trapped."

With her fingers, M connected the dots of their hiding locations to create a triangle with Foley's building in the center.

"When he leaves class, we'll move with him, but we need to keep our distance, so he won't see us, and we need to keep the triangle formation," she said.

"That will work for tracking him," said Merlyn, "but how do we plant the wire on him?"

"Yeah, we can't jump him if we're trying to stay out of sight, right?" asked Cal.

"We're not going to jump anyone," said M. "We're going to let him capture himself. Remember how Professor Bandit said that there were only two types of people in this world?"

"Criminals and victims," echoed Cal.

"Well, the two don't have to be mutually exclusive." M smiled. "Ever heard of a sheep in wolf's clothing?"

"Don't you have that backward?" asked Merlyn.

Before M could answer, Devon and the Flynn twins rushed past them on the sidewalk. Devon didn't seem to notice them hiding in the bushes. She led the sisters up the stairs and into the building with determination. M definitely didn't like having Devon hanging around the scene. Was it a coincidence, or was she up to something?

"That was close," whispered M. "Let's get to our vantage points before anyone else shows up uninvited."

M stepped into the forest and, waiting for Foley's class to end, she flashed back to her last night at home. The weather was different here, wherever she was now. The crispness in the autumn air was gone, and in its place was the stuffy pollen scent of spring. Could she actually be in the Southern Hemisphere?

About forty minutes into the stakeout, students began to trickle out of the front door to the building. First one, then two, but then a steady flow of fifty kids, all dressed exactly like Foley, burst out of the doors and ran in every direction. M could see Cal and Merlyn panic, but they both stayed in position. M scanned the crowd. None of the kids truly looked like

Foley, she noticed. Some were too tall, some were too short. Some had short dark hair, some had long blond hair. But not a single kid matched the Foley she remembered from their first night in the limo. They were all decoys.

She pulled out her map again to study the building. Was there another exit? She quickly found a new path with her finger that looked like it led from this building to the library. But when she looked for the path in front of her, it was covered with trees. Confused, she looked back at the map. The pathway didn't just connect the two buildings . . . it connected the entire campus.

"Underground!" yelled M as she ran from the tree line toward the front door. "He's moving underground, let's go!"

The team sped up the stairs and into the building. They turned down the hallway toward Foley's classroom only to find someone waiting for them.

"Ms. Freeman, Mr. Eaves, and Mr. Fence, whatever brings you to this neck of the woods?" asked Ms. Watts. "I believe our class doesn't begin until tomorrow."

As M frantically scanned the hallway past Ms. Watts, she noticed that Cal's mood changed instantly. He was agitated — scared of something. Maybe he'd had an interesting interview with Ms. Watts, too?

"Um, we're looking for Foley, Ms. Watts," said Merlyn. "He promised to show us around after his class."

"Well, I'm afraid he's no longer here," she said. "But you're free to look for yourselves. Enjoy your day and I'll see you in class tomorrow."

Ms. Watts stepped aside and allowed the trio past her without giving them a second look. M examined the empty classroom. Everything looked normal, or at least as normal as a classroom at the Lawless School should look. The walls were lined with bookcases and various pieces of art, all in detailed wooden frames, which actually reminded her of her own house. The smart board was still on, projecting a list of dates next to names that M had never heard of — except for one name: M Freeman. The date next to it was years before M was born, around the time her parents had met each other. M was lost in thought when Cal called out, "Over here!"

He stood next to a desk where a lone notebook sat open, with its pages gently lifting in a light breeze. And written in the notebook was a note: *Nice try — Love, Devon.*

"Where's that breeze coming from?" asked Merlyn.

In one swift movement, Cal jumped toward a large bookcase against the wall closest to the desk. He grabbed the shelf and swung it aside to reveal a secret passageway.

"Wow, you were right, M!" he said.

"How did you know about this?" asked Merlyn.

"It was on my map," said M.

Merlyn was impressed. "Man, I had no idea these existed. Who knew that Zara would give you that much information?"

It's true, thought M. Why would Zara give her the keys to all the secret passageways at Lawless? It didn't matter now, though, because in the distant darkness, M could hear footsteps. Footsteps she hoped belonged to Foley.

"Let's just go get our mark before those fifty kids realize

we didn't follow any of them," she said as they ducked inside the entrance.

The tunnel turned downward into a steep decline after a few steps in, probably leading underneath the foundation of the building, thought M. LED lights ran along the baseline of the passage, giving off a murky glow. The walls were covered in smooth white tile that accented the creepy psych-ward appearance in the poor lighting.

Soon the group hit a speed bump. The passageway split into two tunnels heading in different directions. Everyone stopped and the sound of their own breaths echoed in the silence. M stood between the two tunnels and listened carefully for any sign of Foley. A muffled squeak followed by an audible stumble came from the tunnel to their left.

"We should go this way, right?" whispered Cal, pointing to the right tunnel. "He's trying to throw us off track."

"No," said M, "that sounded like a real fall."

She raced into the increasingly dark tunnel, followed by Cal and Merlyn. As they ran, the floor lights disappeared and blackness worked its way around them. M slid her hands along the cold walls as they moved forward, making sure they weren't missing any sudden turns or new paths. It was so dark that someone could be hiding right beside her and she would never know it. After several long minutes, M finally saw an unexpected flash of light ahead of them that dimmed back into a thin strip almost as quickly as it erupted.

"That's our exit," she whispered.

As they came closer, the sliver of light became the silhouette of a door in the darkness. M reached it first and slowly inched it open. Light flooded the passageway and the trio shut their eyes tight to avoid the blinding brightness.

M craned her head away from the light and looked back into the tunnel. Perhaps it was the light playing tricks on her, but she could swear she saw a shadowy figure back in the direction they'd come from. But once she rubbed her eyes and looked more closely, no one was there. M remembered the mysterious shoes in Professor Bandit's classroom and suddenly had the feeling that she wasn't ever going to be alone at the Lawless School.

"Where are we?" asked Cal.

"Clearly, you've never been in a library," joked Merlyn, as he stood next to rows and rows of books.

Just like everything M had seen at the Lawless School, the room was impressive. It looked like a cathedral out of the sixteenth century, with deep-colored tapestries hanging from the wall and stained-glass windows casting down an unearthly rosy light. The ceiling floated high above them as the walls arched into a ridiculously beautiful dome.

"He definitely came this way," said Merlyn, pointing at a trail of dusty footprints coming out of the secret entrance.

M walked purposefully to the tapestries along the walls and flapped each one, sending a wave of fabric rippling across each piece of art. Clouds of dust floated from behind the heavy portraits and sparkled in the quiet light of the library.

"What do you think this little thing does?" asked Cal, as he pulled out the wire from Professor Bandit.

"We're going to find out, aren't we?" Merlyn smiled. "But something that small can't do too much damage. It's probably just a bug."

"Okay, Foley's not hiding behind the tapestries and he didn't have too big a head start on us, which means he must be in here somewhere," whispered M. "Merlyn, you cover the aisles. Cal, watch the front door. Don't let anyone in or out and remember what I said about the sheep in wolf's clothing. Sometimes it's okay to be afraid. Now give me the wire and let's get credit for this assignment."

Merlyn nodded in approval while Cal held out his hand. M darted between them, running to the back of the room and climbing up the rear bookcase. Once on top of the bookcase, she could see the entire room. Foley had to be hiding in the Dewey decimal maze. And M knew the fastest way to solve a maze was to destroy it. Steadily she began to rock the heavy structure back and forth.

"What are you, crazy?" yelled Cal from the other side of the room.

The bookcase slowly toppled over, knocking into the next bookcase, and soon the rows all fell like massive dominoes. M hopped swiftly from stack to stack, keeping an eye out for Foley or any other sudden movements.

"There!" yelled Merlyn, from a safe vantage point. "He's running toward you, Cal!"

As the bookcases crashed down, Foley made a run for the door. He jumped in front of Cal and yelled, "Cal, let me outta here and I'll get you anything you want."

"Cal!" screamed M. "Don't let him past you. I've got the wire!"

Cal hesitated, with his back arched and looking ready to pounce, but then, suddenly, he stood up and stepped aside from the door. "You are going to owe me big time for this," he said to Foley as he hastily ushered the mark through the exit. "I'll hold them off for a few minutes, but that's all the time I can give you."

Cal stepped back into the room, shut the door, and turned his attention to Merlyn, whose jaw had dropped.

"You let him escape!" cried Merlyn. "I thought you were on our side. Professor Bandit is going to have our heads for this!"

"Relax," said M as she rode the last bookcase down into the front of the room. She landed gracefully. "He can't get too far. Right, Cal?"

A grin flashed across Cal's face. "Yeah, something tells me we've got him right where we want him."

"I'm not sure what just happened, other than a few thousand dollars' worth of damage to this room," said Merlyn, "but I think you guys had a plan all along that you didn't let me in on, right?"

M pushed open the front door to show Merlyn their prize. Foley was frozen solid in a running position.

"No way," Cal said with awe. "I've heard of freeze rays before, but that tiny wire did this? That's so cool!"

"Can you explain this to me?" asked Merlyn. "'Cause I really thought Cal had gone over to the dark side . . . er, well, the darker side, I guess."

"We fooled Foley into capturing himself," said M with a smile. "I never actually took the wire from Cal, but I announced that I had it so that Foley would think the wire was with me. Then we needed Foley to trust Cal, to believe that he was wicked enough to betray our cause and help him escape."

"So Cal only pretended to go bad. He was a sheep in wolf's clothing," realized Merlyn. "You double-agented him! Genius!"

"What can I say," admitted Cal. "I'm a natural. With a simple pat on the back, I planted the wire on Foley and he apparently turned into a Popsicle. But I have one last question for you, M. Are there any rooms that you aren't going to totally destroy today?"

Merlyn and Cal started to laugh, and M let out a smile. Then, as she turned to look at the chaotic mess of books, tables, and shelves laid out across the library floor, she couldn't help but laugh, too. Something had clicked into place during their hunt for Foley. M had begun to feel at home in this strange new world. She felt like she belonged at Lawless — especially having made her first true friends.

Unfortunately, though, when the librarians and security guards arrived on the scene, having friends with her didn't make much of a difference.

"What happened!?" screeched the librarian as her look of intense shock passed back and forth between the immobilized student in the hallway and the rubble of books that covered the floor.

"Excuse me, Ms. Freeman?" a security guard interrupted. "Dr. Lawless would like a word with you. Please come with us."

Friends were great, but when you're called to the principal's office, you must go it alone.

CHAPTER 10
FROZEN OUT

West building seven was beautiful on the outside and down-right creepy on the inside. The well-tended bushes and tree-lined sidewalk façade were inviting enough, but as soon as M entered the front hallway, a feeling of dread overcame her. The walls were bare, stark, and unfinished like a parking garage under construction. Every footstep echoed through the cavernous void until the sounds drifted into a forbidding silence. It was the harsh reality behind a Hollywood set, a space reserved for the crew only, where strangers were not welcome. It was hard to believe that this skeleton of a building housed Fox Lawless's office.

Three floors up, M was led into a room filled with ratty old books covered in dust . . . the kind of dust that took years to accumulate. Historical dust. M shuddered as she surveyed the wall-to-wall shelves, imagining how big the spiders lurking in their filthy nooks must be.

The office was large and small at the same time, disappearing into shadows at every corner. The only light in the room glowed green and sickish atop an oversized desk that could have doubled as a lifeboat.

M took a seat in a large leather chair next to an empty stone hearth. Across from her sat Dr. Fox Lawless Jr. The red-headed headmaster had surrounded himself with antique collectibles at every turn — a standing globe with outdated borders, chairs with handcrafted legs that ended in carved claws gripping the floor, and an ornate chessboard with marble pieces in the middle of an ongoing battle. M's eyes were flitting around the room so fast, she felt like a hummingbird moving from flower to flower for some sign of life. Lawless tracked her eyes and smiled slyly as he gently tapped his fingers on a lone book that sat on his desk. He was obviously enjoying the moment, though M had no idea why.

Don't first years always get in trouble? Isn't that part of being a first year? Especially at the Lawless School, thought M. *Isn't trouble, like, everyone's middle name here?*

More people came into the room behind M. She was not surprised at all when she turned to see the rest of the entourage. Ms. Watts, Zara, and Professor Bandit stood and watched, a solemn audience to the proceedings.

The scent of soot and the sound of Lawless's water-torture-style tapping filled the air around M. It was almost too much to bear. If she was in trouble, she would rather have it out in the open and over with instead of facing this tedious silent treatment.

"Sir," started M, "am I in trouble for hurting Foley? Will he be all right?"

"Mr. Foley is fine," said Lawless.

"Good. I was worried. He looked, I don't know" — M struggled for the best description — "frozen."

"Observant, Ms. Freeman," said Lawless. "The device you planted on Mr. Foley is what we call the deep freeze. A brilliant device, this thin strip of metal simply arrests the muscle control of anyone it's planted on by sending a light but resounding shock through the system. The effects are a paralysis that lasts only for a few hours. Such a wondrous little contraption, isn't it?"

The headmaster shifted his focus from M to the back of the room. He picked up a letter opener and played with it absentmindedly yet menacingly in his hands.

"As to whether you are in trouble, though, well, that depends on you, Ms. Freeman. Over your first couple of days on campus you have crashed one of our planes, wrecked our runway, gutted the air-conditioning system in our student center, and treated our library like your personal playground. You've shown such over-the-top actions resulting in such destruction . . . that if I didn't know any better, I'd swear you were a Fulbright."

M balked at the thought. She wasn't anything like the masked team of monsters that had attacked her the other night.

Lawless could see her defenses rising and quickly added, "But luckily for us all, you are your father's daughter."

He let the sentence dangle before her. M had heard this before from Ms. Watts, but she didn't fully understand what it meant, especially since she was just now learning who her father really was.

"Your father," Lawless continued, as if reading her mind,

"was one of our top students. During his time at the Lawless School, he planned unimaginable thefts. Oh, he was the stuff of criminal legend."

Tenderly, Lawless opened the book on his desk to a marked page and turned it toward M. She stared at a page of pictures from another time and in some of them she saw her father. Well, a much younger version of her father. In one, he stood in front of the same building in which his daughter was currently trapped, surrounded by twelve other students. His long hair hung in his eyes, a contrast to the well-trimmed, receding hairline she remembered. The laugh lines around his mouth had been erased, but his smile was exactly the same — confident, easy, and loving. The headline above the photograph read *The Masters*.

But that wasn't the only thing that caught M's attention. In one of the other photographs she saw someone else familiar — a young and strikingly beautiful Ms. Watts, with her arms around M's father in what was obviously a more than friendly embrace.

"I wish you could have seen him, Ms. Freeman," said Lawless. "He saw in the world not limits, but ways beyond those supposed limits."

"Is this a yearbook?" asked M.

"They all are, my dear." Lawless nodded as he waved his hands around the room. "Dating back as long as this school has been in existence. The people in these pages are the most dangerous minds that have ever walked this earth."

"What does 'the Masters' mean, Dr. Lawless?"

"Oh, your father had many friends here," Lawless said, seemingly dodging the question. "He was even lab partners with Professor Bandit, did you know that?"

Lawless slid his finger across the page and pointed to a small, skinny boy with dark, penetrating eyes. He stood in the rear of the group photo, blending into the background. If Lawless hadn't pointed him out, M would never have guessed that this tiny husk of a boy was Bandit.

"Yes," said Professor Bandit from behind M. "Your father and I disagreed on a great many things, but he was an excellent partner. He was full of ideas, both good and bad. And, you see, even though he's departed, I can never forget your father. He made me what I am today."

The back of M's leather chair squeaked where Bandit braced it, leaned closer, and walked around to face her. M tried to avoid eye contact with him, but his sinewy hand wrapped around her jaw and gently lifted her eyes back up to meet his.

"He did this to my eyes," Bandit whispered with calm assertion.

His right eye was greenish yellow, while his left eye was a deep blue. But as he held her in his gaze, M looked closer. The hues of his eyes shifted like brilliantly vibrant clouds, while his black pupils anchored each iris, calm amid the twisting colors like the literal eye of a beautiful but violent hurricane.

"I'm sorry, sir," M said while mustering her courage against the madman's glare. "But I am not responsible for whatever my father did to you."

"Ah, why apologize?" Professor Bandit laughed. "Do you even know what these eyes can do? It wasn't some horrible accident. No Bunsen burner flaring acid into my face and driving me into a life of crime. After all, I was born into the life of crime just like everybody else here. No, what looks like a genetic mistake was one of your father's most insane inventions. These are skeleton keys. They unlock optimal security systems by confusing iris recognition software. This was what your father and I worked on during our senior year at Lawless. He wanted to develop the formula further, to temper it with glass or plastic to create contacts that could be inserted and removed at will, but where's the fun in that? I pushed him to let me be the lab rat and voila, these are the new windows to my soul."

Bandit's cold stare bore through M.

"But you are right," he said viciously, letting go of her chin. "You are not responsible for what your father did. Which means you deserve no reward for his merits. I would like to see you removed from our campus immediately."

"Don't be too harsh, Len," Ms. Watts scolded. "All M has proven so far is that she has more raw talent than a good deal of our students. She just doesn't know how to control it. And I feel like she has not come to fully embrace her situation yet. But can you blame her? She doesn't know yet what it means to be one of us. She's been left in the dark for her entire life. We can't turn on the bright lights and not expect her to be blinded."

Professor Bandit closed his eyes. "Acting out is tolerable to a point, Ms. Watts. But I believe that Ms. Freeman is a hazard to herself and to others while she's here."

"She's not acting out," snapped Zara, rising from her seat. "Dr. Lawless, if I may, M's not acting out at all. She's risen to every challenge she's been given. Let her stay and we'll teach her the Lawless way."

M couldn't believe what she was hearing. Was Zara really defending her to Lawless and Bandit? And why was Ms. Watts trying to keep her at the Lawless School, when she had already warned her not to come in the first place? The room was silent and still once more, but the mood was heavy.

Lawless leaned back in his chair and nonchalantly spun the standing globe beside him. "Round and round and round she goes," he said to himself, "and where she stops, nobody knows." Then quickly he brought the spinning globe to a halt with one powerful hand and turned his full attention back to M. "Freeman will continue on with her studies at Lawless," he announced. "But, my dear, you *will* learn to be a true Lawless student. That is to say, you must keep your head down and stay out of trouble until you are ready to make trouble without leaving behind such disaster in your wake. I know you were at the commencement when I told you that Lawless students are ghosts. You will learn to be unnoticed and terrifying. You will cease leaving trails of destruction behind you that even the deaf, dumb, and blind could follow right back to our door. If anyone can learn to be a master criminal, it's you. You are your father's daughter, after all. And we should be the ones to teach you."

Ms. Watts and Zara pulled M out of her chair and escorted her from the room, but not before Lawless called out, "Besides, Ms. Freeman, you've been so much fun already. I can hardly wait to see what else you have in store for us."

M felt powerless as she was dragged down the hallway by Ms. Watts and Zara, their hands firmly cinched around her arms. She was like a child stuck between two angry parents.

"I thought you were watching her, Zara," Ms. Watts said crossly.

"I know what I'm doing," Zara snapped back, "but I can't help it if you've assigned me damaged goods. She acts like she has no clue what's going on and then out of nowhere she reacts to these situations faster and more ruthlessly than anyone I've ever seen. She's out of control."

"Then it's your job to *teach* her control," Ms. Watts reprimanded as they exited West building seven. The sun was already behind the mountains, but the day was not ready to let go. The still-bright twilight washed across the campus as students gathered outside.

"You wouldn't let a lion loose in a classroom without a lion tamer," asserted Ms. Watts. "Be the tamer, Zara, or I'll find a new one."

Without looking back, she stormed off into the evening, leaving Zara and M alone. Other students were scattered across the open lawn and while it seemed like none of them was paying attention, M suspected that all of them were chomping at the bit to get the gossip on her.

"Listen, M." Zara sounded calm and collected. "It is painfully obvious that you don't understand a lot about our school, so let me fill you in on the new rules. Rule number one: Don't be you. You are dangerous. Just be like a regular student for a change and see how things go. Whenever you find yourself asking, 'What would M do in this situation?' try doing the opposite."

"But —" M started.

"Ah! Right there," interrupted Zara. "M would be argumentative about this, but a regular student would realize that her guardian was trying to teach her a lesson and she would listen."

M held herself back. In light of everything, she still wasn't ready to leave the Lawless School just yet. As crazy as the whole experience had been, she felt an excitement that she hadn't felt before. True, her old life was cozy, but this new life was dangerously fun. Plus, in the past three days, she had already discovered more about her father than she had in the past six years. And M had a feeling that there were far more mysteries to uncover here.

Zara continued, "Rule number two is always remember rule number one. Just go to class and learn what they are teaching you. You'll have plenty of time to exercise your talents, but let the school hone your skills. Give us a chance. Now nod for yes."

And M nodded without delay.

"Excellent," said Zara. "Now let's go back to our dorm room before these jackals think you're in trouble with the headmaster."

"Aren't I?" asked M.

"Far from it," Zara said. "For whatever reason, you're Lawless's pet project this year."

CHAPTER 11
GARDEN VARIETY DISTRACTION

Tuesday. Tuesdays used to be routine for M. They had always started at 5:30 A.M. M would shower, eat breakfast, and arrive at the library for history and social theory by 7 A.M. After a three-hour study session, M had her morning tea and was allowed to catch up on the daily events. Sure, it was always the daily events that her tutors gave her to focus on, but it felt good to read about real life outside of her own home. The rest of the day followed with geography, linguistics, a late lunch, advanced math, and ended in a haze of homework.

M had no idea what awaited her on her first Tuesday at Lawless.

The birds were singing outside and the sun was faint, which meant the clouds that had rolled in the night before were still present. M had hoped the night sky would give her a hint about the school's location, but she hadn't been able to see a single star.

M closed her eyes again and pulled the blankets closer. On her back, she stared up at the unfinished wooden slats on the underside of the top bunk. It was like being trapped in a coffin. She stretched her arms up and touched the bottom bunk ceiling with uncertainty. Was it a dream? The slight imperfections in the bristling knots told M otherwise, and she let her arms fall back down.

She ran her hands carefully over her knees, shins, elbows, and forearms. They burned with a dull ache after yesterday's chase. The bruises were definitely blooming just beneath her skin. Holding her entire body still, M tried to meditate and settle back into herself.

"Early bird gets the worm, M," Zara said, walking in through the bathroom door. "Or in this case, the hot water. See, the Lawless School is beautiful, picturesque, and distinguished and all, but let's call a spade a spade. This place is old and the plumbing definitely needs an update. If you're not up by six thirty, then there's a cold shower in your future."

M struggled out of her new bed and made her way to the bathroom. The decor was definitely outdated. At the sink, she twisted the hot water handle until it almost came off. As Zara had suggested, the hot water was dead and gone. M splashed her face with cold water and got ready for the challenge awaiting her on this first Tuesday of her new life.

Gym.

Gym was a class that M had never experienced, but from the little she knew about it, it was usually the least popular one in school. She imagined it was what fully separated the geeks from the jocks, a strange realm of broken dreams where being picked last meant everything. And the very fact that anyone had to study math after breaking into a panic-induced sweat brought on by a game of dodgeball just seemed inhumane.

What could they possibly have in store for her at a Lawless gym class? Running a 5K while being chased by police?

Dressed in nylon shorts and a baggy T-shirt, M made her way over to the cafeteria where she met up with Merlyn and Cal, who were already eating and deep in conversation.

"No way," argued Cal. "Diamonds are the world's hardest material."

"They're pretty, but they lost out years ago to wurtzite, boron nitride," Merlyn said as he turned his attention toward M. "What are you wearing?" he asked her.

"What? It's shorts and a T-shirt," said M, suddenly self-conscious. "I've got gym today. Isn't this what people wear to gym?"

"Oh yeah, sure, like I always wear my lab coat and safety goggles to chemistry." Cal laughed. "And then change into my apron for home ec."

M turned bright red as she sat down, eager to change the subject. "How's Foley?" she asked.

"He's fine," answered Merlyn. "He came back last night after I was asleep, but he was up and moving around this morning. I think his ego took the biggest hit. We really caught him by surprise. Lucky thing that you knew about the secret passageway."

"Yeah, lucky," she said.

The truth was that M was beginning to think luck had very little to do with it. Zara hadn't given her the secret passage-ways on the map. M had studied the map again last night. Red lines and blue lines zigzagged across it, running through different buildings without keeping to the designated grid. She would have noticed those lines as soon as Zara had given her the map. But if not her guardian, who had traced out the hidden paths? It had to be the mysterious lurker in Professor Bandit's classroom. They'd had the opportunity. So what was the motive?

But M had to give up this train of thought. She had made herself a promise that she would stick to the Lawless lesson plan. She owed it to her father to at least try to fit in.

"Who's your gym teacher?" Cal asked M.

"Um, Ms. Frank," she said. "You guys know anything about her?"

Merlyn and Cal both stifled a laugh. "Yeah," Merlyn said after he caught himself. "Yeah, Ms. Frank is . . . well, Ms. Frank is . . ."

"Ms. Frank breaks people down for the fun of it," Cal finished. "If you've heard the story of Humpty Dumpty, Ms. Frank forced him up on that wall and convinced him to jump. She's got issues. But the good news is that you'll never find yourself in a worse situation than what she has in store for you. That's how she trains her students."

M wasn't sure if Cal and Merlyn were pulling her leg, but they hadn't lied to her yet. Maybe they were people she could trust?

M finished a large breakfast while they told her the more infamous stories about Ms. Frank. How she stole a set of Houdini's handcuffs and chains from a folk museum and used them on her first years. How she was known for always breaking at least one set of teeth and several bones each year.

Some people claimed that she was physically unable to feel pain, which meant that she couldn't comprehend anyone else's pain. But most important, they told M that she was one of the most insightful teachers at the school, if you survived long enough to learn anything.

Conveniently, the gymnasium was in the student center, mere steps from the cafeteria. But it didn't look anything like M had pictured. There were no basketball hoops, no volleyball nets, no bleachers, and no signs of sports anywhere in the room. Its bright white walls were cold and sterile under harsh, buzzing lights. The open floor where the class had gathered was so hard that it was painful for M to just stand on. M was also pained to see that the other students were dressed in everyday clothes. She stood out like a thrift store victim at fashion week.

"Clothes make the criminal, M," teased Devon, "but what you're wearing should be illegal."

M knew better than to rise to a bully's bait. It was time to take control again, just as she'd done with Zara back at her house upstate. So M gave Devon a big smile and squealed, "Devonator! We've got two classes together now! How totally total!" Her voice echoed and her shoes squeaked in the large room as she ran over and sat down next to Devon, who looked more annoyed than surprised.

"Ruffians!" shouted a small woman, who entered the room and closed the doors behind her. Walking with the grace and power of a cat, Ms. Frank paced around the class as she spoke. "Ruffians. Thugs. Hooligans. You aren't dainty criminal masterminds in my class, you got it? You are muscle, not mental. You are brawn, not brains. You are grunts, not glory. You will learn to jump off buildings without any thought of what's beneath you. You will learn to crash through windows without getting a scrape. You will learn that scars are your only friends and that the best scars come from the people that you thought were your friends.

"Now look around this room. We call it the Box. It's a place of nightmares — I'm not going to sugarcoat it. We don't play in the Box. Playtime was over the minute you kissed Mom and Dad good-bye and stepped onto the plane that brought you to me. The Box is very real and will hurt you if you let it. But if you can make it through the Box, you can make it through anything out there in the wild — Fulbrights, FBI, Interpol, Scotland Yard, CIA, KGB, anything. So let's get at it, ruffians. Who wants to bleed first?"

Ms. Frank was certainly candid about her lessons; M picked up on that immediately. And the old M would never have done what she did next. She raised her hand to volunteer.

But someone else beat her to the punch. Another girl held up her hand at the exact same time.

"Looks like we have a tie," said Ms. Frank. "You'll both get a chance. Juliandra Byrd, you're up first, followed by Freeman."

"Just Jules, thanks," the girl told Ms. Frank, as she walked toward the middle of the gym floor. Jules was thin and fit, with a nest of tightly curled dark hair. She wore a bright pink jumpsuit that radiated against her dark almond skin. Her long legs and gangly arms might have looked awkward when she was standing still, but when she moved, her every movement was measured and precise.

As the girl took position, Ms. Frank silently ushered the rest of the class up a set of stairs that led to a separate, smaller room with a glass window overlooking the main floor. Once everyone was inside, Ms. Frank closed the door and walked over to a computer panel by the window. M figured the room had to be some sort of control booth for the Box.

The class flocked to the window and watched the girl below. Jules looked so small and alone in the cavernous room, but her body language was completely confident.

"Escape the Trans-Siberian Railway," Ms. Frank commanded through a microphone, and she pressed a series of buttons on the control panel. Suddenly, the huge room below began to flicker and change. The walls came alive like giant TV monitors, and instantly Jules was transported to a snow-laden mountainside. Trees, with black branches that sat heavily under several feet of snow, replaced the blank walls, and a set of railroad tracks twisted and turned around the mountains. The floor where Jules stood lifted off the ground, raising her into the air and shaking her violently. The background images on the walls began to move — the Trans-Siberian Railway was storming down the tracks with Jules on its back.

Wind whipped from out of nowhere, blowing Jules's hair in every direction. Watching as the girl's breaths turned to white clouds, M regretted her decision to wear shorts even more than before. But Jules was unfazed. She kept her balance as the rickety train roared down the track. The turns on the sides of the mountains around her disappeared, dropping steeply into bottomless falls of a white abyss, buffered only by trees and frozen snow that whirred past, threatening avalanches if anything disturbed their winter slumber.

Once a straightaway showed up, Jules seized the opportunity and raced ahead, skipping lithely from one train car to the next until she reached the last car. She made her way down from the roof onto the rear platform of the caboose. M watched as the earth under the train rushed by. The ground in the room was moving! And if the ground was designed to mimic a train traveling about thirty-five miles an hour, hopping onto that ground was not going to be easy. Still, Jules slowed her breathing into steady streams of steam and once calm, she leapt into the snow. Her landing was perfect; there was virtually no snow cloud when she touched down and what little there was, she used to her advantage by rolling into it, and the bright pink jumpsuit instantly vanished in the white backdrop. Then skipping like a stone on water, Jules bounced and slid with ease until regaining her footing.

The control room erupted in cheers and clapping.

"Virtually perfect," said Ms. Frank, above the applause. "But where do you go now, Ms. Byrd? The temperature is below freezing, night is on the way, and the only thing harder than leaping off of a train at full speed is trying to climb back on to one. For your next trip in the Box, remember to wait for a sign of life before you leap into the wild. A village, a barn, a lodge of some kind — look for anything made by humans, or else you will find yourself hunting for shelter while the Fulbrights or something worse hunts for you."

And then without missing a beat, Ms. Frank pulled an about-face and announced, "Now it's your turn, Ms. Freeman. But not dressed like that."

Ms. Frank walked over to a closet and pulled out a black jumpsuit, similar to what the Fulbrights had worn.

"Put this on," said Ms. Frank. "We wouldn't want to break those knobby knees on the first run now, would we?"

M pulled on the jumpsuit, which felt way too snug, and walked down the stairs to the center of the room, suddenly very afraid of what she had agreed to do. When she passed Jules, the girl gave M a half smile that M couldn't read. Perhaps it meant "good luck." Perhaps it meant "top that." Perhaps it meant "there's no way you can plan for what comes next." She'd seen how adept Jules had been, perched on the speeding train. And even though M was beginning to think she was pretty smart at this criminal gig, she also knew that she was pretty clumsy. There was a high probability that the only thing that would smart after this test was her body. And her ego.

"Subway at rush hour!" called out Ms. Frank over the loud-speaker, and the room went silent.

The smell was the first thing M noticed, rising around her like piles of trash. Then the room went dark and the floor lifted beneath her. At first she stood, planting her feet to keep her balance as the ground beneath her became a speeding train. Then she realized that the ceiling was closing in on her as well.

Quickly she dropped onto her belly and felt the cold metal bouncing underneath her. Sweeping her fingers across the floor — now the roof — M found tiny ridges to grip and started to crawl toward the front of the train. Lights flickered from all around and the wind howled in patterned intervals as the poles between tracks flew by. M's plan was simple. Hold on for dear life, wait for the next stop, then roll off the roof and onto the platform as if she were just another passenger. Then get lost in the crowd.

But when the headlight from an oncoming train illuminated the tunnel, it outlined a terrifyingly familiar silhouette. Crawling toward M was a team of Fulbrights, moving fast. M flipped around and shuffled toward the back of the train. She could hear the Fulbrights kicking and clawing behind her, but thanks to the wind, she picked up speed and reached the last car in no time. Rolling over, M could see that the Fulbrights were almost on her. Weighing her options, she looked at the tracks beneath her, darting away like teeth ready to shred her to pieces if she leapt down. *Always jump before you look*, her father used to say. She always thought he was teasing her in that Dad way that every father shares with his children, no matter how embarrassing. But now his words seemed like a great idea.

The rattling of the oncoming subway blasted past her and M quickly rolled over the side of her train and pushed with all of her might. Propelling from the first train and between the poles, she slammed onto the roof of the train traveling in the opposite direction. She looked up just in time to see one

Fulbright attempt the same stunt and clock himself on the separation poles. Rushing away to safety, M knew the feeling of victory wouldn't last long. This was the Box, after all.

After what felt like forever, M realized that her new train was not making local stops. She careened through open platforms filled with gawking onlookers, as the air horn on the subway blared its warning in her ears. The train had to stop eventually, she thought, but what would be at the end of the line? Just then the subway hit an incline and M found herself riding up from below the streets of New York and onto a bridge. Scaffolding and traffic whizzed by in every direction. This was her chance to escape. With room to stand, she forced herself up against the wind and pawed for the closest overhead metal beam. When she finally latched onto one, her palms burned and she felt like her fingers had been separated from her hands. The subway slithered unrelentingly below her dangling legs, but M managed to pull herself to safety. She climbed onto the beam and slid carefully above the motorized hum of bumper-to-bumper cars, trucks, and the motorcycles that zipped through the cracks in the traffic. The Box was way too real, she thought.

When she reached the bike path, M dropped down and began walking away from the city. As she walked, she wondered when the test would be over. Jules's test had ended as soon as she landed in the snow. Did the simulation end only when you either succeeded or completely failed? Apparently, she had done neither.

Her knees, elbows, and especially her hands throbbed as

she continued across the bridge. M thought about asking Ms. Frank if the test was done, but New York City still surrounded her. And that's when she heard the airplane.

Sputtering above the water, a single-engine plane lifted even with the bridge. With stacked wings that were attached by poles and a propeller whirring at its nose, the plane looked like it had flown in from another time.

"Why did it have to be a plane?" M asked herself.

New York City and the bridge started to flash as if M were watching an image on a television screen freeze, then cut in and out. One second, the Empire State Building glowed against the dark sky, the next, everything disappeared except for M and the plane now beneath her. Free-falling, M braced for impact on the bottom of the Box, but crashed on the top wing of the plane darting through the clouds.

"Hold on!" came a voice from the darkness, and suddenly another student had jumped onto the opposite wing. It was Jules. Quickly, she shimmied across the wingspan, holding out her hand to reach M.

No sooner had M clasped Jules's hand than the plane turned into a death roll, flipping M and Jules upside down and tossing them into the air. Both students smashed against the wall of the Box, which cradled them as they slid down to the floor, and the lights finally came back on.

"Alive is good," said Ms. Frank through the speaker. Devon's laughter echoed through the room as she stood at the control panel above and waved excitedly to the crumpled pile of people that was M and Jules.

"But next time," Ms. Frank continued, "let's aim to stay on the plane until you either land or seize control from the pilot. And, Ms. Byrd, keep to your own missions from here on out."

M and Jules untangled themselves and checked to make sure everything on their bodies was still in place.

"I'm Jules," said Jules.

"I know," said M, gathering her breath. "I'm M."

"I know," said Jules. "The whole school knows who you are. You're better in tight places than wing walking, eh?"

"Airplanes and I don't always agree," M said.

"That's the story going around," replied Jules, "but I thought you handled your event about as good as anyone could have." She helped M to her feet. "Is it true you didn't know about this place, like your parents didn't tell you anything?"

"Yeah, I guess," M answered shyly. She still had a hard time talking about her parents under the circumstances. "Your parents, what's their story? They must be, like, master overlords of high-flying evil."

"Something like that," said Jules. "We come from carnival circles. Trapeze artists, high-wire walkers, contortionists, knife throwers, that kind of stuff. Anything that can be performed without a net, the Byrds are the first to try it."

"Keeping up the tradition in the Box, too, eh?" noted M.

She smiled. "Maybe we'll get to team up again sometime."

"Right, but next time, let's make it closer to the ground," said M as they walked upstairs and rejoined the class.

That night, when M and Zara were back in their room, M

told Zara about her day, with a special focus on Devon and her insane desire to sabotage everything M did.

To her surprise, Zara came to Devon's defense. "Don't blame her for taking the controls. Ms. Frank always does that on the first day. It's a tradition."

"So I should trust Devon, then?" asked M.

"Whoa, no way," said Zara. "I said don't *blame* her. But you shouldn't trust her, either. She's got it in for you. Besides, you shouldn't really trust anybody here. They're all thieves and liars, right?"

"Does that include you?" asked M. She couldn't help thinking back to the message in the envelope.

"Maybe," said Zara without taking a moment to consider the question. "I could be a long grift waiting for the right time to spring a trap on you." Then pausing, she added, "Besides, I'm still deciding whether or not to trust *you*."

To avoid any awkward silences, M charged on. "What was your first experience in the Box?" she asked.

Zara flipped over in her bed and hung her head over the edge so that her hair fell around her upside-down face. "Eiffel Tower elevator in the rain. It was not romantic, and to this day I hate the lights of Paris."

M laughed, wondering if this was the sort of conversation that would pass for normal in the months and years ahead.

The two girls carried on like this late into the night, swapping stories as the moon rose above them and moved through the stars like clockwork. It felt good. It felt as if they were almost becoming friends. Almost.

CHAPTER 12
BLIND SPOT

In the weeks that followed, the fallout from the Box affected M more than she could have imagined. She began to notice every door around her, every window, every potential hiding place or dark corner where she could dash to in an emergency. But the emergency never came. Her lessons even reached beyond the real world and into her dreams. M began "sleep escaping" — which was like sleepwalking, except she was trying to break out of intricate mazes and undefined rooms that she dreamed up every night. She became accustomed to waking up in the oddest places around her room. Curled up in the window frame, tucked under the desk; if there was a tight space in the dorm room, M had found it and hid there until her roommate ushered her back into bed. Zara promised that this happened to every first-year student in Ms. Frank's class, which M was at least able to confirm with Jules.

"I woke up on top of my bookcase last night," confessed Jules. "And it was so much more comfortable than my bed! I think something is definitely wrong with me."

The best outcome of M's gymnastic sky ride was that it had brought her and Jules together. If there was one thing

M had learned in her short time in this new world, it was that a true friend was hard to find at Lawless, but M had easily fallen in with Jules. The two of them, along with Merlyn and Cal, were like their own clique in a sea of far weirder and probably more diabolical cliques at school. Most first years seemed to keep their distance from one another and focus on their studies. But a few first years tried desperately to get to know the different subsets of second years better. Those kids followed older students around like prepledges, doing random acts of menial favors for each clique . . . with predictably bad results. An Ident might need a glass of water, but only from the fifth-floor bathroom in the boys' dormitory. Or a Smooth Criminal might need an alibi, so could he use your name? Okay, that's great, until you become the fall guy and get called into Lawless's office for an infringement you didn't commit. M decided to stay away from that mess and stick with her smaller, tamer crew. *Steer clear of weird*, as her mother would say. Not that M had much time to wonder what her mother might be doing — or stealing — now. M's old, quiet, lonely life was a thing of the past.

"I heard Derrick Hollows gave up his Social Security number to the Cops," said Cal.

"Is that true?" asked Jules.

"Oh yeah, it's true." Merlyn laughed. "Everyone in my dorm was just issued one of these!" He held up a cafeteria ID with his picture on it, but filled with all of Derrick's personal information. "Dinner is on me, Derrick Hollows, today."

M was barely paying attention to her friends. She was too busy reading up on the history of thievery in the UK.

"Did you guys know that thieves used to work with the servants in mansions to coordinate break-ins?" she said, shaking her head in disbelief.

"Um, it's called an inside man. Everybody knows that," said Cal. "That trick's been used since the dawn of time."

"Take it easy, Cal," said Merlyn. "She didn't come from the most forthcoming family."

Zara had been right about M and the Lawless School. She had a lot of things to learn, things that the other students apparently grew up with, hearing stories of great thieves before their parents tucked them into bed. But what M lacked in basic knowledge, she more than made up for in her drive to study and master her lessons.

In fact, the workload of Lawless classes had taken over her life and let loose a wash of days and weeks. One day it was September and the next day November was around the corner. But who had time to notice?

Classes demanded all of M's waking time and attention. Seven days a week, loads of homework and exercises and readings from books that she had never heard of all contributed to her sense that time was flying by.

So far, M didn't have a favorite class. She loved almost all of them. That could have been because she was actually good at them, which didn't surprise anyone more than it surprised M herself.

While Professor Bandit still gave her the evil eye every day, M found his class fascinating. They studied lock picking, cracking into vaults, spying, tracking, how to outsmart lie detectors, and how to detect lies, too. And Bandit, for all of his eccentricities, had introduced M to a mantra that she completely agreed with: "No weapons."

"A Lawless criminal needs only one weapon and it is the greatest weapon in the world: the mind," Bandit would say, tapping his finger against his head. "If you fall back on using any other weapon, you're not a criminal, you're a thug. And there's no room for thugs in our secret underground."

The "no weapons" mantra carried through the rest of M's classes, too. In gym, Ms. Frank never gave the students any weapons when they were in the Box. "You've only got what you've got, now make it work," Ms. Frank would say, before the lights shut down and a student was thrown into whatever bizarre situation awaited.

M's other classes were intense, but covered ground she had already been introduced to while in homeschool. Geography, math, science, they were easy to handle.

But some classes were not at all what she expected. Like drama class. M thought Zara had added it to her schedule as a joke at first, but Mr. Vodun was no laughing matter.

Standing well over six feet, he'd boomed out his opening speech like it was a Shakespearean monologue. "The best actors are prepared to play any part in any scene. None of you are true actors yet, but your journey starts today. Join me and learn to wear a disguise without ever wearing a disguise. Be a chameleon, a stranger on the street one minute, a doctor in need the next. Join me and I'll teach you to be invisible."

Then, wandering through the room, Mr. Vodun had sat in an empty desk next to Cal, who was furiously scribbling away in his notebook. Letting his strong shoulders slump, Vodun turned to Cal and said in an unaffected voice, "Dude's weird."

Cal didn't look up from his notebook. "Dude's cool. Show some respect," he responded, clearly assuming he was talking to a fellow student.

M's hardest class without a doubt had the most ridiculous name: Computer Wizardry. Taught by a kid named Code, who looked young enough to be a Lawless student himself, this class had Merlyn written all over it. A Crimer's delight, the class was meant to cover basic computer hacking . . . only Code's idea of "basic" differed from the majority of his inexperienced students'. Programming codes like Perl and Lisp might as well have been another language to M, and that was only the tip of the nerd-berg. Merlyn loved the class, though, and M loved having him in class for all the help she needed with her homework.

"It's like a puzzle, you know," Merlyn had explained. "If you keep it fun and look for patterns, you'll pick it up. And if you don't, I know you'll always need me in your crew. It's a win-win situation."

Her most stressful class was a tie between storytelling and art history, although for very different reasons. Storytelling was taught by Dr. Gerhardt, an ancient man. He was frail, thin, and wheezed between every syllable he said, but could he ever tell a story. From the first bell to the final bell, Dr. Gerhardt had his students hypnotized and hanging on his every word.

It was his story on the first day of class that captured everyone's attention, including M's.

"The best part of being old," Dr. Gerhardt had begun, "is that you've had the opportunity to collect a great deal of stories. Stories built on the backs of great or interesting people who pass through your life. Looking out on this classroom today, I know I'm building new stories and I'm reminded of a few old ones as well. Oh, some call it fate, some call it life, some call it like they see it, but no one saw this coming. Two little lovebirds grew up together, living a Lawless life. The boy was brilliant, the girl was gifted, and their parents dreamed what every parent secretly dreams: that one day their children would take over the world.

"They started with small wrongs. Child's play, really — palming a pack of gum, sneaking into theaters to watch movies all day for free. It was innocent rebellion, all part of a childhood filled with skinned knees and sugary sweets.

"Soon they graduated to bigger crimes. Lookouts for their parents, the occasional pickpocket, a first bit part in a larger grift. They were both tapped to play the role of a lifetime — tourists in a museum who were separated from their group. Both children cried and cried and raised a ruckus so distraught that almost every single person in the museum came running to their side. Say what you will about the world, but the world reacts to children's tears. And while the staff and visitors calmed the bawling children, their parents made off with millions in fine art lifted right off the wall of the adjoining room.

"The years led this pair to the same desks you sit in now, class. He sat right here, she sat right there, and I sat at the head of the class, probably telling them a similar story to this one. They excelled in storytelling. Stories were second nature to them. What fictions they wove, intricate webs of lies with just enough truth to keep you guessing, to keep you believing what they were saying. In truth the stories were so good that you *wanted* them to be true.

"They excelled in the rest of school, too. The powerful duo ruled their years here with a charm and velvet glove that paved a path for the sharpest minds of our little private party here at Lawless. Pulling together members from every shadowy arm of the school, these two created a group called the Masters. The first of its kind, and a group that has continued to exist ever since — a blending of all the skills and factions of the criminal underworld for one single purpose: chaos.

"And now here we sit, in the same room from where great minds sprung. A show of hands, class, who here has always wanted to join the Masters?"

M turned to see the entire class raise its hands. When she faced forward again, Dr. Gerhardt had his hand up, too.

"I'll admit it." He had laughed, followed by another deep wheeze. "I would have loved to have joined the Masters, too. They do seem to have a great deal of fun. But I digress. . . ."

His voice had trailed off and Dr. Gerhardt had fixed his eyes in a dark upper corner of the classroom. M could not see what he was looking at, or whom, but she had imagined he was seeing old ghosts flicker before his eyes.

M remembered her father's yearbook photo with the Masters group. Did Dr. Gerhardt count her father among his past ghosts, too?

"The moral of my rambling story," he had continued, "is that even the good stories can fall apart. Once our two villainous heroes graduated, they split up. No one knew why, but it didn't matter. They each went on to achieve unparalleled triumphs — robberies, thefts, heists — some of which you will no doubt cover in Professor Bandit's class. They found other loves, started families of their own, and here we are today, together in this room."

The class was dead silent during Gerhardt's dramatic lull. Pens and pencils stopped scratching down notes and the tapping of computer keys had ceased.

"And names, well, what's in a name, as Shakespeare asked. They aren't important to our story as a whole, but they certainly will mean something to a few students in our class. You'll know who you are in a moment."

M had suddenly felt the room closing in on her. It was as if a hand were hovering over her, about to latch on to her and pull her unsuspectingly backward.

"The boy, you see, was named M Freeman," exhaled Dr. Gerhardt. "And the girl was named Lady Watts, although some of you may know her today as Ms. Watts."

There it was. A crushing weight came down on M's shoulders and forced the air out of her. M had had her suspicions about Ms. Watts. And her father may be a lynchpin of Lawless history, but it was still hard to keep hearing his secrets come from strangers, especially when so huge a secret was publicly announced in front of her peers — her friends and her enemies both. M felt invaded. She sank deeper into her desk.

"But the hope is that the good stories," Gerhardt had gone on, "even in their darkest hours, can tell us, the listeners, something we didn't know about ourselves. Even if the stories are utterly fabricated for effect. This is the course of storytelling. Any criminal worth his weight in wanted posters can spin a good yarn, but a Lawless student weaves a tapestry and calls it a work of art."

It was Gerhardt's story that brought a whole new level of weirdness to M's art history class, taught by none other than Ms. Lady Watts. Her lectures were dry and her views on art history barely expanded beyond the pages of beginners' textbooks. M knew more about Da Vinci's work than Ms. Watts touched on in a weeklong lecture on the great master. She bypassed his mad inventions in favor of the simple study of his brushwork, the names and dates of his most popular works, and ways to tell a fake Da Vinci from the real deal. It was clearly a class meant for students who did not need to know much about art, but it felt like kindergarten to M. She knew the lessons backward and forward. Her father had taught her all of this, starting when she was three years old. M remembered when he had taken her to see Van Gogh's *The Starry Night* at the Museum of Modern Art in New York City. She had studied it all day long, the starry bursts unlacing in the sky, the sad cypress trees moping in the midst of a canvas brimming with life. Ms. Watts's take on Van Gogh was that he cut his ear off.

Beyond the arid approach of Ms. Watts's teaching, the now well-known fact that she and her father had been diabolical sweethearts made being in the same room with her uncomfortable for M.

"Um, hello? Earth to M," said Cal, bringing her back to the cafeteria, where she had been sitting in a daze. "What's with the weird face?"

"That's her 'deep in thought' face." Merlyn laughed, mimicking her empty gaze. "She gets that way when she's wrestling with one of Code's codes."

"Sorry, guys," M apologized. "Not sure where I went there."

The workload had been adding up, but it was a blessing in disguise. It helped M stay on track at this crazy school. She had kept her head low, her nose stuck in the books, and her focus on her small circle of friends.

But M couldn't help noting that the cafeteria was buzzing today, and it wasn't just about Derrick Hollows's run-in with the Cops. Dr. Lawless had made an announcement. There was going to be a school-wide test, but none of the first years had any idea when or where or what would happen, and the older students weren't sharing any information. They only said to be prepared for something called the Class Clash.

The clock in the cafeteria read 7:30 P.M. M threw her books in her backpack and stood up.

"Going somewhere?" asked Jules.

"I've got some extra credit to work on for Professor Bandit," she said. "I'm heading to the library to read more about large-scale safes and their triggers."

"Sounds heavy," teased Jules.

As she left the cafeteria, M felt like she was being watched, but since she probably was, she shrugged it off. Outside, the sky was still light and the weather was unseasonably warm and only getting warmer. By this point, she knew that wherever the Lawless School was located, it had to be in the Southern Hemisphere. She had left fall behind at home, and she was facing the end of spring here, heading into what should be a blazing summer.

The paths of campus were empty and quiet. Usually they were crammed with students meeting up after class, lying on the grass, showing off their newly acquired skills, from wirelessly hacking into power grids to swallowing and regurgitating handcuff keys. They made crime look downright nerdy sometimes. But tonight the lawns were clear and a slight breeze washing through the trees was the only immediate sound.

The howl and rustle of the wind sent a shiver up M's neck. *Alone* was something she was not used to at school. She shifted into a hyperawareness, as if she were training in the Box. She picked through the surrounding shadows as she walked until she landed on one that was all wrong. One that was moving with her, step for step, toward the library.

M broke into a run and stole up the stairs of Ms. Watts's building and into her art history classroom. If she was going to be alone, she should be alone in as small a place as possible. The false bookcase swung aside easily as M climbed into the same secret passageway she had followed Foley through earlier in the year. She had kept exploring these underground tunnels, and after running through them so often, she had memorized every path and could travel in total darkness now.

M held her breath and hoped she was wrong about being followed, but then she heard a *click* and the slow dragging sound of the bookcase scratching against the secret passageway floor. She wasn't alone.

As footsteps slid along the hallway, M stood strong, at ease in the darkness that hid her. She gathered from the slow, shuffling echoes with every step that her tail must be another student, probably a boy — only a boy would have such clunky footsteps. It definitely wasn't the same person from her first day at school, a mystery she hadn't forgotten about, but one she hadn't had time to worry about, either.

When the mysterious shape stood beside her, M hit the lights. The small room burst into light, illuminated by a single lightbulb that hung exposed from the ceiling.

"Ack!" hollered Cal as he cringed against the wall and tucked his head into the crook of his arm, like a vampire hiding from the sun. "Geez, there are lights down here?"

"Cal!" M's scream echoed off the passageway walls. "Dude, you scared me to death!"

"Sorry, sorry," pleaded Cal, "I just needed to talk to you and I couldn't do it back at the cafeteria."

"And you thought it would be good to meet me here?" she asked.

"No, I thought it would be good to meet you at the library," he answered, squinting and regaining his bearings. "But then you ran in here, so I followed you. I don't know, I thought you might be in trouble or something."

"I thought I might be, too," said M. "False alarm. What do you need to tell me?"

Cal handed her a black envelope with her name written on it in white ink. "First, this is for you. You've been selected as a captain for the Class Clash and I'm your partner."

M took the envelope and asked, "Why are *you* giving this to me?"

"We've got a, um" — Cal searched for the right word — "a friend in common and I wanted to tell you before you found out."

She did not like where this was going. "What would I *find out*?"

"Well," he started, "to shine more light on the situation, and there's no good way to say this, so please remember that before you freak out or whatever..." His voice faded away. "Look. My dad... his last name is Fence. My mom, though, her last name is Watts... as in, Ms. Watts."

M was stunned. For the first time she noticed the resemblance. How could she have missed it until now? The piercing green eyes, the flat-line lips, the blond hair. It was almost as if Ms. Watts were in the tunnel with them.

"It's a long story," Cal continued, "but if we're going to win the Class Clash, we can't have any secrets between us."

"I already assumed that we didn't. And not because of some contest," she said. She felt the anger building inside her. She needed to make an exit and fast. She clicked the lights back off and darkness swallowed them again. "Did she send you to watch over me?"

"It sounds bad, but it's not like that, M," he pleaded in the darkness. "I had no idea who you were when we met, I swear!"

But M didn't stay around to listen to any excuses. Instead she silently retreated down the mysterious passageway. Cal's voice slipped into a distant echo as she headed back to her dorm with another envelope and another hard truth to face.

CHAPTER 13
CLASS CLASH

Two things had just been handed to M and she wasn't sure if she wanted either of them. The black envelope sat on her dorm room desk. M stared at it from her bed. She needed distance from everything for a minute. Distance from her father's romantic and scholastic past. Distance from her professors, her lessons, her friends, and even from herself, or at least the current role of M Freeman that this school was writing for her. Distance from the new, strange Cal who came bearing a flat black cloud with a wicked scent of something unknown and dangerous.

M was considering all of her options when Zara walked into the room.

"Whoa," she said upon seeing the envelope. "Did you do something awful to someone in a former life, M? You're a Class Clash captain."

"So I've been told," replied M, "by the first honorary member of my crew, Calvin Fence Watts."

Zara winced and made a short sucking sound of air through her teeth. "Ouch, that's a stinger. I wasn't supposed to say anything to you, but Cal is, like, persona non grata."

"You knew and you didn't tell me?" asked M. "Why not?"

"M, I don't tell you how to run your life," said Zara. "Well, maybe I do a little bit, but rest assured there's a long list of things I don't tell you. Cal was one of them."

"At least tell me why he's *persona non grata*, then," demanded M. "I mean, he's Ms. Watts's son, so it seems like he'd be a shoo-in here."

"No, he's got *ronin* written all over him," Zara said casually, as she walked over to M's desk and picked up the envelope. "Rumor is that his dad was a Fulbright. Very scandalous. And Ms. Watts never mentioned having a son. Nobody even knew he existed until last year, when he just showed up to another student's interview."

"Crazy" was all M could say. Say what you want about coming from a family of criminals, but at least she came from a sort of happy and functional home. She couldn't imagine what life would be like with parents who were split between Lawless and the Fulbrights, good and evil, and forced you to choose between the two. But besides the rumors of Cal's home life, there was another word that had caught M's attention. "Zara, what's a *ronin*?"

"What's a *ronin*?" echoed Zara. "What have they been teaching you over the past few months? *Ronin* is what we call the kids that can't cut it at Lawless."

"You mean people can flunk here?" M was surprised. It hardly seemed like anyone would be allowed to attend Lawless and then move on to a normal life.

"Not a lot, but a few do fail," answered Zara. "They're, like, doomed to roam the earth masterless, or some other dramatic samurai term. All ronin are on a watch list. Lawless keeps tabs on them at all times. It's a lockdown life, not something I would wish on anyone. Not that you should be worried about flunking out if someone has bestowed you with this little envelope."

M shifted upright in the bed. The cold wood floor felt nice on her feet. Outside the moon was beaming almost as bright as the sun and the night brought with it some cool relief from the day's hot weather.

"What does it say inside?" she asked.

"Oh, it could say a million things," Zara mused. "I was on a crew last year. We had to steal a priceless canary. You would think that a canary would be an easy target, but it wasn't caged. It fluttered around campus for hours, chirping and singing in the night. To this day, I hate canaries. But I did learn that there's no such thing as an easy target."

M pressed past Zara's flashback. "Why is it called the Class Clash?"

"That's the wild part, M." Zara smiled. "This is the Lawless version of a school dance. Everyone is invited and everyone is given a different task. Several captains are chosen, and they must put together a team to pull off the task. You'll have a week to case the campus, dream up the plan, and carry out the orders."

"So next Friday will be busy is what you're saying," said M.

"Next Friday will probably be the craziest day you've ever experienced in your life," said Zara, still lost in the black envelope. "I haven't even gotten to the best part yet. Each task is assigned to two different captains."

"So I'm automatically competing with another team to score the prize in the envelope," M said. Just when she thought that this school couldn't top itself, it went and proved her wrong.

"Listen, M, open the letter now and think about who else you want on your crew. The rest will come to you, I promise." Zara zipped the envelope through the air to M, who caught it so gracefully that she surprised herself. "See? The less you think, the more intuitive it becomes."

M tore open the envelope and slid out a heavy piece of paper with a single command written on it.

Steal the School of Seven Bells.

She looked up to Zara, confused, but before she could ask anything, Zara chimed in, "Remember, don't tell me anything unless you want me on your crew. And just in case you were considering me for your crew, don't bother. I'm already spoken for."

Without Zara's help, what else could M do? She read the letter once more and then shredded it quickly into tiny, illegible pieces.

Zara smiled. "Smart girl," she said.

In Professor Bandit's class the next day, Cal sat in his assigned seat a few rows behind M and Merlyn. M hadn't figured out how to deal with Cal's big reveal, but she knew that Merlyn needed to come along for the ride.

"Wow." Merlyn blushed. "My first Clash Class. I've got to be honest here, M, I didn't really think I'd be asked to join a crew for this."

"I didn't think I'd be asked to pick a crew, so I know the feeling," said M.

"So what's the mission?" he asked.

"I'm still figuring that part out, but in the meantime I have to talk to you about Cal," said M, but their conversation was interrupted by Bandit, clearing his throat to indicate the start of class. The students all shifted in their seats.

"Over the years, the lessons at this school have changed dramatically as the field and extent of technology has shifted," the professor began. "In a world where it seems that everything is protected by computers, this school has adapted to teach modern crime. But there is always room for human error. And some classics never go out of style."

Then the professor opened the door behind the front podium and rolled in a mannequin wearing a tattered evening jacket. The twinkling of chimes echoed softly through the auditorium.

"This," announced Professor Bandit, "is the School of Seven Bells. It is a symbol of our school. If we had a mascot, it would creep around wearing this."

He leaned toward the shabby jacket and gently tapped seven different places. Each tap set off a tiny chime.

Ting. Ting. Ting. Ting. Ting. Ting. Ting.

"You see, there are seven bells placed in the prime locations where a person carries their valuables. Today it's your turn to take a crack at stealing from each of these pockets without setting off the warning bells."

The entire time Bandit was talking, the tiny bells did not stop ringing. The slightest whisper, the lightest footstep set them off.

"That seems impossible," Merlyn murmured to himself.

"That's our target." M sighed.

"Of course, what fun would a simple jacket of jingle bells be nowadays?" questioned Professor Bandit as he pulled out a remote. He pressed a button and let loose a rare smile. "That's why I've electrified the jacket. Now, when you hear a bell ring, someone will have *their* bell rung."

It was like trying to silence a wind chime in a hurricane. By the end of class, the first years were all scorched thumbs. M had failed miserably, but was at least able to walk up to the jacket unannounced — it wasn't until she tried to steal a notebook from the inside pocket that she was stung with a vicious zap. Poor Merlyn set off the bells from five feet away, and by the time he finally finished his drill, his fingertips were black and his hair stood straight up. And if M had hoped that Cal would be any better, well, no luck there. Cal's shirt actually caught on fire during his first effort.

There was only one student who aced the test: Devon Zoso. Like a wizard who stopped time and froze the bells in place, Devon riffled through each pocket, pulling out wallets, watches, handkerchiefs, notes, and other various hidden goodies. It was frightening how effortless it seemed for her. When she finished,

Devon went directly back to her seat without even looking at Professor Bandit.

If Bandit was impressed with her, he didn't show it. *And why should he be?* thought M. Devon had probably learned everything last year in the same class.

"Now that you've danced with the School of Seven Bells, I want you to master this challenge by the end of the year, or else you will not advance past this class," promised Professor Bandit.

A collective groan rose from the classroom, prompting a second wicked smile from the professor.

"How are we going to steal that?" Merlyn asked M as he ran his hands under the water fountain in the hallway after class.

"We'll need some more help," said M coolly.

Jules was game. M would need her to be the stealthy acrobat of the crew. If the jacket was kept in the back room of the auditorium, they would have to break into the building. Merlyn could keep tabs on Professor Bandit. And Cal, well, he was on her team no matter what, but M was still unsure what to make of him. Ever since his confession, she couldn't help thinking of him in a new light. People tended to notice his lame jokes and goofy manner, but he turned out to be a whip-smart kid who really knew his way around Lawless. The falsely clumsy move he'd made to lift her dorm card on the first day, the fact that he'd stumbled immediately upon Foley's class when they were tracking him, and the speed with which he had found and opened the bookcase entrance to the secret passageway — it all added up to something. M knew that Cal was a lot more competent than he let on. But why he'd disguise that, she had no idea.

Her concerns about Cal aside, their crew was set. Almost.

"Would it be crazy to bring Devon into this?" Merlyn asked everyone at lunch.

"I think those shocks are getting to you!" M quipped. "Did they melt the part of your brain that makes good decisions?"

"Well, she's mastered the jacket," Merlyn explained. "She might know something important that we aren't considering."

"No way," said Cal. "Don't trust Devon."

"Why not?" asked Jules. "What do you know?"

"All the other students here," Cal started, "they make sense. But Devon doesn't."

M was more than ready to take Cal's advice on this one. "Devon's out. I don't trust her, either. We've got our crew."

The week flew by. Dr. Gerhardt kept on with his hypnotic stories, Code's computer lectures became increasingly cryptic, but M's mind was in another classroom, locked away with the School of Seven Bells. It wasn't until Friday, the day of the Class Clash, that Ms. Watts's unusually in-depth lecture on Rembrandt broke M's concentration. Rembrandt was one of M's father's favorite artists.

"Believe it or not," Ms. Watts said to her art history class, "Rembrandt had a close relationship with the criminal under-world. He painted them, actually. Well, he painted criminals once they were deceased."

The lights in the room dimmed and a painting flashed up onto the screen. It was deeply shaded and crowded with eight men dressed like Pilgrims, in black uniforms with white, frilled collars, leaning over an unclothed man, whose arm was being cut open with his veins, muscles, and bones bared.

"The Anatomy Lesson of Dr. Nicolaes Tulp," said Ms. Watts. "It's one of Rembrandt's most well-known works. Dr. Tulp is the gentleman holding the scalpel. The other men are doctors viewing the autopsy. But the star of the painting is the corpse. Aris Kindt was his name, and he was a wanted criminal in the early 1630s for several robberies. As you can see, though, he didn't make it. Still, here he is, captured timelessly and mysteriously in this touchstone sample of Rembrandt's artistic gift. Note the shadows around Aris's face. That detail has been called the *umbra mortis* . . . otherwise known as the shadow of death."

Ms. Watts clicked through several other paintings, each one undeniably Rembrandt in their attention to detail, their shaded darkness, and their realistic, mundane scenes. But that was Rembrandt's strength, M's father always said. Finding the hidden beauty in everyday life and showing its true face to the world.

Finally she landed on a portrait of an odd-looking man with a pin-sized head. His scraggly hair flowed into a mullet and his wispy mustache looked almost like dirt on his face. Whoever he was, he was no Mona Lisa.

"And perhaps it's because of his relationship with criminals that Rembrandt's art has been irresistible to thieves," continued Ms. Watts. "Especially this portrait. Called *Jacob de Gheyn III*, it's more commonly referred to as the Takeaway Rembrandt. I'd like for you all to read up on this painting's history and be prepared to discuss it next week."

The lights flickered back to life and M snapped out of her spell. Rembrandt would have to wait. Tonight, M was going to steal the School of Seven Bells.

She met Jules, Merlyn, and Cal outside of her class.

"What's it look like out there?" she asked.

"We cased the auditorium," answered Jules. "There's no sign of crew B."

"I don't like that," confessed M. "If we haven't seen them, it might mean that they've seen us. When is the Class Clash supposed to start, anyway?"

With a thunderous *boom* behind them, a smoke bomb exploded, spewing a sooty cloud from the art history building that engulfed M and her team. Class Clash was here and it was crazy. Heading over to the auditorium, M ran through a maze of student madness. Zip lines zizzed overhead as masked thieves passed back and forth from building to building. Miniature unmanned drones flew through the air to distant locations, some with extended claws carrying various prizes, like class trophies or priceless volumes of books from the library, and one even flew by dragging Dr. Gerhardt's teacher podium along the ground. When M looked up at the rooftops, she could see them lined with shadows holding remote controls, barking commands into walkie-talkies, or watching the bedlam through binoculars. More smoke bombs were going off as her team finally reached the outside of the auditorium.

"Coast looks clear," yelled Jules over the chaos. "Well, as clear as it's going to get tonight."

"We're going in," said M as she waved her crew inside.

The lights in the auditorium were dead, which made M even more nervous. Everything about the event was unsettling, but when even the simple things didn't work, it was hard to feel like she wasn't walking right into a trap. The smoke outside had blotted out what was left of the evening sun, so the windows refused to shed any more light on the situation. M, Cal, and Jules moved forward, while Merlyn closely monitored his computer for signs of Professor Bandit. He was to stay by the door in case anybody else came along. Jules pulled out her flashlight and scanned every row on the way down the auditorium aisle. There wasn't a soul to be seen.

They reached the back door that stood between them and the School of Seven Bells. It was locked. Cal pulled out a pick and tried to work some magic, but he wasn't as good at picking locks as he had hoped. His pick snapped in half and lodged into the handle with a pitiful *crack* that echoed through the empty room.

Jules patted Cal on the shoulder. "Good try, but it looks like we're on to plan B."

In addition to the windows that edged the ceiling of the auditorium, there was a lone window at the front of the room, directly over the rear door. M and Merlyn had had many debates about what was behind that window. Merlyn was convinced it led to a secret room, but M was willing to bet that it led to their target. Jules put on a special set of gloves and shoes covered in tiny hooks and claws, and then took a deep breath before sprightly climbing straight up the wall like Spider-Man. When she was at the top, she took one gloved finger and traced the rim of the window, which neatly popped out from its frame. Jules stuck her head through the resulting gap. When she pulled her head back out, her wide smile glowed in the darkness. She gave the crew a thumbs-up before climbing through entirely. M and Cal could hear the slight scratching of her gloves and shoes against the wall on the opposite side of the locked door. Then, *click*, the door opened and Jules ushered them inside.

There it was, the School of Seven Bells. It was untouched, left just as Bandit had placed it at the end of M's class. The get still felt all too easy, but M's happiness swallowed up her fears. She was going to win her Class Clash.

Then, smiling at her friends, comfortable in her victory, M grabbed the jacket. And that's when it happened. Coldness shot through her entire body. Her arms locked in place, her face caught on an optimistic grin, while her legs went numb and stung with the icy stabbing of pins and needles.

Though her body wouldn't obey her, M could still see everything that unfolded. Jules and Cal ran toward her, but they were too late. Out of the shadows stepped Devon Zoso and the Flynn twins. Each twin blocked Jules and Cal with an eerie *tsk-tsk*, as if to say, *One more step and your friend is in big trouble.*

"Oh, I had no idea who would walk into my little trap," cackled Devon, "but that it's you, M Freeman, my, that makes this so much sweeter!"

M wanted to run, but her legs were rooted in place.

"I see in your eyes that you have no idea what's going on . . . but you of all people should," explained Devon. "It feels different when you're on the receiving end of the deep freeze, doesn't it? Just ask your pal Foley."

How stupid M had been! Devon hadn't just aced the School of Seven Bells in class, she had planted the deep freeze on the jacket at the same time. Then all she had to do was wait for her Class Clash challengers to capture themselves. Of course, thought M, Devon could have stolen the jacket first and left M to find a naked mannequin, but she was too devious for that. She wanted to be there when her challengers realized they'd lost. She wanted them to know who'd beaten them.

Devon snatched the jacket from M's hand and waved good-bye. "Normally if I said it was great to see you, I'd be lying," she said as she backed out the doorway. "But seeing you like this, well, it's been a delight."

It was Cal who spoke next, which seemed to surprise everyone in the room . . . most of all Devon. "Give it back now and we'll let you leave peacefully," he said.

"Did you miss the part where I won?" asked Devon, who turned and walked away.

"It's shocking that you think you did," said Cal, holding up Professor Bandit's remote — the remote that armed the shock system in the School of Seven Bells. With one click, he set off the jacket in Devon's hands. Instantly, M could hear the hum of electricity, a pulsing, zapping sound, followed by desperate cries from Devon in the next room. M could also hear the shuffling of feet as the Flynn twins tried to help their friend, but each time they touched her, they too cried out in pain. The most frightening thing to M, though, wasn't the sound of screams or bodies writhing on the floor. It was the look of absolute satisfaction on Cal's face.

"We win this time" was all he said, smiling at M, who could do nothing but watch.

M woke up in the infirmary, though she wasn't sure how she got there. She was groggy and every joint in her body ached, but she seemed to have some limited movement back. One look around the room confirmed that the Class Clash took no prisoners. Every bed was filled. Bandages and braces shined in the buzzing, harsh lights like badges of honor. M imagined that every kid in class must have a story about the scar they earned from the Class Clash. She tried to sit up, but a nurse forced her back down.

"Steady as she goes there, missy," he said. "You're in no position to be upright just yet. That deep freeze will stay with you for a while."

"Sorry," she said meekly. "Thanks. I just — I don't know."

The nurse smiled at M. He didn't look to be all that old actually; M could have mistaken him for a student. He wore heavy-rimmed glasses and had a nose that looked like it had been broken once or twice. But his brownish blond hair was perfectly styled, keeping its shape even when he bent down to pick up M's call button, which had slid from her bedside.

Wiping a damp cloth across her brow, he told her, "Listen, for now I'm telling you what the nurses are going to tell the others in here. Relax."

"How many of us are in here?" M asked.

Peering around, he said, "I don't know . . . looks like twenty in this room. Including one Ms. Devon Zoso, who is sleeping off a nasty loss, I hear."

"Ugh, it didn't go as I'd planned it," she admitted.

"It rarely ever does," he said. Then he pulled out a file folder and placed it on the table next to M. "You're going to be in here for a bit, so I thought you could use something to help pass the time. Don't peek at it now, but when you're ready, I promise it's a good read."

As dazed as she was, M knew this wasn't typical bedside manner. And there were other pieces to the puzzle. The guy's hair was too perfect, considering what a busy night it was in the infirmary. And his polished wing-tip shoes were way too fancy for an overnight sick bay shift.

"You're not a nurse," she said. "Who are you?"

"You *are* good," he said casually. "My name's Adam Worth. I'm the head of the Masters for this year. And you, M Freeman, have caught our attention."

"I have been told that I'm attention grabbing," she said weakly. Even with this new bombshell at her bedside, she could feel her body slipping back into the deep sleep of exhaustion.

"Get your rest," said Adam, getting up to leave, "and don't forget to read that file when you're feeling better. Like I said, it's a good read."

And with that, M fell back asleep.

CHAPTER 14
A SURPRISE ENDING

M's stay in the infirmary was hard to put together. Bedridden, she fell back and forth between reality and vivid dreams until it was impossible for her to tell which was which. One minute she opened her eyes to find Jules sitting with her and holding her hand, the next she was having a conversation about everything that happened at the Class Clash with her father at their dinner table at home. She even imagined she was visited by Jones, her mother's butler. And though her dreams felt foggy and distant, her reality felt exactly the same way. All eerie and unsettling.

The deep freeze, it turned out, took more than a few hours to leave her system as Dr. Lawless had first told her. M was in the infirmary for what felt like a lifetime. She spent dizzying hours focusing all of her physical and mental efforts toward regaining control of appendages as small as her big toe. Every bit of movement was a victory, but it sapped M's energy, catapulting her back into her dream state.

She remembered Merlyn visiting and mumbling something about taking notes for her in Bandit's class. Jules visited another time and swore that the coast had really been clear and that she couldn't forgive herself for letting her down.

One day Cal paid her a visit, but M couldn't face him. She pretended to be asleep as he rattled on with apologies, explaining that he hadn't planned to use the remote, but after all, shocking someone as wickedly deserving as Devon didn't seem so bad. If they had been speaking hypothetically before all of this, M might have agreed. But seeing Cal's smug satisfaction at Devon's pain, it just felt wrong.

"Anyway," Cal finished, "I visited Devon and apologized. She's in here, you know? She ignored me, too."

His voice dragged like he had a thousand-pound anchor wrapped around his neck, which was then plunged into a fathomless pit of water. Cal sounded genuinely sorry, but it didn't matter to M. She couldn't get past what had happened.

One thing he said that did strike a chord with her was that Devon was definitely in the infirmary. Hadn't someone else told her that, too? She had a vague memory of Devon by her bedside. She looked awful. Her hair was singed, her fingertips blackened and blistered, but she had a smile that was angelic and beaming. *I'm proud of you, M*, she had said. *I didn't think you had it in you, but you proved me wrong. You are your father's daughter.* Before Cal visited, M thought it had been another fever dream. But now it seemed disturbingly real.

Suddenly her haze fell away and a new name popped into her now-very-clear head: Adam Worth. She wondered if she'd made the whole thing up, until she opened her bedside drawer to find the folder left by her mysterious suitor — along with a set of heavy-rimmed glasses and a fake bulbous nose. She picked up the folder, her mind swirling over the possibilities of what it might contain.

Whatever she'd expected, it wasn't this. Inside the folder was a report that read like an art history major's final thesis, and it covered the history of the Takeaway Rembrandt. Painted in 1632, the portrait was of Jacob, an engraver living a quiet life in The Hague, a city in Holland. There was no picture of the painting in the report that M studied, but she remembered it from Ms. Watts's last class. Whoever he was, Jacob was no looker, thought M. Rembrandt may have been a great artist, but he didn't pick the most beautiful subjects.

The report claimed that there was nothing exceptional about the painting other than its size, which was smaller than other Rembrandt paintings. Experts believed that its small size made it a target for lazy thieves. It was dubbed the Takeaway Rembrandt for a very good reason — *Jacob* was the most stolen painting in the recorded history of art theft. All in all, it had been snatched four times on four separate occasions from the same museum, the Dulwich Picture Gallery in London.

Thieves had used every trick in the book to get at this inexplicably popular masterpiece. The first theft came on New Year's Eve in 1966, when a team drilled out an opening in one of the gallery's side doors. The team made off with more than just *Jacob*, stealing eight paintings in all. But it marked the first known theft of the Takeaway Rembrandt. The paintings were all found a few days later when the London police, known as Scotland Yard, were tipped off by an anonymous caller. Arrests were made, but only of small-time crooks, petty thieves who claimed there was another member of the heist. But the mysterious mastermind was never apprehended.

Seven years later, *Jacob* was heisted for a second time from the Dulwich Gallery, in broad daylight by a visitor who simply lifted the painting off the wall, placed it in a plastic bag, and walked right out of the front door with it. In this instance, the man was arrested minutes after he left the museum. When asked why he had stolen the painting, the thief said only that the piece struck him so much that he wanted to sketch it — so he took it. The police on hand described the man as dazed and confused when they caught him and that, while totally outlandish, his story stayed the same after multiple inter-views. The painting was returned and put back on display immediately.

Jacob was stolen for a third time in 1981, by two thieves posing as visitors to the museum. As one thief distracted the security guard on duty, the other slipped the Takeaway Rembrandt into a hidden pocket in his jacket. Once again it was the only painting targeted, and once again it was recov-ered when authorities received an anonymous tip. This time, *Jacob* was found two weeks later in the trunk of a taxicab.

Finally, after three thefts, the Dulwich Gallery caught on. They upgraded their security system. They even bolted *Jacob* to the wall. But this all proved useless, as the painting was stolen for a fourth time in 1983. These thieves entered from the skylight in the ceiling. They used a crowbar to yank the bolted painting from the wall, which set off the new alarm system . . . but the crew had disappeared before the police showed up three minutes later. This time *Jacob* was gone for three years, but in 1986, after yet another anonymous tip, the painting was found in West Germany, wrapped in paper and placed in three protective boxes sitting in a railway station. No arrests were ever made.

When M reached the end of the report, she gasped at the final line: *Researched and written by M Freeman*. She held her father's own words in her hands. She immediately went back to the beginning and read the report over again.

She had studied Rembrandt in homeschool, but only about his life, his art style, and that style's importance in the canon of art history. She'd never studied the lives of the paintings themselves. And until a few days ago, she had never even heard of *Jacob de Gheyn III*.

As M combed over the report, she couldn't help but feel that she was missing some piece to a bigger puzzle. She'd heard of some paintings being stolen twice, but they were usually extremely famous works, like Edvard Munch's *The Scream*. So what was so captivating about this particular painting beyond any other Rembrandt piece? And why was it important to her father? That's the question that bugged her the most. If she could solve this mystery . . . well, she didn't know what she would get. She certainly wouldn't get her father back. But it felt like something she was supposed to solve. A mystery that her father had left for her. Adam Worth must have realized that, too. Why else would he have given her the report in the first place?

As soon as M was released from the infirmary, she went directly to the library to read up on Rembrandt. Maybe his personal history would hold a hidden secret, she reasoned.

Rembrandt grew up in Holland in the early 1600s. His earlier paintings were of scenes from the Bible. Later, he was discovered by Constantijn Huygens, a poet and wealthy statesman from The Hague. Rembrandt was hired to paint a series of biblical scenes and portraits. These jobs launched Rembrandt's career, and he became a "must have" artist of the era. Often he was hired to paint pairs of portraits for families, friends, or businesses. Given that photography had not been invented yet, the only way to have a picture of someone was to have it painted. Therefore, the more realistic the painting was, the better.

Rembrandt went on to paint many great works throughout his life, but there was still no historical sign as to why *Jacob* was so important. M read and reread over his history, but the Takeaway Rembrandt wasn't even a footnote in the artist's life. It was dismissed in every book as a curious afterthought.

M played with her moon rock necklace, deep in thought. It felt good to have her muscle control back, even for such an effortless movement. The library desk lamp gave off a halo glow around her small study space, and for a moment M felt the whole history of the Lawless School. It was frozen in time, the wooden desks, the dusty, spine-cracked books, the well-worn carpeting. It was like her library at home. She suddenly deeply missed her home. As empty as it had been after her father's death, it was the same fifty-three steps from her bedroom to the kitchen. And when she heard a creak in the night, she knew exactly where it came from and could tell the difference between the house settling into itself and the sound of her mother leaving by the back door.

The creaks in the Lawless library, however, happened often and were untraceable. Even in the midst of her research, M was aware that she was not alone in the library. Not that she should have been; it was the middle of the day, of course students would be there. But the fact that she never saw anyone, only heard the creaks of their footsteps on the floorboards, raised a flag.

"Whatcha reading?" asked a familiar voice from the darkened row to the side of M.

It was Devon. As she walked closer, M could see that she'd had a makeover. Her hair was cut shorter, and she wore silk gloves on both hands.

"Books," answered M. "The kind with words in them."

"You know, no one's ever solved the Takeaway Rembrandt mystery," she said coolly. "I think the books are right; it's just an unlucky fluke."

"It's just an assignment for Ms. Watts," said M.

Devon sidled into a chair beside M, then leaned in and whispered, "Can you keep a secret? I've got you figured out now, and I'm gonna tell the whole world."

Before M could reply, she continued, "You made it look like Calvin Fence was some miscreant extra that you had to deal with on your team, but you needed someone to pull the trigger, so to speak. Are you afraid to fight your own fights?"

"I didn't mean for — I mean," stammered M, "*you* set a trap for *me*. How could I have even known you'd be there?"

"When we're both healed," promised Devon, "we're going to deal with this."

The floorboards creaked again, as an elderly gentleman made his way past the two girls. He was dressed in an old-fashioned three-piece tweed suit that nearly faded into the background of the library's dusty decor. Tipping his bowler hat to M and Devon, he continued down another aisle and the creaks drifted away.

As if reading a cue, Devon gracefully slipped out of her chair and back into the darkness. How could a library be so dreary and dark during the daytime? thought M. It was time to leave.

Back at dinner, Merlyn and Jules were excited to see their friend up and moving again.

"Was it like the worst game of freeze tag ever?" asked Jules. The insensitive joke caught M off guard and she couldn't help but crack a smile.

"From here on out, I'll be 'it,' okay?" she said. "So what did I miss? Where's Cal?"

The table grew quiet again as Merlyn pointed to the opposite side of the room. Cal had moved off to some doomed table in the rear corner. He sat alone, sinking into himself.

"What he did during Class Clash, everybody heard about it," said Merlyn. "Professor Bandit flipped out on him. Weaponizing the School of Seven Bells is apparently frowned upon in this establishment, as is trying to electrocute a student . . . even though Bandit fries students with that stupid jacket every other day in class!"

"He's been put on probation," Jules chimed in. "I kind of feel bad for him."

"Devon Zoso deserves a lot of things, but she didn't deserve that," said M. "She beat us fair and square. She beat *me* fair and square. Whatever Cal's got coming his way, he's earned it."

"Whoa, I like harsh M, she's a straight shooter!" Jules laughed. And just like that, the mood lightened again. M was back with her friends. The mystery of *Jacob de Gheyn III* could wait for now.

That night M decided that she needed to confide in someone who had been at Lawless and knew a thing or two about its crazy ins and outs. And that someone, while she wasn't happy about it, was Zara. When M entered her room, Zara was writing a letter.

"Who are you writing?" asked M.

"Who wants to know?" asked Zara. "Could it be my long-lost frozen roommate?"

"Har, har, hardy, har," guffawed M. "It was nice of you to visit me in the infirmary, by the way."

"Ugh, no." Zara shuddered. "I stay away from that place. Once you go in there, it's hard to get out."

"It's not the mafia," said M. "Hey, can I ask you a question? And can I get an honest answer?"

"Yes and maybe," said Zara, who shifted around to fully face M, suddenly interested. "But perhaps not in that order."

"Okay, well, when I was in the infirmary, I met someone named Adam Worth. Er, well, more like he met me." M blushed. "What's his story?"

"Oh, you've been a naughty girl, M, if you've got Adam Worth knocking at your door." Zara smiled. "Here's what you need to know about Mr. Worth. First of all, that's not his real name. Every year the Masters choose a new leader. No one outside of the Masters knows who that is, only that he or she is only referred to as 'Adam Worth.' Second of all, what did he tell you?"

"Just his name. And that he was head of the Masters. And that I had caught their attention."

"Sounds like he's sussing you out to see if you're Masters material," said Zara. "It's a bit early for them to make their picks, but I can see how you're a special case."

"What do you mean, 'make their picks'?" asked M as she sat down on her bed.

"The Masters is like *the* school club," started Zara. "They choose members from every group to join their ranks. So it's a revolving door: As people graduate, new members are brought aboard."

"And what do they do, exactly?" asked M.

"Well, no one knows *exactly*," said Zara. "Unless you're in the club. And since your father started the club, seems like you would be high on their list of new recruits."

M fell back onto her bed. Her father, the Masters, Adam Worth, Devon, Cal, Ms. Watts, the Takeaway Rembrandt — the population of M's life had become too crowded too fast. She needed to pick one thing and focus on it. She chose Rembrandt.

"Thanks, Zara," she said as she bounced up from the bed and moved toward the door. "I believed almost everything you said tonight."

"I aim to please," said Zara, who had already lost interest and gone back to her letter. "Where are you going, anyway?"

"The library," answered M. "I've got this assignment hanging over me and I'd love to just knock it out."

If the library felt like it was haunted during the day, the dark rooms felt cursed during the nighttime. M shuffled through the aisles of books and the hairs on the back of her neck lifted at every turn. She finally found the book on young Rembrandt that she had been searching for and retreated to her usual desk. It wasn't long before she uncovered her next surprise.

Apparently Rembrandt often painted portraits in pairs. These portrait pairings, usually for wealthy families or wealthy friends, were a sign of true devotion, connecting two people for eternity. It turned out that Jacob was best friends with Constantijn Huygens's younger brother, Maurits Huygens. The two friends hired Rembrandt to paint them. Jacob and Maurits each kept their own paintings with the promise to reunite the works again after one of the two friends passed away. And that's exactly what they did. Jacob died first and his painting was returned to Maurits, but then a year later Maurits died.

And then a strange thing happened. The *Jacob de Gheynn III* was suspiciously absent from every history book M could find for the next 122 years! Its history, where it went — the trail simply died with the original owners until *Jacob* ended up with a random collector in England, who later bequeathed the painting to Dulwich College in 1811.

M was so engaged by her discoveries that she forgot about the eeriness of the library. The creaks had ceased and the books sat motionless in their shelves. It was a cold draft against her back that snapped her to attention. That and the strong hand that covered her mouth and pulled M from her chair into a secret entryway, which shut firmly before her eyes.

CHAPTER 15

STRANGER DANGER

"Shhhhhh." A calming suggestion shushed through the darkness of the passageway.

M was frozen solid again, this time with fear. Every muscle in her body clenched so tightly that she may as well have been a sculpture that someone was trying to steal.

The silence of the passageway was deafening. There was only the sound of M's shoes scraping the stone floor, the clap of heavy footsteps, and the husky breathing of the man behind her. His sweaty palm pressed against her mouth, his fingers laced around her cheek as his thumb anchored against the bridge of her nose.

She knew him, of course. She'd actually seen the stranger earlier that day. The tweed sleeve that brushed over the back of her neck gave him away. It was the old man from the library. How stupid was she to not have fully noticed his play earlier? He had been making his mark, not perusing the aisles in search of books and accidentally scaring off Devon. Geez, were there *any* accidents at the Lawless School?

As she was carefully but forcefully ushered backward, M let go. She relaxed. It was time to stop fighting the Lawless

School and roll with it. It was just like Zara had suggested: Whatever M would normally do, she should do the exact opposite. If that was the goal, then kicking and screaming were out. And it helped that M was tired. She was tired of swimming against the tide, and if this guy were going to be a boat, maybe he was leading her to shore. Even if it were a distant, dank, dark, secreted shore that lay miles away and underground.

By her estimate, they must be somewhere under the patch of trees on the west side of the library. They had already passed several other passageway branches, but had stayed the course, heading straight down a slow slope. Finally, as they rounded one last turn, the hand dropped away from M's mouth and she was set free.

"You're pretty strong for an old man," M said into the darkness.

"You're pretty smart for a young girl," answered a familiar voice, "who decided to go to the library by herself in the middle of the night."

The tip of a match flipped into a little lick of fire, followed by the scent of gasoline from a lantern. When the flame caught, the old man lifted the lamp between them, a small island of light in the dark tunnel.

"Hello again, Ms. Freeman." Her mother's butler, Jones, smiled.

M warmed immediately. A familiar face at the Lawless School was about as rare as a kind face at the Lawless School. What were the odds that she would find both in the same person? She hugged him fiercely.

"Jones! What are you doing here?" she said, pressed against his chest.

"Watching over you, as your mother asked of me," said Jones.

The feet in the auditorium, the mysterious presence in the secret passageway, and now the elderly gentleman from the library — M realized they had all been Jones.

"How in the world did you find this place?" she asked.

"I hitched a ride on your airplane, though I fear that I might have given you a healthy scare, coming out before the gas was released."

"You were the one on the plane!"

Jones nodded. "After you left with your guardian, I tailed you. And when the Fulbrights ambushed you in the field, I seized the opportunity to steal away on board your plane."

"Wow." M let it all sink in. "Oh, wow! Were you hurt in the plane crash?"

"I'm a little dinged up," he said, "but none the worse for wear."

"Not too dinged up to steal my map on the first day," suggested M.

"Guilty as charged," said Jones. "But I needed your schedule. And when I noticed that your map was incomplete, I added in the missing passageways."

"Wait, how did you know about them, if you've never been to Lawless before?" she asked.

"Oh yes, I neglected to tell you that I am a proud Lawless graduate," he said.

Of course he was. Why hadn't M ever considered Jones in her piecing together of her real past? He was the muscle of her family's operation. His chameleon skills were also top notch, especially if this hulk of a man could look as feeble and meek as the elderly man in the library.

This covert conversation was the most she had ever heard Jones say at one time and far and away the most he'd ever said to her. He had been with their family for as long as she could remember. At first, M thought he couldn't speak at all. But as she grew up, she realized that he was a monosyllabic maestro. He said everything you needed to know with as little verbiage as possible. If she needed to know if her father was home, Jones needed only to give her a wink. Where's Mom? A slight head nod toward upstairs said everything. If he did have something to say, he made his words count. It was almost a Zen thing. But here he was, gabbing away in the dark.

"Here," M said, "there's a light switch back here, just let me —"

"No!" Jones interrupted, grabbing her arm. "The lights are on a grid. As soon as one goes on, they'll know someone is here."

Danger filled the room again. "Jones . . ." M hesitated. "Where have you been living the past few months?"

"In the forest," he told her. "I've been moving campsites every night. M, no one can know that I am here. You're not even supposed to know that I'm here."

"Then why the dramatic ta-da kidnapping?" she asked.

"There are truths that you need to hear," Jones said. "These are hard truths and I'll start with the most recent one first. The entire school year I'd had some contact, though not much, with your mother. After you left, there was little time for her. The Fulbrights closed in on the house almost as soon as your car had left the driveway. She escaped, and she kept me informed of her movements. But it's been a month since I've heard anything, and, well, I think she might need my services more than you right now."

"My mother's missing?" asked M.

"Maybe," soothed Jones. "But your mother is resilient. I thought the jig was up after your father's accident. She proved me wrong, though. Kept calm and carried on, she did. We don't know what's happened to her now, but better safe than sorry. I'm leaving tonight, but I needed to see you first."

M nodded as the lantern light flickered against the old tiled walls. She'd lost her father already. The thought of losing her mother shocked her, touching her in a way she hadn't expected. She'd hardly thought of her mother over the past few months. Was she too busy? Or was she so used to her mother's absences over the years that the longest stretch hadn't fazed her in the slightest?

"Before I go, because I know how daunting this school can be, I wanted to tell you to keep a stiff upper lip, M. I've seen everything you've accomplished here. It hasn't been easy for you, but you fit this puzzle better than any of the other students limping around campus. Fox knows this. Your teachers know it. I want to make sure you know it, too. Lawless isn't known for accolades, but you've earned them. And I believe you will be approached soon by someone from the Masters."

"They've already made contact," M blurted out. *Made contact*, she thought, *why am I talking like that?* She was animated and thrilled with her secret discussion with Jones, but she figured she should tone down the thief speak.

"Good," said Jones. "Then you're on track. Get in with them, they will help you discover the truth behind the Takeaway Rembrandt."

"What do you know about the *de Gheyns*?"

"All I know for sure is that your father is gone, your mother is missing, and this is all tied to that painting," admitted Jones. "Whatever is happening, it's important enough to kill and kidnap for."

There was a lull as Jones shifted uncomfortably in the space. *Kill.* The word hung in the air. Her father's crash had always been called an accident, but now Jones had confirmed M's worst nightmare. Someone wanted her family dead. And now the person who had been protecting M for her entire life was abandoning her. She looked at Jones's face. As she studied him, she could see the cost of his journey. He'd lost weight. Half-moon shadows were etched under his eyes and his lips were dried and cracking.

He peered into the darkness, tilting his head and listening to the bottled night air. "There's a lot to learn about your father, I'm afraid. I wish I could have told you everything before your adventure began. As I'm sure you've learned from that blather puss, Dr. Gerhardt, bless his old, well-rehearsed heart, your father and Ms. Watts have a history together. And history is never straight and narrow. It's a tangled web of emotions, as raw as exposed nerves, so that even the slightest brush can send sparks ricocheting in every direction. You know she hates your mother. I don't know whether that emnity extends to you, so play it safe. The more you stay clear of Ms. Watts, the better. 'Nuff said?"

"Yeah, sure," agreed M.

"And now I must take leave," said Jones, without a hint of drama. "Good-bye for the time being, Ms. Freeman. I'm sure our paths will cross again."

"Hopefully in a cheerier place next time." M smiled as she hugged him again. "Hey, how are you going to get out of here and back to civilization?"

"I have to keep some secrets." Jones grinned. "But rest assured there's a world beyond those woods. I'll see you there."

M took in Jones one last time before he capped the lantern flame and they were immersed in a thick darkness. Footsteps led away from her. She stayed and listened as Jones moved on to his next task. Then she walked back the same way she had been dragged, without turning on a single light.

The next morning, M woke up before her roommate, with a resounding confidence she hadn't realized she'd been missing. There was purpose in her world now. *Get in with the Masters.* M had avoided cliques at Lawless, but this was one that she could see herself joining. Especially if her father started the whole thing, why wouldn't she want to be a part of that?

The sense of direction was so reassuring that M didn't let the other information from Jones disturb her. Mother incommunicado? No worries: Super Jones was on the case. Avoid Ms. Watts? Fine. Done and done. Well, except for in art history. And who knew, maybe the Masters could get her transferred. It's not as if she'd learned much in that class anyway.

After a steaming-hot shower, M left early to search the cafeteria for signs of Adam Worth. She sat from the 6:00 A.M. opening until the 8:00 A.M. closing. Jules and Merlyn were there, puzzled over her refusal to join them. Cal was there with his lost-puppy-dog looks from across the room. All the cliques that she knew of were there, too. All of them except the Masters. Did that mean they ate elsewhere? Or that they were blending in with the other students? A clique that split up at mealtimes would be almost impossible to identify.

M wasn't even sure if she would recognize Adam Worth if she saw him again. Aside from the fact that he'd worn a disguise before, her memory of him mixed with those of all of her other visitors. She remembered him having Cal's serious posture, Jules's hands, Merlyn's hair, or Devon's eyes. He was a hodgepodge of persons in her mind, which didn't bode well for her ability to simply identify him in a crowd. He'd known what he was doing, visiting her when he had.

After a lunch spent spying through the cafeteria again, M lost heart. She saw the same students over again, and none of them was her mysterious Adam Worth.

The day went on. She practiced hot-wiring cars in Professor Bandit's class, only to find herself wondering if Adam had broken into the infirmary to see her. In Dr. Gerhardt's class, while listening to alibi tapes from famous criminals who were exonerated of their crimes based on their bulletproof stories, M wondered what stories Adam might have told the nurses if he had been caught next to her bed.

She was becoming obsessed — and what was worse was that she knew it and didn't mind at all. Her new mission made the Lawless School make sense. It gave her a direction, a compass in the middle of a whiteout blizzard.

But as much as Adam Worth and the Masters gave her, they did not show themselves. The semester went on. The spring weather turned decidedly into summer heat, and M's classes became more and more involved. Ms. Frank taught her the ropes of how to properly latch a grappling hook on a roof's edge. M broke circuits, she cracked codes, she cut through windows with diamonds, and she stole silently into houses while robot-children decoys listened for the slightest creak in the floor. She picked locks and learned the sweet sensation of tumblers unhitching — the hum in her fingers and thumb felt magical, as if saying, *Open sesame!*

As time crept ahead, M never took her eyes off the students around her. Adam was here, she knew it. And she knew she would find him. She couldn't explain why or how she knew it, but it was the same feeling as walking through the doorway of her Lawless interview months ago. The Masters held a promise of something bigger: another world, another life, another person whom M was more than ready to become.

"Hey, Miss Distant," said Merlyn one day in the cafeteria.

"Huh?" said M, who was searching through the sea of diners. "Oh, sorry, did you ask me something?"

"Uh, yeah, he asked you to pass the salt, like, ten times," said Jules. "What's up with you, M? You act like you're looking for ghosts."

"Here," said M, absentmindedly sliding the saltshaker to Jules.

"Wow." Jules laughed.

A loud rumble from beneath the earth made all the trays, plates, and glasses clink and bounce nearly to the floor. Everyone was used to it by now. It was the construction crew rebuilding the landing strip inside the mountain that M had ruined in her less-than-aerobatic crash landing. She cringed every time another massive machine went to work in the cave. The new and improved M didn't like to remember the feeling of being so out of control.

"What kind of contractor do you hire to fix a secret lair?" asked Jules.

"Blind ones?" guessed Merlyn.

"Deaf, dumb, blind, and desperate ones," added Jules.

"M Freeman!" yelled Merlyn, finally catching her attention. "If you're not going to try to keep up with our witticisms, I'll have to ask you to leave the table."

"Sorry, guys," said M, "I'm just out of sorts."

"Hey, are we ever going to make up with Cal?" Merlyn

motioned over to Cal, still sitting by himself in the corner. "'Cause Jules is cool, but I need, like, a guy friend around here, too."

"M, what he did at Class Clash was wrong," agreed Jules, "but he was trying to protect you in his own doltish way. He seems really torn up over it."

"It's clear that something weird happened between you two," said Merlyn.

M had kept Cal's secret family history from her friends, but she wasn't the best poker player when it came to how she felt about him.

"We know something's up," admitted Jules. "Just know you can talk to us if you need to, whenever you're ready."

M was just about to express her gratitude when a bleating alarm suddenly blared through the cafeteria. As soon as it stopped, an announcement followed over the speakers.

"ATTENTION STUDENTS: A NATURAL GAS LEAK HAS BEEN FOUND, DUE TO NEW CONSTRUCTION. PLEASE LEAVE THE PREMISES IMMEDIATELY FOR OPEN AIR."

Students jumped up and rushed for the door. M and her crew shuffled through the herd outside, into the blisteringly hot sun. Awkwardly enough, they ended up right next to Cal.

"Is it hot enough for you out here?" asked Cal, in an obvious attempt to break the ice.

"Well, it's better than suffocating on noxious gas fumes," said Jules.

"You know," added Merlyn, "I'd be more worried that a gas leak in a construction site would lead to —"

BOOM! A giant eruption shook the entire campus, and a plume of dense smoke spewed in the distance.

"An explosion," finished Merlyn after he had fallen to the ground.

"ATTENTION STUDENTS: THE GAS LEAK HAS BEEN FOUND AND DEALT WITH ACCORDINGLY. YOU MAY HAVE NOTICED A SMALL EXPLOSION. REST ASSURED THAT THIS IS UNDER CONTROL AS WELL. YOU MAY NOW RETURN TO YOUR REGU- LARLY SCHEDULED CLASSES."

M stood up and watched the black smoke lift outward and upward, carried off in a downwind current. "How is it that no one knows about this school?" she said to herself.

Then, from behind her, came an answer: "They say the greatest trick the devil ever pulled was convincing the world that he didn't exist."

It was Adam Worth, stepping out of a crowd of shell-shocked students trying to go back to class after two near-death experiences. He smiled a smile that reflected the sun with certainty and a hint of madness — the dangerous, charismatic kind of madness. "And the devil learned that from the Lawless School."

"And just who are you supposed to be?" asked Jules.

"I'm sorry," said Adam. "My name's Ross. Ross Peters. I'm a third year. You're Jules Byrd, right?"

"How do you know that?" she asked.

"From your high-wire act in the Box." Adam smiled. "Your video went viral. Everyone in school is talking about it. How did you manage to keep your balance in those winds?" Then, before Jules could answer him, Adam turned his attention to Merlyn. "Oh, and you're Merlyn Eaves?"

"I am?" said Merlyn in a paranoid tone.

"I'm a big fan of your cartoon destroyer," Adam said. "Brilliant stuff."

"You saw that?" Merlyn blurted.

"What's the cartoon destroyer?" asked M.

"It's this crazy virus that recodes computer files to become cartoons!" Adam laughed. "It's totally amazing, like, one minute you're looking at your report on *Oliver Twist* and the next minute, *BAM*, it turns into a cartoon that plays once and then erases itself."

"Looks like the clique has a fan," Cal grumbled.

Adam turned in his direction. "Now, you I don't know. My name's —"

"Yeah," interrupted Cal. "Ross Ross Peters. I heard you the first time."

"Anyway," said Adam. "I have to talk with M. Do you guys mind if I steal her away from you for a minute?"

"Go on, guys," said M. "We'll meet up later."

With that, Adam ushered M back into the crowd of confused students. And though none of her friends could see the smoke screen that Adam was running, M saw it immediately. And it broke her heart to know what it meant. The Masters had come for her, and now it was time to leave her friends behind. But it was for the best.

At least, that's what she told herself.

CHAPTER 16

BECOMING A MASTER

"I'm glad you came," said Adam as he guided M back into her new home. The Masters building was hidden at the campus's edge, not far from Fox Lawless's own West building seven. Since it was tucked back into the woods, M hadn't seen it before, and it definitely wasn't on her map. "Everyone's waiting for you inside."

On the way, Adam let M in on a few secrets about the Masters' abode. Not only did the Masters have their own dorm, they also had their own cafeteria, their own classrooms, their own gym . . . they even had their own Box. It blew her mind that there could be more than one Box in the world.

M smiled and looked around at her new surroundings. The hallway was painted a rich red and lined with photographs. Toward the front entry, the photos were grainy, yellowish, and brownish scenes of young students in old-fashioned clothing posing with various paintings, gold bars, or monstrous jewels as big as their hands. As they moved farther down the hallway, the student pictures upgraded from black-and-white images to Polaroids to color photos. It was a criminal time capsule. A love letter to heists.

"Is that guy holding the *Mona Lisa*?" asked M, pointing to one photo.

"Ah yes, 1911, that was a good year," answered Adam.

"So these photos are like a Lawless walk of fame?" asked M.

"Every Master has his day," said Adam. "You'll have yours, too. But I'm getting ahead of myself."

"Well, they can't all be Masters, right?" asked M. "I mean, didn't my dad start this clique?"

"We like to think of the school's greatest graduates as retroactive members," said Adam, "but this club was your father's baby."

"Is there a picture of my dad here?" inquired M as her eyes flickered up and down the hallway, searching for her father's shaggy-haired image.

"He's down here." Adam walked M to a picture of her father with the young Ms. Watts, holding none other than the Takeaway Rembrandt. "Your father was obsessed with that painting. No one here knows exactly why."

"Not even Ms. Watts?" asked M. "Seems like they shared a lot of things back then."

"It would seem that way, but I've asked Ms. Watts countless times about the painting's significance to your father. She claims to have no idea," said Adam.

"And you believe her?" asked M, keeping her eyes on the photograph.

"I don't know," he answered. "That's why I keep asking her every now and again. See her in this photo? She knows something. Something she's not happy about."

It was true. Even though she was smiling, Ms. Watts's eyes were not. She was trying to be happy for the camera, but the flash captured a worried, concerned, put-on-a-good-face snapshot.

"You could ask her yourself, you know," said Adam.

"I'd rather not," admitted M.

"Suits me," he said. "Anyway, I think we're done with this hall of history. Are you ready to meet your future?"

"Let's do it," said M as she walked through the set of heavy wooden doors at the end of the hallway.

The next room was a small antechamber. Adam took a moment to prep M. "The rest of the Masters are in the next room. Not a lot of people make it this far into our home. Please treat everyone you meet here with respect. It's come to my attention that a few of our members have crossed your path already, so you'll see some familiar faces. Don't be alarmed."

Then he opened the doors without waiting for a response.

"Welcome, M Freeman," he announced to the waiting crowd.

The ballroom was monstrously large and incredibly regal. Windows lined the walls, and where there were no windows, oversized works of art were hung. The closest thing M could compare it to would be something out of the French palace of Versailles. The furniture was draped in luxuriously vibrant velvet coverings. There was a fireplace at the opposite end of the hall with a fire roaring, even though it was hot outside. It reminded her of her own fireplace back home. But there was very little time to take in the view, as the twelve members of the Masters descended upon her in a flurry of introductions.

"M," said Adam, "I'd like you to meet everyone. Stephanie Lee. She's our human computer."

Stephanie was smaller and looked younger than M. She bowed bashfully before fading into the line of other Masters.

"This is Rex Sykes. He's the muscle," said Adam.

Rex was the exact opposite of Stephanie. He towered over the rest of the Masters and cast a shadow across the room that looked less like a boy's and more like a mountain's.

"Angel Villon. He's the good hands man."

Angel offhandedly flipped a coin into the air that became, midtwirl, a tiny ball of fire that he caught and blew out between his fingers . . . leaving a new coin behind.

The rest of the introductions was a complete onslaught of names, descriptions, and sample showcases of each kid's talent. After Angel's fireball, it was hard for M to keep up. Until Adam introduced her to a pair of girls whom she already knew.

"Meet the Flynn twins, Lucy and Kitty . . . or is it Kitty and Lucy," Adam joked. "It doesn't totally matter who's who here, since their strength is in how they work together. You see, M, these two are the best safe crackers I've ever met."

M begrudgingly shook their hands. The Flynn twins were Devon's guardians. They had been on Devon's team during the Class Clash and had stood by when Devon gave M the deep freeze. Was it a means to an end? Did they know that M would meet Adam in the infirmary? She wouldn't put it past the

Masters to plan that far out in advance. Still, anyone who was friends with Devon didn't sit well with M.

"And now that the formal introductions are over," said Adam, "on with the fun! M Freeman, will you do us the honor of escaping this room?"

"Excuse me?" asked M. "You want me to escape from here?"

"Yes, please," said Adam. "And don't mind us, we'll just be standing guard by the front door and observing you."

A sound of moving machinery echoed through the room, and heavy iron shutters slowly lowered to block the windows. M noticed that the Masters had all moved behind her, leaving the rest of the ballroom open for her to explore. She wasted no time, picking up the lightest-looking chair that could do the heaviest amount of damage to the windows and chucking it at the glass before the iron curtain fell. Unfortunately the chair merely bounced off the window. It had obviously been rein-forced, and M guessed they all would be. Next she shifted several pieces of furniture, checking for hidden exits in the floor. Nothing turned up. That's when it hit her: the fireplace. She walked down the length of the room to the fireplace. A discolored stone in the hearth was an obvious trigger. She stepped on it and the fire ceased, giving her just a moment to flit through the flue before the flame erupted again.

On the other side of the fireplace, waiting for her, was Ms. Watts.

So much for steering clear.

"Congratulations, Ms. Freeman," said Ms. Watts. She smiled. "You've passed your first test. And now you must prepare for your second and final test: Steal something. Anything in the world. The target is completely your choice."

"I am going to steal *Jacob de Gheyn the Third*," said M with certainty.

Ms. Watts's eyes flared, but M couldn't read the emotion that lit them. "Very well. You will have the entire group of Masters at your disposal, so plan accordingly. You will leave in the morning. Your prep time starts now."

Adam and the other Masters came rushing through the deactivated fireplace, cheering for the new recruit. They took M to dinner at their special cafeteria and then led her to her new room. Once away from the Masterful crowd, M lay down in her bed. She could barely breathe, she was so excited . . . and scared. Was she ready for this? A real-life crime? M had reached a point of no return. She needed to make a firm decision tonight, because it would be impossible to unsteal that painting. In fact, it would probably be impossible to ever quit the dangerous path she was spiraling down.

But she brushed all of her mixed emotions aside. She didn't have time to worry about anything else besides dreaming up an airtight plan to steal the Takeaway Rembrandt by tomorrow. Her mind was made up the second she stepped through the fireplace. M Freeman was going to be exactly like her father: a master thief.

M's eyes had just closed when her alarm went off. Groggy and bleary eyed, she lifted her head to find Adam standing in her doorway.

"Ready?" he asked, with a smile. He looked genuinely excited, like this was what he lived for. Maybe it was, thought M.

He led her downstairs. The staircase kept spiraling past the main floor, down and down and down until they reached what looked like a broom closet. The room was small and barely fit both M and Adam. With a wink, he closed the door and the room started to move, gliding forward and throwing M off balance. She righted herself immediately. When the room finally stopped moving, Adam opened the door to another descending staircase. M went first, walking calmly down the stairs. At the bottom there was a second airplane hangar with, of course, an airplane. The rest of the Masters stood before it.

"What's your poison, M?" asked Adam from behind her.

"Adam, Angel, and Rex," M said with certainty. "You're the team."

"Excellent," said Adam. "Shall we to the robbery?"

"Um, but," started M, who suddenly remembered her last insane plane ride. "Um, can somebody give me the pixie dust before I get on the plane?"

"Of course," said the Flynns as they stepped forward.

Suddenly, the air around M was full of yellow dust. She blinked her eyes feverishly, but her eyelids were becoming too heavy to keep open. M felt herself fade into a deep, deep sleep. The last thing she saw before drifting off was Adam pointing to the plane. And as if in a hallucination, M heard herself say, "Okay," and felt herself walking slowly toward the dark steps.

CHAPTER 17
TAKEAWAY

The London sun was gray in the sky, highlighting a new world covered in piles of dirty snow. M's eyes took a moment to adjust to the grimy brightness cast from the sky and reflected from the ground, and that's when the frigid temperature hit her. The cold air came as a shock to her system as white clouds erupted from her open mouth. M shuddered and started breathing deep. It felt like she was taking her first breaths of real air after being in outer space. She hugged herself to get warm and noticed that she was wearing a large black parka and layers of clothes. She was in an open airplane hangar, with a limousine waiting for her. *Another limo*, she thought to herself. *How is this inconspicuous?*

"Ah, you're back!" called out Adam, from inside the limo. "Come and join us!"

M shuffled across the hangar and into the limo where she was blasted with hot air. Her crew was all there. Angel looked bored, Rex looked ready to crush something, while Adam reveled in the bitter cold. But as soon as M slid inside, she saw there was one extra member whom she hadn't expected. Ms. Watts.

190

M tried to sound nonchalant. "Ma'am? What are you doing here?"

Ms. Watts smiled slyly. "Why, Ms. Freeman, of course students attending any off-campus field trip require a chaperon. And after all, your father didn't found this little club all on his own, you know. Now what is your plan?"

While M wasn't happy to have Ms. Watts's shark-toothed grin along for the adventure, she wasn't about to let the teacher rain on her entrée into the Masters.

"The plan," M began as the crew perked up and gave her their full attention. "I'm calling it Locked In. But before I go into it, we need to make a stop."

The traffic moved slowly in the London morning. How otherworldly it felt to drive on the other side of the street! M kept looking left, at the people walking along the sidewalk, while on her right, lines of cars backed up for miles, wrapping around the ancient stone churches that seemed to be on every corner. The street signs flashed by, blue circles with white arrows, guiding the limo along, taking M through an unknown city. It was her first time traveling abroad. Well, aside from her time at Lawless. M tried to not be overwhelmed by the newness. She had a job to do, after all.

The limo double-parked in front of the London Graphic Centre, an art supply store, and M ran inside to purchase the most ornate midsized frame they had, along with a giant art book filled with famous pieces, four stainless steel eighteen-inch rulers, spray paint, and a pack of lightbulbs. She paid for it all with her club card. It felt really good to use the card finally, like she was officially part of the underworld now. Dad would have been proud. As she waited for the cashier, she wondered what would happen if the card didn't work. Would they call the police? Would they call the shady bank that funded this club card? But the flashing APPROVED at the register put her worries to rest.

Back in the limo, M laid out the whole plan, every step, every beat, every single movement that she needed her players to play. She had imagined that her plan would take the whole ride to describe, but as it turned out, everyone understood it on the first description. Was it too simple?

"How can I help?" asked Ms. Watts.

"You can't," said M. "You weren't part of the plan."

"So improvise." Ms. Watts smiled. "Isn't that your specialty?"

"Look," said Adam, "I dig your plan, except for the spray paint. There's no way any gallery would allow spray paint inside. That's a big red flag. Why not let Ms. Watts handle the security cameras?"

M didn't like it, but Adam was right about the spray paint. Even if they could hide the canisters out of sight, the constant clicking they made when they jostled was a dead giveaway. "Okay," M agreed begrudgingly.

"You won't regret it, M." Ms. Watts smiled again. "I promise. Oh, and just in case something unexpected happens, everyone take a cell phone." She passed around phones to the whole crew. "My number is programmed in here as *Mom*. Think of it as your panic button."

Clearly this was not the best time for M to start doubting herself, so she channeled her father. *Keep calm, carry on*, he always used to say, though he said it over things like spilled milk or a brief power outage. Would he say the same thing about an international art heist?

Eventually they made it to the Dulwich Picture Gallery in South East London. The building looked like something that belonged on the Lawless School campus. It was riddled with classic archways and the roof was filled with expansive and intricate skylights that looked like rows of greenhouses. Angel and Rex left the car first and waited on a set of benches outside the entrance. They had drinks, which weren't allowed in the museum — the perfect excuse for not entering right away. As they sat and sipped their piping-hot beverages, M and Adam breezed into the museum.

The entrance was filled with portraits rich in history and dense with color. M and Adam separated in the first room. M recognized a few works immediately, but most of the paintings were both familiar and foreign to her. Saints, farmers, royalty, the subjects ranged greatly, but all held the same depth of realism, the same striking detail. These artists had poured their hearts and souls into these pieces. They showcased the creases in every subject's brow, the length of every hair, and the landscape told as much of a story as the main character in each piece. M thought about how the *Mona Lisa* was as respected for the detail of the landscape as it was for the famous muse and her mysterious smile.

M stepped farther into the museum, which was bathed in natural light, thanks to the skylights above. Looking upward, she wondered which skylight the last thief had crashed through to steal the painting. It was a long way up to the roof from down here. Whoever stole that painting had some strong rope-climbing skills. Even Ms. Frank would have appreciated the forty-foot free climb.

Luckily, the gallery wasn't too crowded for a . . . what day was it, anyway? thought M. How long had their flight been from Lawless's Never Never Land? Not that it mattered now. She was here, the coast was clear, and she was going to steal that Rembrandt.

M wandered through the gallery, pausing in front of a few paintings so as to not be too suspicious. Going straight to her target would look bad, a rookie mistake. The dark red walls flowed down the length of the museum's main hallway. At one end, she could see Adam getting into position. On the other side of the hall, Angel and Rex were deep in discussion over a random painting. Angel's long trench coat swayed as their conversation became louder and impassioned. They were attracting attention. The plan was working.

Security guards drifted past M, casually moving toward the front room to keep an eye on Angel and Rex. Finally, M walked through another archway into the Dutch collection wing. It was small, only one room, with amber-brown wainscoting at the base of the wall that matched perfectly with the green wallpaper. It was as if she were stepping into the forest around Lawless. But there, right in front of her, was the Takeaway

Rembrandt. It *was* small! M studied the painting directly next to it, another Rembrandt piece called *Girl at a Window* that was twice as big. She steadied her hands, which were shoved into the pockets of her parka. The adrenaline was kicking in. On the outside, M was a young student silently taking in the beauty of these great pieces of art, but on the inside, she was a ball of nerves. The muscles in her legs tensed. All she wanted to do was run, run anywhere, she was just so anxious to move. This must be what an athlete feels like before the big race. All she could do now was stay in position until the referee shot the starting pistol.

POP! came a loud, shattering explosion from the back room. *POP! POP!* It was Adam throwing the lightbulbs against the floor, but to an untrained ear, it sounded more like gunshots. The game was afoot. Guards left their posts and ran back to see what was going on, and that was M's cue. She swiftly pulled her hands from her pockets, and the metal rulers slid down from her parka sleeves. She knew that the Takeaway Rembrandt was bolted to the wall. Using the rulers like crowbars, M ripped the painting, frame and all, from its moorings. Instantly the silence of the museum was cut by a blaring alarm that was completely ear shattering. M was not prepared for how loud it was, even though she knew the siren was coming.

This was Angel and Rex's cue. From under his trench coat, Angel pulled the ornate frame she'd bought earlier. And Rex, well, Rex just ripped the closest painting down with his bare hands and they both ran through the front door. Confused, the guards ran in every direction, not knowing what to focus on first — the mysterious noise from the back room or the two thieves who had stolen artwork from the front room.

Luckily the Dutch wing was off the main hallway and therefore afforded M a lot of privacy. She traced the back edge of the Rembrandt with a ruler and quickly separated the painting from its frame. *Jacob de Gheyn III* was painted on a sturdy piece of oak wood, which was normal for portraits painted before the mid-sixteenth century, when canvas paintings came into fashion. *Thanks, Mom and Dad, for teaching me that!* thought M. Whoever thought it would pay to know such random things?

Tossing the frame aside, M stuffed the painting into a large pocket in the back of her parka jacket. Without looking up, she dropped the rulers down a grate in the middle of the room. People were darting by her, running for the door, but no one was looking in her direction. They just wanted out of the mayhem, which was exactly what M was hoping for. The more madness, the less people would pay attention to what was really happening. Quickly, M fell to the floor and screamed at the top of her voice, "HELP! STOP! THIEF!" and then she fainted dead away.

A set of guards came to M's aid immediately. Over the high-pitched alarm, she described exactly what had happened. How a man who conveniently fit the precise description of Adam Worth had come into the room after the blasts from the other room. He had pushed her aside, then took something metal out of his pockets, pulled a painting clean off the wall, and ran out.

"Don't worry, miss," said a guard with an air of pride. "The gallery's on lockdown and we've got cameras everywhere. We'll get him."

Let's hope Ms. Watts really handled the cameras, M thought. If not, then Operation Locked In was going to become Operation Locked Up in no time flat. M followed the guard's pointing hand back to the small black bowl at the top of the room. It was a 360-degree camera and it would have seen everything.

"Thanks, sir," said M, getting to her feet. "I, um, I should get going 'cause I was supposed to meet my mom and she's going to wonder where I am."

"I'm sorry, miss, but because you're a witness, we'll need to keep you here until Scotland Yard arrives," said the guard.

"But you have the cameras, don't you?" asked M, hoping to inch her way out of this bad situation.

"Aye, but this is standard procedure. The police will want to have your report firsthand," he answered.

"Yeah, firsthand," agreed M.

The painting started to tap on M's back, like an awful reminder that her plan was shot and that she was most definitely going to jail. Sweat started to form at her brow and trickle down the back of her neck. *Please don't ruin the painting with your own sweat*, she thought. The room was suddenly hotter than a sauna, but it could have been her guilty conscience making her burn up.

She could hear the sirens fast approaching. Even their police cars sounded foreign.

M braced for the possibility of being arrested. What would it feel like to be caught red-handed? What would it feel like to have her hands cuffed? Did Scotland Yard use the same kind of handcuffs she'd practiced with at Lawless, or did they have some fancy new kind of handcuffs that she had never seen? The questions were coming faster than any of the answers. *Keep calm. Carry on.* It was the best advice in this situation. A level head lives to steal another day.

The museum suddenly flooded with police, both in uniform and in plain clothes. M was kept in the Dutch wing with a guard on either side of her. A detective had moved her from the middle of the room into a white chair that had been just beneath the Takeaway Rembrandt. She held her breath and counted to twenty to try and relax as she watched the police walk back and forth through the hallway. Soon one officer made his way over to her.

"Miss," began the officer, "my name's Chief Inspector Banks. I understand you're a witness. First may I ask if you're okay?"

"Yes, sir," said M, "just startled."

"Art theft is always startling," said Chief Inspector Banks. "Especially when you live through it. What's your name?"

"M Freeman."

"Miss Freeman, may I ask how old you are?"

"Twelve, sir," answered M.

"American, too, I'm guessing?" said the inspector. "So where are your parents?"

"Just my mother, sir," said M. She immediately jumped into an intricate lie. "She's in a meeting across town. I wanted to come see the gallery. It beats watching TV in our hotel room."

"Do you have a number where we can reach her?" he asked.

M smiled. Ms. Watts was going to come in handy after all. She dialed Ms. Watts's emergency number — the cell display showed *Mom* — and gave the inspector her phone.

He stayed in front of M and waited for someone to answer before beginning to speak.

"Hello, may I talk to Mrs. Freeman? Yes, this is Chief Inspector Banks of Scotland Yard. Yes, yes, your daughter is fine; she's just had a bit of a scare, I'm afraid. I can't give you the full details over the phone, but could you come down to Dulwich Picture Gallery? We have your daughter here and want to ask her a few questions. It would be best if you were here when we do. Yes, ma'am, I understand and I will see you soon.

"Well," he continued with M after hanging up, "your mother is on the way now. I'm going to wait to ask you questions until she arrives."

And with that, he turned and walked out of the room, leaving M and the Takeaway Rembrandt to sit and stew until Ms. Watts showed up. Watching the police walk back and forth through the archway, M took her seat as a small sign of hope. The inspector had put her in a chair that allowed her to look at what was happening. If they knew more than they were letting on, they would have moved her to the secluded end of the Dutch wing without a full sight line into their comings and goings. M saw other witnesses being led from the back room to the front room and back again. They were probably walking the police through their museum visit so the police could rule them out as accomplices to the crime.

Chief Inspector Banks was gone for what felt like an eternity. M tried to keep her back as straight as possible. The last thing she wanted to do was ruin the painting she was trying to steal. She must have looked extremely uncomfortable, mostly because she was extremely uncomfortable, holding such an unnaturally rigid position. But if anyone noticed, they didn't say anything. Finally, M could hear Chief Inspector Banks speaking to someone.

"Yes, ma'am, your daughter is extremely lucky," said the inspector. "Although in art theft cases, bystanders are rarely hurt. The art is the target, not the person admiring the art."

As they walked around through the archway, M tried to not be repulsed by the thought of acting like Ms. Watts was her mother. But in the end, it didn't matter. And it didn't matter because it wasn't Ms. Watts who accompanied Chief Inspector Banks into the room.

It was her real mother, Beatrice Freeman.

CHAPTER 18
ONCOMING TRAFFIC

M's eyes nearly popped out of her head at the sight of her mother. It had been five months, but almost nothing had changed. Her hair was still up in a neat bun that shimmered in the natural light from the skylight above. She wore a sharp gray business suit cut perfectly to fit her tiny frame and it was accented by a large necklace made of layered silver circles locked in a pattern that imitated a ruched scarf. She hardly looked like she had been on the run as Jones had told M earlier. She simply looked marvelous.

Ignoring the inspector, Mrs. Freeman kept her eyes keenly on her daughter, opened her arms, and started sobbing. "Oh, M, you're okay, thank goodness!" She scooped M up into a hug, and forgetting all about the oak panel painting in her parka, M hugged her mother back. It was an embrace that M hadn't experienced in a long time. Hugs like this were few and far between. But none of that mattered now. She was back in her mother's arms.

Which felt great, until her mother leaned in and whispered, "Follow my lead."

Mrs. Freeman was the first to let go, and turned to face the inspector. "So if you have camera footage, then why are you still holding my daughter here like a criminal?"

"Well, Mrs. Freeman, she is a firsthand witness," said the inspector, with authority.

"And has she told you what she saw?" asked Mrs. Freeman, with just as much authority.

"Yes, she left a statement with museum security," confessed Chief Inspector Banks, "but, ma'am . . . this is embarrassing and confidential, but the camera system was wiped out right before the attack."

It took all of M's remaining energy to contain her excitement and still seem like a witness to a crime instead of a criminal who was about to walk out free with the very piece of stolen art on her person.

"We have a hit on the three thieves. They are in the previous video, including the one that your daughter has identified as the culprit of the Rembrandt," finished the inspector.

"Then what more do you need from us?" asked Mrs. Freeman. "You have our number, you have our names, and you have our word that we're in no hurry to leave the country. I am here for several months, curating an installation at the Tate Modern."

"Ma'am, if you will excuse my prying," said Chief Inspector Banks, "but it seems odd to me that you would have a background in art, have a daughter involved in an art theft, have an alibi in place, and know enough to tell me that you are staying in the country. It seems all too well rehearsed."

"Inspector," M's mother said sharply, "your insinuations are slander. Why wouldn't my daughter take an interest in art if she's surrounded by it? Now, I would prefer that she did not labor away visiting such ancient galleries when there are so many exciting modern art opportunities around London, but she is keen for the old masters. And I've seen more than enough police dramas to know what information you'd want from us. Can we leave or shall I phone our lawyer?"

"We have your number and your flat information, so you're excused for now," relented the inspector. "But just in case you remember anything, here's my card. We'll keep in touch."

"I have no doubt you will, Inspector," replied Mrs. Freeman as she handed his card to M. "Come on, dear, don't dillydally. Scotland Yard has their man to catch, lest we get in their way."

And with that, M's mother took her hand and they walked through the crime scene and out of the front door scot free.

Outside, the sun was sinking behind the London skyline. M's mother had a limo waiting, and once in the safety of the backseat, M could finally breathe again.

"What are you doing here?!" she asked as they pulled away from the museum.

"Well, saving you, of course," her mother answered. "I should be asking you what you are doing here."

"It's a long story," confessed M. "I thought you were in trouble?"

"Don't be silly, M," answered her mother. "Why would I be in trouble?"

"But Jones —" started M before her mother interrupted.

"Really, being a suspect in an art heist, M!" Her mother shook her head disapprovingly. "I know you didn't do it, but I really wish you had. I would have been so proud. Really, what am I paying that school of yours to teach you? Certainly not to be a mere accomplice to the crime, I hope."

M's face flared as she prepared to rage against her mother . . . but something was off. Her mom had basically given her a full security pat down during their hug, so she *had* to know about the painting. Something was wrong. She was covering something up. *Follow my lead,* she had said, so M was going to.

"How has the Lawless School been?" asked her mom.

"Good," said M, deciding to keep her responses brief.

"Excellent," replied her mother. "I'm hungry. You must be, too. Driver, take us to the Lion's Den, please."

The Lion's Den turned out to be an upscale restaurant, exactly the place she imagined her mother would dine. As they walked through the glass doors, M felt completely out of place in her giant parka. But it didn't matter; her stomach had started gurgling and growling as soon as her mother mentioned food. Who knew stealing would work up such a healthy appetite?

"Your jacket, miss?" asked the maitre d'.

"No, I'll keep it on, if you don't mind," said M. Even though that was the last thing she wanted to do.

"Of course," snipped the maitre d'. He showed them to their seats, opened the bottled water on the table, and filled their glasses. "Bon appétit."

The restaurant wasn't crowded, but M couldn't shake the eerie feeling that she was being watched. Looking around the room, she took a sip of her water. It tasted heavenly. She'd had no idea that her mouth had gotten so dry. As she put down her glass, her mother handed her one of the large menus.

"Oh, you'll like this place, M," her mother said, smiling. "You must try the hamburgers. They're off the map, but they're the original. This was one of your father's favorite restaurants. It used to be a hole in the wall back when this neighborhood was just a bunch of empty warehouses. You wouldn't have even known anything was here, unless someone gave you a hint. Anyway, trust me, get the hamburger. It's much better than the copycats in the touristy area across town."

"Okay," responded M. Her mother was being super weird. Sure, they'd just finally been reunited over a stolen painting after her mom had gone missing and M was off at a boarding school for thieves, which normally would call for megaweirdness. But this was something else. It was like she was talking in code, stressing different words in what she was saying, like *hamburgers*, *off the map*, and *copycats*. Whatever her mother was trying to tell her sounded like gibberish.

Finally M couldn't stand it any longer. She blurted out, "No, you know, we can't just keep acting like everything is normal between us. It's not normal. Why didn't you ever tell me? About Dad, about you, about Lawless?"

"You were young, dear," her mom explained. "You were so young and your father, he never wanted you to know."

"Why not?" pushed M. Her mother was trying to calm her down, but she was getting really angry now. "Didn't I deserve the truth?"

Her mother positioned the menu in front of her mouth so that M could only see her eyes. "Your father and I argued back and forth about telling you. I always thought you should know. But it was your father's secret to keep more than mine. I suppose I got used to the secrecy.

"And, M," her mother shifted into a whisper, "something happened between your father and the Lawless School. I don't know what and he would never tell me. I had hoped their involvement in our lives was a thing of the past."

M's anger was getting the best of her. The corners of her mouth curled down uncontrollably, her eyes went glossy with tears. "Why are we here, Mom? Why are we acting like it's not crazy that we're sitting in a glamorous restaurant after you magically appeared out of thin air? You haven't seen me in five months and you just happen to find me in London on the day that I stole —"

"M," her mother shushed her sharply, cutting her off midsentence.

Even with the menu blocking half her mother's face, M could see the same tears building in her mother's eyes, ruining her mascara. Then, as she looked past her, another detail clicked into place. Fourteen tables, two by the front window, the waiters with flower lapels, the service entrance to the right, the stairs leading to the bathrooms downstairs . . . this was the same restaurant Zara had flashed during her original interview!

"I'm so sorry for everything, M," her mother said. And then she whispered, "Run."

Fulbrights crashed through the kitchen doors en masse. Immediately M flipped the table away, flinging her water glass and plate at the two closest assailants. The tableware crashed against her targets and she slipped past them, bolting for the front door. Two more Fulbrights lunged for M with flying tackles. They had her dead to rights, but luckily they rammed into each other first, allowing her to just squirm out of their grasps.

Now only the maitre d' stood between her and the front door, with an army of Fulbrights at her back. M rushed forward, ready to crash through the thin waiter, only to find the maitre d' wanted no part of what was going on. He slithered backward and M shattered through the glass door. She made a mental reminder to thank Ms. Frank for teaching her how to do that without getting hurt, before getting up and running into the street. It had looked like there were no cars coming, but, of course, she was in England . . . where everyone drives on the wrong side of the road!

Cars started furiously honking as they ripped past the small girl in the black parka. Lights flickered as the high-pitched squeal of swerving tires echoed in the night air. M was frozen in place, waiting to be struck by the oncoming traffic until one car pulled to her side and the passenger-side door flew open.

"Get in now!" cried Zara.

M leapt into the car and Zara put the pedal to the metal before the door had shut, leaving M's mother and a team of angry Fulbrights behind in the proverbial dust.

CHAPTER 19
ZEE ZCHOOL OF ZEVEN BELLZ

"How did you find me?" asked M, windswept from her insane escape. The last person she'd expected to hitch a ride with in London was Zara Smith.

"Those friends of yours back at school," Zara started before whipping through a crowded roundabout. After a series of honking horns, she continued, "They're attached to you, you know. They came by and asked me if I'd seen you. I hadn't. So I found you."

"But why?" asked M. "Why come all this way? Did you know I was in trouble?"

"I had a hunch," she said without taking her eyes off the road. "M, I'm your guardian. It's my job to guard you. Even in London."

"That restaurant back there, that was the same restaurant you showed me in my interview, wasn't it?" asked M.

"The Lion's Den is usually a Lawless safe house," said Zara. "They flash that picture in every interview."

Another roundabout rushed toward them and she breezed around the four-lane roadway without pause.

"I guess it's not a safe house anymore," said M.

"Fulbrights ruin everything," agreed Zara as she ran a stoplight.

"Where did you learn to drive?" asked M, clutching her seat with white-knuckled fear.

"Getaway Driver's Ed." Zara smiled.

"Okay, well, we've gotten away now," said M. "Maybe we can be inconspicuous from here on out?"

Zara eased up on the gas. "So, anyway, your first-year pals gave me those puppy-dog eyes, and I knew I needed to find you. I went to Ms. Watts first, but surprise, surprise, she was gone, too. So I hacked into the club card security system, saw that you bought some interesting items in London, and here I am."

Suddenly M remembered the painting. She couldn't believe she'd sat this long with it against her back. She quickly shifted out of her parka and placed it across her lap. Her back was wet from sweat, which was suddenly cold without the jacket, but it felt amazing to not have a work of art for a back brace. And even though Zara had come all this way to help, M wasn't ready to let her know about the Rembrandt yet.

"So what's the next step?" M asked as they drove on.

"Food, obviously," said Zara. "Unless you had a chance to eat, back at the Lion's Den?"

"No, there wasn't a lot of time to chat and chew," confessed M.

They pulled into a grocery store called Tesco. The lights were loud and buzzing and the food looked almost like the food at home, but slightly different. The potato chip flavors were crazy! Lamb and mint, ketchup, roast chicken. Who bought these things?

"Have you ever had a ploughman's wedge?" Zara asked as she tossed M a prepackaged sandwich. "You'll love it. Oh, and try some of those prawn-flavored crisps."

"*Prawn* as in shrimp?" asked M.

"Trust me," she replied. "They sound awful, but they're completely addictive."

In the end, Zara was right. The ploughman's wedge was amazing and the prawn chips, while they took a few bites to get used to, were great. M topped off her feast with a Double Decker chocolate bar.

The busy skyline of London quietly gave way to a lurking landscape of rolling hills and withered forests that M imagined medieval knights on horseback could gallop from at any given moment. Night fully settled into the Arthurian backdrop, and apparently M's run of luck continued as they had dodged the worst of the inner-city traffic, according to Zara.

"We're making great time," said Zara.

"Great time to where?" asked M. "Are we meeting up with the others?"

"No," she answered. "I have no earthly idea where your Masters crew slithered off to."

M couldn't help it — she felt hurt that Adam had left her behind to be captured by Fulbrights. Was this how the Masters worked? One for all and every thief for herself? M had hoped it would be different. That maybe the Masters would have been the ones speeding across the English countryside to save her life.

"I have a friend in France," Zara continued. "We're heading there now. It'll buy us some time to figure out how to get back to Lawless unnoticed. The Fulbrights will be on full alert after your little excursion."

"Wait, what if I don't want to go back to Lawless?"

"You don't have a choice anymore, M," Zara answered. "That ship has sailed."

"No, I mean, what if I don't want to go back there immediately? I have some unfinished business to wrap up first."

"Hmm," said Zara. "I guess I'll see what I can do. But either way, first stop is France."

"How do we get there?" asked M. "I thought England was on an island."

"And you'd be correct," said Zara. "We're taking the Chunnel."

The Chunnel was a passenger train that ran under the English Channel, connecting England to mainland Europe. And while M wasn't giddy at the thought of traveling almost half a mile underwater, it sure beat floating six miles above the ground in an airplane.

They ditched the car in a parking lot and loaded into the train. M had to put her parka back on, and either she was getting used to the Rembrandt, or she'd lost the sense of feeling in her back, because it felt great to be warm again.

"Got your passport?" asked Zara, with a smile.

"Oh no!" gasped M. "I don't have a passport! We flew in to some sort of private airfield to get here."

"Here." Zara handed her a passport. The picture of M was in place and all her credentials were there, including several stamps from other countries — countries M had never actually visited. "I toyed with the idea of becoming an Ident early on," she explained. "It didn't pan out, but I learned a thing or two. Thank me later."

The time on the Chunnel flew by. M tossed her parka over her as a blanket and fell into a deep sleep as soon as they took their seats. When she woke up, Zara had some more goodies for her to snack on.

"How do you know this place?" asked M, still groggy with sleep.

"I lived in London and Paris for a while," she said.

"Your parents were criminal psychologists, right?" asked M.

"What?" Zara responded. "Oh yeah, they are, so — uh — but we moved around a lot."

M had finally found a topic that made Zara lose her cool. But she decided to file away the chink in the armor for now rather than risk angering the person who had helped her escape the Fulbrights.

"Sorry," said M. "I mean, I get it. Parents are weird. So, are we in France yet?"

And almost like magic, the train surfaced and the windows suddenly looked out over the dark French countryside. If it weren't for the light cast by the train, M would have thought they were still underground. Snow covered everything in sight, gleaming and glowing as the train glided through the night.

Outside, the air was cold and smelled of ice and the salty ocean. Zara and M made their way to the train station's parking lot.

"What now?" asked M.

"Pick a car, M," said Zara as she gestured to the full lot, "any car."

Within seconds they were on the road in a blue Toyota Camry. Surprisingly, it was an easy target. The keyless car barely had a chance against Lawless technology. Zara had pulled out a small black box, waved it over the door handle, and the Camry opened itself up to them. Then, with a push of the start button, the car fired right up. There was no other way to describe it, thought M, except: It was pretty cool.

M tried to stay awake, but the night driving coupled with an onset of jet lag knocked her right out. She woke again to the light crunch of tires on a dirt road. The trees were lilting over the path as if peeking to see what was happening in the world below them.

"Almost there, M," comforted Zara. There, it turned out, was an old cabin in the woods somewhere in the French countryside. Before exiting the car, Zara held up a hand-drawn map and read it by the light of her cell phone. She seemed assured of her directions and gave M a warm smile. "Yep, this is the place."

Getting out of the car, they headed up to the cabin. The lights were all out except for a lantern that hung in the front yard, near a small porch. The house looked exquisitely French in its rustic quality. People in the United States dreamed about having a quaint home like this built somewhere in New Hampshire or Montana or Northern California. But this one was authentic, down to the squeaky floorboards on the porch.

"You sure that your friend is home?" asked M.

Before Zara could respond, the front door slowly opened. "Zara Zmith, you have vays of surprising an old voman," said a shaky, matronly voice.

"Madame Voleur, forgive us, but we had no choice," answered Zara.

"You alvays have choices, dear," said the woman, in a thick French-German accent. "Let us hope zat you have chosen visely. Now come inside out of zee cold."

Madame Mallory Voleur looked at least ninety years old. She was small, shrunken even, folding into her body in a way that only years of living can allow. Her hair was wrapped in a head scarf reminiscent of a fortune-teller's and her home was crammed with knickknacks ranging from saltshaker collections to taxidermy statues of small animals.

As she shuffled and led the girls into her home, her breathing was audible from across the room. "Ms. Freeman, it is nice to make your acquaintenze again," Madame Voleur said, without turning around.

"I'm sorry, Madame, but have we met before?" asked M.

"Vell, you ver much younger," she said as she turned and smiled gently at M. "A baby. I do not expect that you vould remember. But I knew you right avay tonight on my steps. You see, you have your mother's eyes. Sit, we have much to discuss."

"Madame Voleur is a little off the beaten path," Zara chimed in, as they all sat down. "M, you know by now that not every criminal goes to the Lawless School. Your mother, for instance, was a self-made thief. She learned from the school of hard knocks, which happens to be taught by Madame Voleur."

"*C'est vrai*, it's true," said the woman. "Your mother vas one of my best pupils. She loved crime, but she loved your father, too."

M was not prepared to uncover more about her mother's past tonight. She wasn't prepared to talk about her father, either. As she sat in her chair, she took everything in. Her first art theft, being detained by the police, seeing her mother again for the first time in ages, only to have the reunion broken up by Fulbrights . . . Maybe it was the lack of sleep, but M felt suddenly overwhelmed. The family ghosts were everywhere in this French shack. Had her mother sat in this same seat? Had her father been in this room at one time when she thought he was on a business trip, evaluating a stamp collection in Des Moines?

M started to cry. She couldn't help herself. It began with one tear, a tiny leak, and then the dam burst.

"Chin up, *miette*," cooed Madame Voleur. "There is no crying in crime."

"I'm sorry," sniveled M. "Excuse me a moment."

She got up and went through the first door she could find. It was a bedroom filled, again, with beautiful oddities: delicate

Fabergé eggs, snow globes, and a disturbingly complete collection of Beanie Babies. M wiped her eyes and sat down on the iron-posted bed, which heaved and sank with her weight. What in the world was going on? Had her own mother tried to throw her under the Fulbright bus? Or had M run to save herself when her mother had needed her most? It felt like M had lost either way she looked at it.

And that's when she saw the jacket. Madame Voleur had a School of Seven Bells jacket on a mannequin in the corner of the room. M walked over to it softly, carefully, making sure to not allow the bells to ring out at her approach. It was strangely comforting, this jacket. It was something she knew, something that she could control. So she leapt into the exercise and lost herself. Like clockwork, she moved swiftly, picking all seven pockets in a continuous, fluid motion. She pulled out a wallet, a gold watch, handkerchiefs, notes, cash, documents, and a coin purse, all without sounding off a single bell. The room was as silent as a tomb.

Until Madame Voleur said, "Zee Zchool of Zeven Bells is an oft-overlooked classic."

M jumped and jerked her hands away from the jacket violently. She hadn't heard the old woman walk into the room and now she was standing right next to M. The seven bells chimed softly in the dark room. "Sorry, Madame, I —"

"Do not worry, *miette*," said Madame Voleur. "Ziss jacket is not electrified like your cruel school's version. People do not learn well through punishment, in my experience."

M relaxed, as Madame Voleur continued, "Zee Zchool of Zeven Bells vas created by my family, believe it or not. Years ago, of course, before there vas a Lawless School. Your mother had the same silent hands. You vill not vant to hear ziss, maybe, but in time, perhaps you vill."

"I was with her tonight," said M. "When the Fulbrights came. I left her there. I escaped without her."

"It is hard," said Madame Voleur, "for thieves to love anyzing. Zee first rule vee teach is to be unattached to zee zings of ziss vorld. Ziss is how thieves get caught. But your mother loves you very much. You did not leave her. She allowed you to escape."

Zara, ever an entrance maker, poked her head into the room with an announcement: "Okay, Ms. Watts and the others are on their way. They'll be here in the morning."

"How on earth could they find us?" asked M.

"Bread crumbs and cell phones." Zara smiled, clearly proud of herself. "I left them a trail of bread crumbs by paying for everything with my club card. Then I sent a text to myself and like it was a flare in the night, they triangulated us and texted me that they're about to board the Chunnel."

"Wait, if you have a phone, why didn't you just call them?" asked M.

"Who uses a phone to talk anymore?" said Zara. "Besides, I'm sure the airwaves are crawling with cops looking for a certain stolen painting." She winked. "There are no secrets at Lawless, M. Congrats on your first heist."

With that, a third wave of exhaustion swept over M. It was late and everyone was tired, so they all went to sleep. It was just like being back in her dorm, thought M before she drifted off to sleep. Except now Zara was snoring right in her face in a shared bed.

The sunlight in the morning was so jarring to M that she woke up completely bewildered. Through the window, sun rays lit up the room and fell right on her pillow, which never happened in her bottom-bunk-bed cave. She squinted her eyes in the bright haze between sleeping and waking up. She saw a shadowy figure sitting in the chair across the room. As she rubbed the sleep from her eyes, she heard Ms. Watts's familiar and unsettling chirp: "Good, you're awake. We need to talk."

"What?" said M, sitting up in bed. Zara was fast asleep beside her still.

"Let's see that painting," Ms. Watts insisted.

"Before we do that," said M, as her head finally cleared the cobwebs, "can you tell me why I was left to rot with those Scotland Yard detectives? Or why *my mom*, who I haven't seen in months, waltzed in to the rescue? Or why she then took me to a Fulbright convention, where I was the guest of dishonor?"

If Ms. Watts was surprised at this line of questioning, she didn't show it. "After Angel and Rex followed you into the gallery, I fuzzed the camera feed. Then all I could do was wait for our rendezvous, but as far as I knew, everything had gone as planned. Except for Rex stealing an actual painting — that was rather impulsive of him. But we used the lemons and made lemonade, putting that painting on a train heading for

Liverpool. The detectives will hunt in the wrong direction for a while.

"Once Adam, Angel, Rex, and I met back up, we waited for your phone call, but it never came," continued Ms. Watts. "Angel and Rex thought you might have skipped out on us, but I told them you're a special case. And I was right, as usual. Somehow, your mother pinged my cell number and forwarded all incoming calls. I don't know how, why, or what she was even doing in London, but if Fulbrights were involved, then you're lucky to still be with us."

"Yeah, lucky," said M. "So why wouldn't the Fulbrights want Scotland Yard to bust me?"

"The Fulbrights don't work with Scotland Yard," answered Ms. Watts. "In my experience, Fulbrights handle everything by themselves. Fewer witnesses that way. Now let's see that painting."

M did not feel good about showing her the painting. The whole time Ms. Watts spoke, she had an intense thousand-yard stare. It was the stare a thief has when they're thinking less about what they're saying and more about how they are going to steal what they've come for. There was no way she was going to leave Ms. Watts alone with the Rembrandt.

M pulled her coat out from under the blankets of the bed and carefully removed the painting.

It was beautiful in the natural French light. For such a dark and seemingly straightforward painting, she could see every painstaking brushstroke. How did this much attention to detail not make Rembrandt blind? At the top left corner of the painting was Rembrandt's signature and the date of the painting, 1632. M's hands were shaking. Not because the painting was so old, but because this very painting had also been held by her father. He had seen all the same artistic intricacies, felt the same weight of the wood in his hands. She wondered if he had been shaking this much when he stole it. The connection was strong and it felt like she was holding her father's ghost in her hands one last time.

Ms. Watts broke M's spell by taking the painting from her and flipping it over to look at the back of the wood.

"Who speaks Latin here?" called Ms. Watts.

Out of the crew in the next room, Rex, oddly enough, was the one to answer Ms. Watts's summons. No wonder he didn't have much to say, thought M; he spoke a dead language.

On the back of the painting there was a Latin inscription. Ms. Watts made this feel like a teaching moment, but it seemed to M that her teacher was hunting down a secret. She kept her eyes on the older woman as the rest of the Masters filed into the room.

"It says that this is Jacob de Gheyn the third, and it calls the painting his last gift at his death," said Rex. "But it's not addressed to anyone. Who's it a gift to?"

"Maurits Huygens!" exclaimed M. The other Masters had trickled into the room and looked confused by this new, strange name, so M told them the story of Jacob de Gheyn and Maurits Huygens.

"But if the paintings are a pair, why aren't they kept together?" Adam wondered aloud.

"And why isn't anyone stealing the Maurits guy's painting?" came a question from a bed-headed Zara, who was stretching behind the group.

"Because the previous thieves didn't do their homework," M said excitedly. "They couldn't figure out the next step. The Takeaway Rembrandt is only the first clue to a bigger prize! We need to find the Huygens portrait."

Adam pulled out his cell phone and within minutes said, "Guys, I know where we're going next. Hamburg, Germany."

"What's there?" asked Angel.

"Mr. Maurits Huygens, of course!" M smiled.

This wasn't an art heist anymore. It was a treasure hunt. The same hunt her father had been on before her.

But as the group was getting excited, M thought of her mother again. "I can't go with you to Germany," she announced. "My mom is in danger. She's my family. She's my priority."

Adam started to plead with M, but Ms. Watts, who had been strangely quiet for some time, interrupted him. "M, you won't find your mother in London. The Fulbrights will take her with them."

"Take her where?" asked M.

"To Germany, of course," Ms. Watts said, with certainty. "That's where they will try to stop us from stealing *Maurits Huygens*."

CHAPTER 20

GO WILD

It didn't take long for M to decide that she was going to steal a second painting. It was never even a question. Her mother was trapped and M had a golden opportunity to save her, all while following in her father's footsteps.

And she certainly hadn't forgotten about what she'd learned about her parents while at the Lawless School. Zara had told M that her parents first met in Hamburg, Germany, while on a heist. M could guess exactly what they were trying to steal: the Takeaway Rembrandt's companion. But why? What was so important about this pair of paintings? And why hadn't Ms. Watts been there to help her father steal them?

As everyone else was busy taking turns showering at Madame Voleur's cabin, M stared intensely at the *Jacob de Gheyn III*. Besides the Latin, it looked like any other old Rembrandt. But it was important. It had to be. Why else would her father steal it? M scoured the background of the painting to see if she had missed something, some landscape beneath the deep black shadows, but she couldn't see anything.

"Sometimes it is not the painting zat is vorth stealing," said Madame Voleur from behind M, as if she could read her thoughts. She had kept herself scarce while the Masters and Ms. Watts were in her house. M could sense that Madame Voleur wasn't too keen on the Lawless School.

"Your friends," she continued, "I am afraid zey bring you trouble. Zere are great mysteries in ziss vorld that vee are not meant to discover. Your friends, zey do not agree. Zey vant everything, no matter zee consequences. Now vhat is it you vant?"

"I want to find my mother," M whispered.

"Zhen find your mother, you vill." The old lady smiled. And as Madame Voleur took the *Jacob de Gheyn III* in her aged hands, she continued, "I vill make sure ziss is returned to zee rightful owners."

"But, Madame Voleur..." began M, but then the floor behind her creaked, announcing the presence of Ms. Watts.

"Best not overstay our welcome, M," she said. "Thank you, Madame Voleur, for your...hospitality. But we need to be going."

"Yes," agreed M. "Thank you, truly."

"*De rien, miette,*" Madame Voleur replied as she carefully stored the painting in a trunk across the room.

Ms. Watts and M rejoined the others, who were dining on fresh bread, cheese, fruit, Nutella, and pâté.

"I was thinking," M said to the group, "the Fulbrights will be looking for us in Hamburg. We'll never be allowed near the painting."

"Thanks, Debbie Downer," said Zara.

"No, I mean, they'll notice *us*, but they wouldn't notice a second crew." M smiled. "Could we make a call to Lawless?"

Twenty-four hours later, M paced a hotel room in Hamburg, waiting for Zara's cell phone to ring.

It had been a long day of travel. They had decided to drive across Europe, reasoning that it would be easier to stay under the Fulbrights' radar that way. In fact, driving from France to Belgium and into northern Germany had been as trouble free as driving from Connecticut to upstate New York. If they had flown, certainly their six fake passports would have been a giant red flag to the Fulbrights. Plus they would have had to deal with airport security, which could mean giving their purpose for visiting Germany. And M didn't think that "stealing a national treasure" would be a satisfactory answer.

But driving meant ten hours in a cramped car full of people — one of whom was Rex the giant. By the time they'd found a hotel on the outskirts of town and everyone had unpacked from the sardine can of a car, M wanted nothing more than to crawl into one of the hotel beds and sleep.

She was up at dawn, ready to mastermind her second heist, hoping it would go better than the first.

"Foley landed this morning and went straight to the site with his team," Zara informed the team.

"Which of the Masters did he bring with him?" she asked.

Zara and Ms. Watts traded a look.

"What is it?" M asked.

"The Masters might be compromised, M," Ms. Watts explained.

"They're exactly who the Fulbrights would be looking for. So Foley has brought your friends for support instead."

"What?" exclaimed M. "Support? You mean bait. Merlyn and Jules have never been in the field before. The Fulbrights will eat them alive!"

"I certainly hope not," Ms. Watts replied. "Foley has also brought my son, Calvin. You may be close to your friends, M, but I am closer to my son, I assure you. Now we all have something at stake."

Zara's cell ring broke the awkward silence that followed. She put it on speakerphone. "Hello?"

"Zara, it's me," said Foley. "Do you have a computer?"

"Yes, we have one here," she answered as she unpacked a laptop.

"Good, I'm sending you an IP address now. Let me know when you're up and running."

Once they typed in the address, the computer screen blinked and the next thing they saw was Cal standing in front of a white building with Greek-looking pillars.

"How do I look?" Cal laughed as he struck a pose like a Greek god's between the pillars. "I thought we were in Germany, not Mount Olympus."

"What are we looking at, Foley?" asked Ms. Watts.

"This is the Kunsthalle Museum," answered Merlyn, who pushed his head into view and pointed upward. The camera swiveled up to follow his lead and revealed the museum's title marquee over the front entrance.

"Ta-da!" Cal said with a magician's affect.

"I was speaking to Mr. Foley," Ms. Watts responded gruffly. "I am familiar with the museum. What are we looking at in terms of Fulbright activity?"

"We look to be safe at the moment, Ms. Watts," said Foley. "But to make sure, we'll need your eyes, too. There are cameras built into our contact lenses. These cameras will send exactly what we're seeing back to you. I'm sharing the full signals now."

Instantly the computer screen came alive with four different points of view. All of M's friends were there and they looked absolutely giddy. She'd never seen Jules smile so broadly — it probably felt good to get away from the school for a little while, even though that meant going to the frozen streets of northern Germany in January.

"We also have ear monitors, so we can communicate with you if we need to," continued Foley. "We're splitting up now."

The four of them headed into the museum, breaking up into pairs. Cal and Jules went to the gallery of nineteenth-century artists — which, of course, Rembrandt wasn't, but they were the scout team looking for anything that seemed out of place. Foley and Merlyn went directly to the old masters collection.

After walking past a healthy dose of patron saint paintings, Foley finally found the portrait of Maurits Huygens. In a black frock and white collar similar to Jacob's, Maurits Huygens wasn't the most attractive subject in the world, either, but he had a mystery about him. His eyebrows and goatee showed the same delicate hand that came to signify Rembrandt's artistic style. The collar was daintier, with more lace details, almost like he was wearing a doily around his neck.

"Is this guy any relation to Christiaan Huygens?" Merlyn asked.

"What are you talking about, Crimer?" asked Zara.

"Christiaan Huygens. The scientist? Big-time influence on Isaac Newton? He was, like, one of the first astrophysicists."

"Sorry I asked," said Zara.

"What should we do next?" Foley interjected.

"Look at it for a minute, Foley," said M.

"M?" whispered Merlyn, Jules, and Cal simultaneously.

"Is that you?" continued Merlyn in a hushed voice. "Because if it is, you've got a lot of nerve —"

"Shut down the chatter!" interrupted Ms. Watts. "Focus on the task at hand."

Something was different about this painting, and M couldn't put her finger on it just yet. "Look at it and talk to Jules about something other than the painting. Both of you keep your eyes on it, but don't seem too interested in the piece."

As Foley and Merlyn chatted away, M studied the painting from both of their points of view. Something was off here, but what? She almost asked Zara to mute their banter for a minute, but then Foley said something that caught her attention.

"Foley," she said. "What did you just say?"

"Nothing. I said I'm hungry," he answered. "And I'm wondering if Hamburg is known for its hamburgers. Is this where they were invented or something?"

Her mother's awkward words at the Lion's Den came back to M in a wave.

You must try the hamburgers. They're off the map, but they're the original.... much better than the copycats ...

"It's a fake!" M said with a gasp.

"How can you tell?" asked Ms. Watts.

"How can you not tell?" she countered. "His body is pointing in the wrong direction. If this is a portrait pair, then he should be facing the accompanying piece. In this painting, though, he would have his back turned to Jacob de Gheyn. It's an obvious mistake if they're together, but apart, it's hard to pick up on.

"Listen, I know this sounds crazy," M continued excitedly, "but I think this is what my mother was trying to tell me in the Lion's Den. 'Hamburgers' was code for Hamburg. 'Better than the copycats' equals the fake *Maurits Huygens*. And 'off the map, but they're the original' equals the real painting!"

"M, you sound like *you're* off the map," said Merlyn, who was shushed immediately by Foley.

"Okay, everyone out now," commanded Ms. Watts. "We'll be in contact with a rendezvous point soon."

The cameras signaled down, and Zara snapped the laptop shut.

"M," said Ms. Watts with a hint of desperation in her voice. "Did your mother give you any more leads? Do you have any idea where to look now?"

"I think I do," said M. "Is there a warehouse district in Hamburg?"

· · ·

The Speicherstadt was a massive warehouse district built as an extension of the Hamburg port in the late eighteen hundreds. Sitting between a series of canals in the port, it comprised a massive brick wall of buildings that stretched the length of several city blocks. Boats were able to dock right next to the warehouse buildings, where goods could be loaded into the storage spaces straight from the hulls, and vice versa. Large pallets of coffee, spices, carpets, and other goods were lifted by a system of pulleys that nested in the buildings' rooftops.

It was an awesome sight and even cooler when it was lit up. M and the others arrived in the early evening, just as the lights came on, giving the scene a sense of majesty. The ground was covered with snow and the canals were littered with chunks of ice that slowly slushed and crushed in the current. M could hear the ice cracking as the wind funneled through the buildings, off the frigid water, right into their faces. Another hour in this wind and their noses would freeze off.

"The magnificent disappearing M Freeman, I presume," said Jules, when M finally appeared on the bridge leading to the warehouse district. Merlyn, Foley, and Cal stood beside her, shivering in the cold.

"I missed you guys!" said M, lighting up with a huge smile.

"Aw, we're just here for the extra credit," joked Merlyn.

Jules elbowed him in the ribs. "M, this is no joke. We've been seriously worried about you. You can't disappear on people like that."

M dropped her eyes. She wasn't used to weighing other people's feelings when making decisions. But she was beginning to see what a responsibility it was. "I'm sorry, you guys. I got so caught up with everything. And it all got a little out of hand."

"Yeah, well, you're forgiven," said Merlyn. He looked sheepishly at M. "Just don't go pulling anything like that again. I mean, Cal wouldn't shut up with his constant M talk — 'I wonder what M's doing now,' or 'Do you think M would like this shirt?' or 'M would have thought my lame jokes were funny.' Dark days, M, dark days."

M turned her attention to Cal, who stood off to the side and wouldn't look at her directly. Instead his gaze followed the icy canal below as it snaked into the distance. M knew what that thousand-yard-stare meant all too well. She'd treated Cal the same way after the Class Clash, when she'd been furious with him. Nope, Cal wasn't going to forgive M as easily as the others had.

It was Adam who broke the silence. "Guys, we're happy you're here. And I want to apologize about making off with your best friend. I mean, it was for the Masters, so . . . No harm, no foul, right?"

Cal finally looked up. He took a step toward Adam and said, "Listen up, Ross, Ross Peters. If you mess with my friends again, I'll personally knock your block off."

"Goody goody," Zara said. "I hate to interrupt the tender reunion, but can we ditch this winter wonderland and snatch what we came here to snatch before frostbite sets in?"

"Yeah, why are we here, M?" asked Jules.

Shaking off Cal's cold shoulder and hot-headed protectiveness, M addressed the crew. "My mom gave me a hint back in London, but I didn't realize it at the time. The *Huygens* has to be here somewhere."

Everyone set across the bridge on to the Speicherstadt's sidewalk. Though the sun was just setting, the lights of restaurants, old stores, and various museums were fully lit, the area busy for a winter night.

"Whoa! The Hamburg Dungeon Museum!" cried Merlyn. "We oughta hit that on the way back."

"That's enough from you, Mr. Eaves," scolded Ms. Watts, and he quieted down immediately. "Now where do we go from here?"

"We could split up," suggested Adam. "We'd cover more ground that way and draw less attention."

Splitting up was the last thing M wanted to do. She had been trying to put the pieces of the puzzle together, but she had hit a dead end. Her mother gave her a little info to jump off from, but not the exact location of the painting. What was the next step?

"What was the date on the front of the *Jacob de Gheyn the Third*, again?" asked M.

"Sixteen thirty-two," said Zara, smiling. "You don't think it would be that obvious, do you?"

"It makes sense," said M. "If I were hiding a piece of art in an oversized warehouse, then that's how I'd find it."

"Can you two let us in on the plan?" asked Foley.

"The painting we want is in warehouse space number sixteen thirty-two," explained M. "Now how do we get in?"

"Leave it to me," replied Angel. He effortlessly skipped up a set of frozen stairs to the closest door and picked the lock in one swift motion. "After you."

The crew entered the darkened warehouse and was immediately struck with an overwhelming aroma — a mixture of coffee and various spices.

Merlyn coughed. "What is that smell? It's like the worst restaurant ever!"

"People keep all kinds of stuff here," described M. "I bet it's a great place to keep perishable goods in the winter, since it's basically like a massive meat locker."

They pushed farther into the rustic hallways. The wood floors were well-worn and old. Tracks from trolleys and overloaded handcarts had made uneven grooves in the floorboards. There was no escape from the cold here. Although the building protected them from the chill wind, their breaths were still visible in the dark of the warehouse, and their fingers still tingled.

The numbers started low, but they went higher as the group went along. At least they were heading in the right direction, and at least 1632 looked to be on the first floor. M had studied the structure from across the river and she wasn't keen to be too high off the ground in such an antique building. There was something about all the cranes that surrounded the structure. Trendy new apartment complexes were sprouting up around this part of the city, but the bare building frames and silent cranes just accented the height of the Speicherstadt. They looked like skeleton arms ready to reach in and pluck out whatever they wanted. She shook off the thought and continued the search.

The number 1632 was crudely painted on a wooden sliding door with nothing more than a padlock keeping it closed. It was not high security. In fact, it was the polar opposite. This was more like breaking into a school locker than stealing a missing Rembrandt.

"This doesn't look good," said Ms. Watts. "Adam, tell me what's behind that door."

Adam pulled a pair of binoculars from his bag and stared at the wooden door. "I'm not seeing any heat sources, Ms. Watts. I think we're clear. Just let me check for electronics or alarms." He flipped a switch on the binoculars and looked up and down the hallway. "Affirmative, nothing there."

"But we walked by tons of high-security systems on almost every other door in this hallway," noted Jules. "Why would anyone put anything important here and only use a padlock?"

"Because they want you to believe that there's nothing important in there, so you'll walk past it," answered M. "It's a bluff. My parents told me about spaces like this. Warehouses where museums and collectors keep their valuable paintings during transit. They're rooms with the least amount of security so that they attract the least amount of attention. Always off the beaten path, under the radar. I think this is it."

As soon as she finished, Rex bit through the padlock with a pair of bolt cutters and slid the door open. The room was huge, filled with trunks and unmarked boxes as far as the eye could see in the fading sunlight coming in from windows high above.

M clicked on a light switch inside the room. The industrial lights in the ceiling flickered and rattled to life with a sputtering buzz and a sickly glow.

Her eyes fell on a set of crowbars placed against the far wall. She took one up and pried open the nearest box as the others gathered round. The lid popped open to uncover a nest of packing material. She fished through layers of waterproof paper shreds and synthetic straw strands, then unwrapped the first find: a Picasso sketch in a plain frame. Next was a Degas portrait of dancers, followed by a landscape painting that M hadn't seen before, but judging by the ornate details of the thick frame, the piece must have been valuable.

"Okay, this is the place," said Ms. Watts, unmoved by the beauty of the uncovered paintings. "Remember that the Rembrandt is our target. Anything that's not our target isn't worth our time. So everyone grab a crowbar and get cracking. It's going to be a long night."

One by one, the boxes offered up their treasures. Da Vinci, Michelangelo, Renoir, Matisse, each piece spilled out of the carefully packed boxes into the stale air of the warehouse room. They were looking for a masterpiece in stacks of masterpieces.

Merlyn and M teamed up to search through the back of the room, going pallet by pallet as the evening stretched into night. They fell into a comfortable rhythm that lasted until Merlyn turned over one trunk and jumped back in terror.

M gasped. "What is it?"

"Dead rats!" Merlyn gagged. "Oh, that smell is horrid."

The stench rose quickly into the open air of the room, over-taking the scent of damp wooden crates. M held her nose and looked for a window to open. The windows were all too high to reach, but there was a docking door that led out to the water, so she cracked it open to let in some fresh air.

The inner canal was right beneath the doorway, where boats could pull in and unload. An ingenious plan, except for one thing: winter in Hamburg. The inner canal was frozen solid. M stood six feet above a fixed slab of ice with gallons of swirling water flowing silently underneath.

"Looks like no delivery today," said Zara from over M's shoulder. "Let's keep looking."

Resuming the search, M picked through crate after crate and picked splinter after splinter from her freezing hands until she cracked open a small box that held only one piece. She unwrapped it to find a blank canvas in a frame. What in the world was a blank canvas doing here among the masterpieces?

"What did you find?" asked Merlyn.

"I think this is it," she said as she placed the empty canvas down. "I need a knife over here! Someone, a knife?"

"Here," said Rex.

M took a small knife from him and carefully cut around the edges of the canvas, pulling it away to reveal the real *Maurits Huygens*. It had to be. The brushstrokes were identical to those of *Jacob de Gheyn III* and the positioning was correct.

M was speechless as the group gathered around again. Carefully she turned the frame over and peeled away the paper backing to get at the actual painting. It was made from the same type of wood as its partner portrait, still sturdy after all these years. M's excitement at the discovery instantly gave way to confusion as she flipped the painting from front to back.

"Where's the message?" Ms. Watts snarled as she wrested the painting away from M. "It has to be here!"

"Try a black light," suggested Adam, who handed her one — like an evil little Boy Scout, ever prepared.

Ms. Watts clicked the black light on, but only dust particles were revealed.

"Fire," suggested M. "Do you have a lighter?"

Adam handed her a lighter. Of course he had a lighter. He probably had anything she wanted in that Pandora's backpack.

"Wait, we just found it and you want to torch it?" asked Cal.

"It's a trick I learned from your mom," M said, remembering her first mysterious note from the Lawless School. She held out a hand to Ms. Watts. "May I?"

The teacher narrowed her eyes as if wary, but she handed over the painting. M carefully traced the flame across the back of the wood panel, and words began to rise from the charred background.

Jonathan Wild.

And, below that: *Black Museum.*

A number was appearing beneath the words, too, but it blistered up from underneath the layers of lacquer very slowly.

"Come on," said Ms. Watts.

"Who is Jonathan Wild?" Merlyn asked, but then the world suddenly went black.

Well, if not the world, then at least the entire warehouse district. Darkness fell all around the crew, and the room went painfully still.

"Please tell me that Germany has rolling blackouts," said Cal, but M knew better.

"Go, go, go!" She started the command as a whisper but was screaming by the end, as she saw the movements of shadows in the pitch-black room.

Before the others knew what was happening, the darkness was dashed away with a flare explosion that erupted in an intense burst of light, temporarily blinding them all.

The Fulbrights had arrived.

M clutched the painting to her chest. She quickly blinked her eyes open and shut in the darkness, trying to regain her sight. Slowly the bright spots began to fade. And when they did, she saw the final number on the painting: *1714*.

But that wasn't the first thing on M's mind now. She could feel the Fulbrights' presence, as scuffling footsteps poured through the front door into the room. She took a deep breath. Even though it would be smartest to escape and save the portrait, her friends were in danger. And she wasn't going to leave them behind again.

As she listened to the Fulbrights' movements, their tactic became clear. They were going to force the Lawless students back and pin them against the frozen water. And their plan was working. M could see Ms. Watts run toward the canal door. The full moon reflecting off the frozen river cast an eerie glow — it wasn't exactly inviting, but it was their only exit. Looking around her, M spotted Jules and Merlyn, still stunned from the blast, but Cal was nowhere to be seen. She gathered Jules and Merlyn and led them through the dark rows of crates.

Rex made first contact with the Fulbrights and it looked like something out of an action movie. He literally picked two of them up from behind and cracked their heads together. Five more Fulbrights jumped him in retaliation, but they were bucked like babies off a bronco's back in a rodeo.

Angel and Adam were less direct in their assault, sliding around the room out of sight and then striking from the shadows to take the Fulbrights down, one by one. M also heard a struggle behind her and assumed Zara and Foley were holding their own. But she wasn't going to turn around and find out. She led her friends to the opening overlooking the canal.

"What now?" asked Merlyn.

"We jump," M said as she looked out over the empty stretch of ice.

"We what?" whispered Merlyn.

"We jump and run across the ice to the warehouse on the other side," she answered.

Suddenly an explosion from behind launched them all into the air. M landed on the ice with a crushing thud and the painting skidded away from her. Merlyn and Jules were flung onto the river nearby.

A fire raged behind them in the warehouse. M's heart sank. Scores of priceless paintings were burning before her eyes. But one could still be saved.

"Get that painting!" commanded Ms. Watts from the safety of the warehouse across the canal.

M saw a shadow dart onto the ice. It was Cal. He slid toward the painting, with his hands outstretched, and snagged his prize. She could see the pride in his eyes as he grabbed the painting and held it up like a trophy. She could also see how surprised he was when the ice cracked beneath him and the canal swallowed him whole.

"Cal!" screamed M.

"The painting!" screamed Ms. Watts.

M dashed to the hole in the ice and dove into the water. It was an unearthly feeling, like nothing she had ever experienced before. Instantly her entire body went numb and her muscles seized up. She fought to open her eyes underwater, which gave her the most intense brain freeze ever. She peered through the murky depths for any sign of life, but the canal was moving fast under the ice. Cal could be anywhere, and she was being dragged along with him. Her lungs began to burn as the rest of her body froze. She tried to surface, but there was only ice overhead.

And against that ice, floating nearby, was a motionless, shadowy form. It was Cal! M's adrenaline kicked in as she swam over to him and looped her arm around his waist. Feverishly she kicked against the ice ceiling that separated her lungs from all that glorious German air. But the ice did not give. She was trapped.

She heard a rhythmic stomping sound. She closed her eyes and listened to it beat louder and louder. It must be her heart. She was listening to her heart take its last beats. It was the most horrible and lovely music she had ever heard. And on the last beat, the water churned around her, bubbles all around, and she felt as if she were rising into the open air.

There was a pressure on M's chest. Even pulses were forcing something out of her. Was it her soul? The pulses were followed by someone's mouth blowing air into her, followed by more pulses — until M threw up a gallon of water.

Lying down on the ice, she blinked her blurry eyes, trying to figure out who had saved her. When she finally focused, a Fulbright mask was staring back at her. He was on his knees next to M, with an exhaust of white clouds puffing from his mask. Then, apparently satisfied that she was going to live, the Fulbright ripped off M's moon-rock necklace.

Catching her breath in the cold air, M sat up and watched the Fulbright escape with her necklace across the frozen ice. Then she turned to look for Cal, but another set of Fulbrights was dragging his limp body back into the shadows.

Slowly the sounds of the night returned to M as Merlyn, Jules, and Zara ran over to her. She must have floated far downstream when she was underwater. They were by the bridge where they'd all met on the way to the warehouse.

"M, are you okay?" asked Jules frantically.

M's lungs burned and her hands had turned blue. How long

had she been underwater? She nodded to Jules and lay back down on the ice. The night sky above them looked so peaceful. How could anything under this beautiful a sky go so wrong?

Surrounded by warehouses draped in flashing shadows from the fire in the distance, M stood with the help of her friends, and they took off in the opposite direction before anyone else came looking for them.

CHAPTER 21
THE MASTER PLAN

The house wasn't much to look at, but it was safe, according to Zara. Just outside of Hamburg, in a forest fit for Grimm's fairy tales, the remaining crew — M, Zara, Merlyn, and Jules — sat on the back porch, watching the sunrise. The light filtered through the trees like a searchlight, as the car they had stolen sat idle in a shed behind the house.

Cal was gone, captured by the Fulbrights. Foley, too. Zara had lost him in the scuffle and later saw him being forced into a helicopter as the Fulbrights made a quick escape.

And poor *Maurits Huygens* — sunk to an icy grave at the bottom of the canal. What would subtemperature water do to a four-hundred-year-old oak panel painting? *Probably nothing worse than the fire that had torched the other masterpieces stored in the warehouse*, thought M. So far in this adventure, the score was good guys one, bad guys one, priceless art zero.

Not to mention that her mother was still missing. M felt like she couldn't do anything right. This whole disaster was her fault.

Reports of the fire had swept across the news feeds. The BBC said that the cause was unknown, but that it was presumed to have been started by three teens whom the police had caught on the scene. There was little doubt in M's mind that those three teens were Adam Worth, Angel Villon, and Rex Sykes.

M was wrapped in an oversized blanket, still struggling to warm her arms and legs. Her hair was icy from the river water, but the feeling was slowly flowing back into her fingers, which gripped a steaming cup of tea. She didn't want to drink it as much as she wanted to hop inside it and thaw out.

She broke the silence. "Ms. Watts left them behind to take the fall, didn't she?"

"They knew what they were getting into," said Zara.

"But Ms. Watts sure didn't help them," spat M. "She played us. She played us and I still can't figure out why."

"M," offered Zara, "I haven't been totally honest with you. Can we talk?"

Zara looked pointedly at Merlyn and Jules.

"Anything you want to tell me, they deserve to hear," M said firmly. "We're all in the same sinking boat now."

Zara exhaled dramatically and shot Merlyn a look. "Fine. But you better not be blogging any of this, Crimer."

Merlyn put up his hands. "I'm a hacker, not a gossip columnist."

"Where to begin?" Zara asked herself. Her legs were bouncing, rhythmic and steady, and her eyes flitted over the horizon. "I'm not who you think, M. My parents weren't criminal psychologists. They weren't even big-time thieves. When I was little, we backpacked across Europe, city to village to city, pulling strictly small-time jobs. Wallets, food, the occasional local bank . . . It was all, I don't know, like some crazy adventure."

M listened silently to her guardian, the girl she'd been warned not to trust. The girl who had saved her life at least once.

"We were constantly on the run. I didn't have any friends. I mean, most of the time no one even knew my real name. But I had my parents and I had my dreams — dreams of the Lawless School. My father, he used to tell me bedtime stories of famous Lawless criminals and their perfect heists — and I would fantasize about joining them, stealing diamonds and artwork and leaving Interpol scratching their heads. But we weren't Lawless criminals. We didn't warrant that kind of attention."

Zara paused, looking out at the dark forest before beginning again. "I suppose I became obsessed. I stole newspapers, looking for clues to fresh Lawless crimes. Cargo trucks mysteriously disappearing from mountain overpasses, secrets sold to rival countries, anything odd or out of place in a news story, I clipped the articles and started a scrapbook.

"It was a childish hobby at first, but it grew into an elaborate map of Lawless footprints and fingerprints that stretched around the entire globe. And then, when I turned eleven, the Lawless School showed up at my door, in the form of a man named Dr. Gerhardt."

244

M blinked at the name. If Gerhardt had visited Zara, why hadn't he shared *that* story with the class?

"He was so cool, you know?" Zara continued. "He just walked through the front door of our rental house. He knew my name, my parents' names. I mean, just the fact that he knew where to find us — we'd only moved there two weeks earlier."

M could hear the emotion in Zara's voice. Whatever secret history she was sharing, it was a story that she hadn't told often.

"He asked to speak with me alone and excused us from my parents. Walking outside, I thought this was it, my big ticket. My Lawless fairy godfather had come to whisk me away to the fabulous life of crime I deserved. But he only asked me for my scrapbook. I gave it to him. He flipped through it once, slipped it under his arm, and told me to forget about the Lawless School forever. 'We don't want you,' he said. Then he stepped into a waiting limo, leaving me on the sidewalk with nothing.

"Needless to say, I was devastated. I locked myself in my room, but my parents kept picking the lock to make sure I was eating. It didn't matter. My future was over before it had begun.

"But then my parents called a friend — they called Madame Voleur. She took me in and built me back up."

If Merlyn or Jules wondered who Zara was talking about, they kept their questions to themselves. M watched the older girl intently. A smile had broken out on her face, but it wasn't a happy smile. There was longing there, and pain. Zara's story wasn't over yet.

"Madame Voleur trained me in the same way that your tutors trained you, M. Except I knew all along that I was being groomed for a life of crime. And I almost managed to forget all about the Lawless School. Until I turned twelve, and someone new showed up at our door. Ms. Watts.

"She told me that the school'd had a change of heart and that I could attend if I agreed, at some point, to give them a favor in return."

"What was the favor?" asked Merlyn.

"To be my guardian," guessed M.

"They gave me a report my first day at the Lawless School," Zara admitted. "It was your life story, M. And the rest is history."

"Why is M so important?" asked Jules. "And why are you just now telling her that Ms. Watts had some weird interest in her?"

"Yeah," agreed Merlyn. "What kind of a guardian are you, anyway?"

"I'm important because Ms. Watts didn't know the next step after the Takeaway Rembrandt," said M with certainty. It was suddenly so clear. "My dad ditched Ms. Watts, didn't he?"

"Yeah," admitted Zara. "After he stole the Takeaway Rembrandt, your father cut off all ties with her . . . and with the Lawless School, too."

"Because of where the Takeaway led him?" asked Merlyn.

"That's the best theory we've got," said M. "He was able to follow the trail from *Jacob* to *Maurits*, but he didn't pursue it any further than that, and he didn't want anybody else at Lawless figuring out where the trail ended, either. He replaced the second portrait with a fake so that *Jacob* led to a dead end. But my mother knew the truth."

"Why not just torch *Maurits*?" asked Merlyn.

M shook her head. "My dad was an art lover. He'd never destroy a Rembrandt, no matter what. And I'm beginning to think . . . it's possible he wanted me to be able to complete the job."

"It must be a treasure," Jules said. "It was his way of making sure you'd be taken care of."

"Maybe," said M. "All I know is we need to finish whatever my father started, before Ms. Watts or the Fulbrights beat us to it."

"So who is Jonathan Wild?" asked Jules. "What's his role in this?"

Zara spoke up again. "Jonathan Wild was known as the King of Thieves. He lived in London in the late sixteen hundreds and the early seventeen hundreds. You see, in London during that time, crime was rampant. There was no police force back then, just a loose policy of a neighborhood watch. 'If you see something, say something' — that kind of thing. Well, Wild came along and saw a unique opportunity. He became what was called a thief taker. In this role, he was hired by the victims of a crime to capture criminals and return stolen goods. In return for his work, he was paid handsomely by the grateful victims — and by the state, who arrested the criminals. And usually hanged them."

"So he was like a bounty hunter," suggested M.

"Something like that," said Zara. "But Wild was playing both sides. He was a criminal on the side. He became the head of the thief takers *and* the head of the criminal underworld. Nothing was stolen in London without Wild's knowledge, and nobody was caught unless he decided to turn them in. He ran the city completely, had a monopoly on all that was good and bad."

"It didn't last, though," continued Merlyn, who had searched online for Wild while Zara was talking. "Eventually he was caught trying to help a thief escape from prison and the whole truth came out. The sheriff and the mob boss were one in the same."

"How do you know all this, Zara?" asked M.

"From Madame Voleur," she answered. "And you won't find the rest of the tale on Google, Merlyn. The story goes that in jail, Wild became obsessed with larger crimes, like megalomaniacal, end-of-the-world stuff. What else did he have left to lose? He was stuck in prison until his execution, so Wild began to read science books from the library. Starting with alchemy, he worked through hundreds of books until he stumbled onto an astrophysics theory by some scientist. The theory was very hypothetical, untested, and buried in a mess of incomplete thoughts."

"Did you say astrophysics?" asked Merlyn. He started typing again.

"That's the connection," said M. "I'd bet anything that sci-entist was Christiaan Huygens!"

Merlyn nodded. "Who, it just so happens, was the son of Constantjin and nephew of Maurits."

"What was the theory about?" asked Jules.

"Essentially," said Zara, "Wild came to believe that by mixing the right combination of extraterrestrial elements, one could create a black hole."

"A black hole." M gasped. "On Earth? Why would anyone do that?"

"Um, did I mention that he was crazy?" asked Zara. "Anyway, by the time Wild reached out to his old gang about his doomsday plan, there had been a division among the ranks. Members of Wild's crew had split into different groups : . . . and that's how the original strands of the Lawless School and the Fulbrights were born."

"Both groups can be traced back to one person?" asked M, amazed. She had somehow assumed that this battle between "good" and "evil" had gone on forever, without beginning or end.

"According to Madame Voleur," said Zara, "Wild's crimi-nal crew found one of the two ingredients quickly. But they couldn't get their hands on the second piece. Over the course of years, Wild's *umbra mortis* theory was lost, and he was never avenged."

"The shadow of death," M whispered. "That's the name of Rembrandt's shading style for dead bodies in his artwork. It's a perfect description for a black hole, too."

"But the theory was lost," echoed Merlyn.

"Lost or hidden?" asked M. "What if Wild had somebody plant a hidden map to his madness on the backs of the two Rembrandt paintings — just waiting for the right criminal to figure it out? The timing works out. The paintings went missing around 1642 and resurfaced after Wild's death."

"Zara," said Jules, suddenly agitated, "I'll repeat myself: Why did *you* wait so long to tell us about this? Are you crazy?"

"Hey," said Zara, "the whole criminal underworld knew that the Rembrandt paintings led to some great secret — but I always assumed it was a treasure, maybe a cache of hidden masterpieces, not some mad scheme by the long-dead Jonathan Wild . . . not . . . ."

"The end of the world," finished M. "Does Ms. Watts know, do you think? Is she hunting for treasure or a weapon?"

"I think your father hid it from her for a reason," said Zara. "And she used you to find exactly what she wanted."

There was an awkward silence as the crew let the ugly truth settle around them.

"Wait, I know what a black hole is, but what can it do?" asked Jules. "I mean, is it that destructive?"

"In space, it's not too bad," answered Merlyn. "It's a vortex of gravity from massively crushed matter that is so strong, it swallows everything around it — including light itself."

"Yeah, totally not horrifying," Zara said sarcastically.

"So what happened to Wild?" asked M.

"Hanged by one of his friends at a public execution," said Merlyn. "Whoever says that history is boring has no idea what they're missing out on. This stuff is crazy."

"Hmm, then what's the Black Museum?" asked M. "That name was on the back of the painting, too. And it's no museum my parents ever mentioned."

"Wow," said a startled Merlyn from his computer. "I found it, but you're not going to like it. Over the years in England, Scotland Yard amassed a collection of criminal weapons and paraphernalia. As the collection grew in storage, it developed into the Black Museum. But it's better known as the Crime Museum now."

"Oh, I've heard of that place," added Jules. "They're supposed to have actual letters written by Jack the Ripper, right?"

"It has all sorts of criminal evidence, apparently," he answered. "Scotland Yard detectives used it for training purposes back in the eighteen hundreds, as insight into the criminal mind and its modus operandi."

"Sounds like a great place to hide a secret," admitted M. "But how did it end up there?"

Zara threw her hands into the air and shrugged her shoulders. "No idea, I swear."

"Okay, well, all signs point to the Black Museum as our next and final stop," said M. "Where is this place, anyway?"

"That's the kicker," said Merlyn. "It's in Scotland Yard headquarters."

The air went out of the conversation.

"So we'll break into Scotland Yard," said M.

"We break into Scotland Yard to find what?" asked Jules.

"Item number 1714," said M confidently. "Whatever that object is, it used to belong to Jonathan Wild and it's half of his loony doomsday equation. We have to get it before anyone else can. Now, if Wild had one element, did he even know what the other one was?"

"Yeah," said Zara, "but it was completely unattainable at the time."

"Can people get it now?" asked Jules.

"Sure, but the idea was far-fetched," said Zara. "Listen, Wild's theory involved striking the moon with a comet to create a black hole big enough to consume Earth."

"Zara." M jumped up. "Did you say the *moon* was one of the two elements?"

"Yes," she said. "It was bonkers to think anyone could swipe even just a piece of the moon in the eighteen hundreds. Getting a scrap of meteorite was plausible, but the moon was safely out of reach."

"Not anymore," said M, wringing her hands nervously around her neck where her necklace used to be. "The Fulbright at the Speicherstadt stole my necklace. The one with the moon rock!"

"Good, then," exclaimed Zara. "According to your file, your father spent his time finding existing moon rocks and secretly destroying them. Your moon rock must be one of the last on Earth. If it's with the Fulbrights, that means Ms. Watts won't be able to get it."

"Still," said M, "I think we all know Ms. Watts and can agree it will be best for everyone if we get to item 1714 first."

"So we're going back to London," said Merlyn.

"We're going to steal from the Black Museum," said M. "And I know just how to do it."

CHAPTER 22

UNDER COVER OF BROAD DAYLIGHT

Merlyn, Jules, Zara, and M checked into the Crime Museum under their own names. Usually the museum was off limits to anyone other than the police, but exceptions were made for those who got permission from one of Scotland Yard's finest. And as M had predicted, Chief Inspector Banks — whose card she'd held on to since he'd detained her — had been more than happy to put her and her friends on the list. All she'd had to do was call and ask him for the favor. He was in a good mood, since the Takeaway Rembrandt had been recovered and three thieves (matching M's descriptions) had been arrested in Germany while attempting another art heist.

The first thing she noticed about the Crime Museum was that it was small. It fit inside two rooms, but those two rooms were crammed full of evidence of past English crimes. Early lock-picking tools, knives, and concealed weapons, like an umbrella fashioned into a gun and walking sticks that served as sheaths for secret swords, lay locked behind glass display cases. The creepiest thing about these weapons was that they had all been used in actual crimes, which made M shudder. *True criminals don't need weapons*, she reminded herself.

Professor Bandit had said so early in the school year. These weapons, this room, everything here was dedicated to the study of madmen.

As the curator led them around the room, everyone looked for any sign of item numbers among the museum's collection, but they couldn't find anything. There must be a manifest somewhere, labeling each display. The curator had a small office off the front entrance. M figured that must be where it was kept, but they were in the thick of the museum tour now, so they might as well enjoy it.

For such a small museum, it was a very involved tour. They learned about the history of English crime and English justice. And the lessons required a strong stomach. The stories were gruesome, disturbing, and worst of all, real — from the killer who boiled his victims in acid to the gory details of Jack the Ripper's unspeakable crimes. M had no desire to see the *umbra mortis* added to this list of atrocities. She needed to get that manifest and find the missing element.

When the tour finally ended, the group split up to canvass the area. Merlyn kept the curator busy with a barrage of questions. Zara roamed through the exhibits, looking for anything vaguely meteoritelike. Jules faded back toward the front while M slipped into the curator's office unnoticed. Riffling through files, M searched every drawer quickly and quietly. She didn't dare touch the computer. It was probably password protected to the nth degree, but M had a feeling that the Crime Museum was the kind of place that prided itself on keeping a paper trail.

"Bingo," she whispered as she clicked open a locked drawer in the main desk. She pulled out the list and flipped through the numbered exhibits. But there was one problem: The list didn't reach number 1714.

M replaced everything and walked out of the office. "Trouble," she said to Jules. "The manifest doesn't go up to 1714. That number isn't what I thought it was."

"Just great," huffed Jules. "I sat through the entire gross-out talk for nothing. So what now?"

M shrugged. "We keep looking."

They joined the others, poring over the odds and ends of the museum. M wandered the rooms, searching at first for what looked most out of place, but this was a crazy museum. Nothing looked out of place.

Finally, something caught M's eye in the weapons section. It was a gentleman's walking cane, crafted out of wood with a decorative brass handle. On the tip of the handle was a smooth amber rock that looked like a tiger's eye, with a single letter inscribed on it. The letter *W*.

"What's this?" M called out to the curator.

"Oh, this piece has a wonderfully mysterious origin," the curator responded, obviously happy to escape Merlyn's unending questions for a moment. "This was the first item ever entered into the Crime Museum, before it was even an official museum. There was an old inspector who collected evidence and weapons back in 1869, starting with this innocent-looking cane right here. Believe it or not, it's not tied to any known crime."

"No crime?" asked M. "Then why is it in the Crime Museum?"

"Because it was the first of its kind," the curator continued excitedly. "If you look at the base of the cane, you'll see a blade. That blade retracts when the handle is turned. Quite dangerous, wouldn't you say?"

M leaned down to get a closer look at the slim blade that was unsheathed from the cane's bottom. The blade was heavily rusted. It looked like any other old weapon worn out by age. But engraved onto the retractable blade was the number 1714.

"So you don't know who this belonged to?" asked M.

"No," said the curator. "But I would venture a guess that whoever had this weapon had a name with the initial *W* . . . or *M*."

"Oh, I . . . I read it as a *W* for sure," said M.

"Ah, yes, *W* when the weapon is armed," said the curator. "But *M* when the blade is concealed."

M studied the amber stone in the handle. It was obvious. It was the meteorite. M had found her mark.

She eyed Jules, motioned toward the cane, and thanked the curator for the tour. Then she left the museum. It was no use being caught at two crime scenes, after all. But she had left a special present in the curator's office air vent — two smoke bombs. When they went off, Jules would pull a fire alarm, Zara would do a smash-and-grab, and they'd all join the rush out of the building before anyone knew what was happening.

That was the plan, anyway.

A blaring bell rang out through the hallway as M hustled to get out of the Scotland Yard headquarters as fast as she could. The hallway filled with men and women who were equally eager to evacuate the building, if for other reasons.

She was almost to the entrance when she saw Chief Inspector Banks shoving through the crowd, against the tide. He walked past her without blinking an eye. His face was blank and he was unfazed by the alarm or by the people moving around him in the opposite direction. M had seen that look before. He'd obviously been dosed with the Lawless special blend of mind-control gas and he was heading right toward the Black Museum. On a mission for Ms. Watts, no doubt. M had no choice — she doubled back to keep an eye on the sleepwalking inspector.

She saw her friends coming up the hallway, walking away from the museum with purpose. Zara carried the cane — it was rotten luck that their mark was too big to conceal. M tried to get their attention, but it was all she could do to push through the crowd.

Chief Inspector Banks got there first.

With one punch from the inspector, Zara dropped the cane and Banks grabbed it. Merlyn and Jules recovered from their shock and tugged at the man, but they were like gnats attacking a boulder. He brushed them aside easily.

Banks stormed back down the hallway, clutching Wild's cane, and barreled past M without stopping. She switched directions and chased him outside. The sidewalk was cluttered with police and other Scotland Yard employees. Fire trucks with lights flashing stood at the ready, parked outside. But that didn't stop Banks. He plowed a path through the crowd, heading directly toward a fire service command car, which idled just in front of the legion of fire trucks. M made out the driver instantly. It was Ms. Watts. Banks made the handoff and the command car tore into the open road.

"What just happened?" asked Jules. "Was that a cop?"

"He's working for Ms. Watts," M said. "We've been scooped."

Zara had already dashed to the nearest available police car and opened it with her special wireless tool. M, Jules, and Merlyn jumped in as Zara sounded the sirens and gave chase.

The cars raced through the clogged inner-city streets filled with double-decker buses and taxis. Weaving in and out of traffic, the command car was big and built for tough riding. Ms. Watts blasted across a roundabout, clean through Parliament Square. A huge cluster of birds flew into the air and people scattered in every direction. Zara was unfazed and followed suit, crashing through a set of outside tables along the way. One of the chairs slammed into the front windshield and spiderwebbed the safety glass. The road disappeared in a splash of white cracks until M kicked the remaining glass out of the way and the London wind swept through the police car.

Ms. Watts made a vicious right turn that nearly flipped her car, but she held it steady on two wheels until the torque pushed the body back down and her other two tires reconnected with the road. Zara made the same turn and lost control of the rear of the police car, fishtailing dangerously into the sidewalk. Wobbling back into gear, she pushed forward and kept on, full speed.

As they blistered past Big Ben onto Waterloo Bridge, helicopters whirred above the cars, their shadows looming along the roadway. The Fulbrights were near.

"Where is she going?" yelled Merlyn, from the backseat.

"No idea!" hollered Zara coolly. "It's a great ride, though!"

Once on the other side of the bridge, Ms. Watts swerved into oncoming traffic, forcing cars into Zara's lane. Zara dodged and wove through the traffic until she caught back up with the command car. As she pulled alongside Ms. Watts, she turned strongly into her, ramming her car and sending her into a skidding stop.

Ms. Watts jumped out from the car with the cane and ran into the city streets. M joined the footrace. M was fast, but Ms. Watts was faster. Luckily, she took a wrong turn and led M to a dead end.

"Give it up, Ms. Watts," cried M. "The Lawless graduate never needs a weapon. Especially one as dangerous as that cane."

"Oh, shut up, kid!" huffed Ms. Watts. "I'm going to end this here and now. Every Lawless student *is* a weapon, you dolt. And you get used all the time. Steal the Takeaway Rembrandt. Steal the *Huygens*. You've been our greatest weapon in this hunt, and you didn't even know it!"

"Well, I don't want to be a Lawless student anymore," said M. "I've seen what you're capable of. You were willing to let me take the fall at the Dulwich Picture Gallery. You were willing to let your son drown. And now you're willing to let millions of people die. For what?"

"For chaos, of course!" shouted Ms. Watts. "For the bragging rights to the most audacious crime ever committed. Look around you, M. What are these people to you? These strangers sipping tea and watching TV — they're fodder.

"And don't you mention Calvin," she continued. "I've done much worse than that, M. Much worse! I loved Calvin. I loved your father, too, you little brat."

M's mind was racing. She kept her eyes on the cane swinging in Ms. Watts's hands, but for the first time, she was hearing Ms. Watts very clearly.

"Y-you," stammered M. "You did it. You killed him, didn't you? You killed my father!"

"What else could I do?" spat Ms. Watts. "That fool was destroying the moon rocks. I couldn't let that happen. They weren't his to destroy! I tried talking to him, hoping to spark back to life the wicked man that I fell in love with so long ago, but he had withered away into some petty-level family twerp."

Ms. Watts paused, pacing back and forth, breathing heavily. She wiped the spittle from her chin, smiled darkly, and turned back to M. "So I planted a bomb on his plane and the rest is scattered just over the hills of the Lawless School."

The confession hit M like a bullet to the chest. *The cane*, she thought, *keep your eyes on the cane*. "It's over now, Ms. Watts," she said calmly. "Whatever happened to my father happened. And because of that, I know what it's like to lose someone you love. I wouldn't wish that horrible feeling on anyone. Even strangers. Even you."

M took a cautious step toward Ms. Watts as if she were approaching a hungry lion. She barely heard the footsteps coming from behind before the puffs of yellow smoke wafted around her like the London fog.

"I'll take it from here, Freeman," said Zara. "Ms. Watts, we need to get everyone back to Lawless *now*. The Fulbrights are on our trail."

The reality of Zara's double cross faded into the dead-end street as a waking dream drifted over M again. Her heavy eyelids shut and everything went black.

CHAPTER 23
COMPROMISED AND CLASSIFIED

M woke in total darkness. Her lips were chapped, her throat was a dry desert, and she had a horrible headache. She tried to move her arms, but they were bound tightly behind her back. Sweat crawled down her neck and the heavy winter layers that had kept her warm in London now clung uncomfortably to her skin.

"Hello?" She coughed. "Is anyone there?"

"M?" Merlyn's hoarse voice replied, from somewhere else in the room. "Are you okay?"

"I guess," said M. "Where's Jules?"

"Byrd, Juliandra. Present and captive," joked Jules.

M couldn't see her friends in the darkness, but knowing that they were there made her breathe a sigh of relief. *Misery loves company*, she thought. Everyone sounded just as tired and worn out as she felt.

"Anyone know what happened exactly?" asked M.

"Here's a recap," began Merlyn. "Your guardian is a really bad driver and a pretty bad person. After she wrecked the cop car, she trapped us in the backseat, which was totally child-criminal safety locked, by the way. *Um, where was that lesson, Professor Bandit?* Oh, and then she blasted us all with yellow smoke. Apparently so she could cart us to the darkest room in the world."

Based on the distance of her friends' voices and their echoes, M figured the room was large. They were all seated far apart from one another, and no one was moving — Merlyn and Jules were tied down, too, no doubt. M kicked her legs forward, feeling for anything that might be around her, but she was met with nothing more than empty air and the expansive floor.

An audible *click* popped like a PA speaker turning on, followed by the white noise of dead-air radio silence. The airy, empty tone seemed to go on forever. It invaded M's head, putting her on edge for whatever was going to come next. Finally a computer-generated voice announced: "Scan complete. Welcome, Lady Watts."

High up above them, a light turned on in a small window. It was the only light in the room and flashed as brightly and viciously as an explosion. Ms. Watts stepped up to the window and her silhouette was a monstrous beacon beaming into the shadows below.

"Students," Ms. Watts began with a smile, "it's so nice to have you here with me today. As you've no doubt gathered, you do not have the upper hand anymore. You actually never did. So please don't try my patience. Ms. Freeman knows the location of a lunar rock. I now require said rock for a very specific purpose. The choice is simple: Give me the rock and you live; don't and you die."

"It's yours," bluffed M. "I have it down here. Just let my friends go, okay?"

Ms. Watts began laughing maniacally. "Are you really going to lie to me, M? I know the rock from your necklace is gone. If it were on your person, I would have stolen it back in London. No, what I need from you is the location of the second rock."

"What second rock?" M's question echoed through the room. "There's only the one. I swear."

Ms. Watts regarded her coldly for a moment. "Well, well, well," she said at length. "It seems your father kept more secrets from you than I'd thought. Students, I fear Ms. Freeman is no longer of any use to me. And therefore neither are you. I'll be sure to let your parents know that I gave you a chance to help before you died. Parents do get so emotional about their little ones going away to school for the first time. Now please, go gentle into that good night, stiff upper lip and all that."

As Ms. Watts backed away from the window, the floor beneath M jolted and rocked. The lit window above began moving closer to them. No, they were moving closer to it! The floor was pushing them upward toward the ceiling.

They were in the Box.

"Ugh, I didn't see this coming," said Merlyn, from his corner. "Accepted into the Lawless School and then turned into a pancake. Now that's criminal."

M strained against her bindings. There had to be a light at the end of the tunnel — other than the lit window above them, crawling ever closer. "Merlyn, could you reroute the program to call this crusher off?"

"Sure, if I wasn't trapped in here with you," said Merlyn despondently.

"Jules, I hear you wrestling with those handcuffs. Any luck?" asked M.

"I'm double chained," answered Jules. "It'll take more time."

M tried rocking back and forth, but her chair was bolted to the floor. The white noise of the speakers had been replaced by the sickening sound of the floor scraping against the walls in its ascent to a dark but presumably dead end of a ceiling.

"Now I know what trash feels like," Merlyn said to no one in particular.

"Everyone bend forward!" shouted M, as the ceiling came into sight. She ducked her head down as the space of the room closed in on itself. The back of her chair caught against the ceiling. The floor stopped momentarily, but she could feel the chair straining against the compacting force. It wouldn't be long before the chair was reduced to a pile of toothpicks — and they would be next.

With a *pop*, the speakers filled the room with white noise again, followed by another announcement. "Scan complete. Welcome, Lady Watts."

"Great, she's back to gloat," strained Merlyn.

"She probably wants to watch," said Jules.

M could see her friends now that the window was level with them and the light washed over the room. She was happy to see the confident looks on their faces. They were absolutely defiant, refusing to give Ms. Watts the satisfaction of seeing their fear. They glared spitefully at the window, and M turned to do the same.

But Ms. Watts wasn't there.

Instead, Professor Bandit stepped into the control room. He shook his head at the sight of his students and pressed a button. The floor paused, but didn't lower. The chairs stayed locked in place with the back of M's head planted firmly on the ceiling. She let out a sigh.

"It is not in my nature," announced Professor Bandit, "to help students. But this is a special occasion. I see you're in a pinch and I'm not sure this punishment is altogether warranted. Ms. Freeman, I asked that you leave school earlier in the year. I truly wish you had taken my request to heart."

M remembered her meeting with Dr. Lawless and Professor Bandit after she had single-handedly destroyed a wing of the library. Bandit had wanted her kicked out of school, but Ms. Watts had lobbied to keep her there. M shook her head slowly. She had thought Ms. Watts believed in her when no one else did. As it turned out, that was part of a bigger plan all along.

"I am afraid that we are all in a proverbial pickle now," continued Professor Bandit. "It is frowned upon for Lawless faculty to interfere with one another's capers, and so I cannot help you further. Ms. Freeman, your father unfortunately gave you the key to unlocking an evil weapon capable of unspeakable damage. What's worse is that you've put that key in the hands of someone willing to use it. I trust you and your friends will make this right, given the opportunity. So here is your slim window. Do not disappoint me."

Professor Bandit gave M one last hard stare, then dramatically turned and left the room. The speakers went silent again and the students were alone.

M tugged her body forward and felt the back of her chair give. With an appalling snap, the chair broke in half and she hit the floor face-first. Her knees burned and her nose throbbed from the landing, but she was free.

"Everyone," she said as she rolled over. "The chairs are fractured. You should be able to break out."

But Jules and Merlyn had already made the same discovery. Their eyes met and collective smiles broke out across their faces. Jules swept her bound arms under her legs and unlocked the handcuffs quickly. Then she freed the rest of their locked wrists and they all hunched toward the control room door next to the window. The floor had almost elevated past the doorknob, but they were able to push the door open and shimmy down into the room. And not a moment too soon, because as soon as they were safely out of the Box, the floor jolted again and pressed firmly against the ceiling, crushing the chairs with an awful sound like bones breaking.

"He wasn't exaggerating about the time frame," said Jules.

M nodded, looking back at the slab of concrete that blocked the window where the open Box used to be. "We've got to find Wild's meteorite and end this now."

They ran out of the room and were met with the brilliant summer sunshine of the Lawless campus. They had been trapped in the Masters' dorm. *Of course the Masters would host this madness,* thought M. *This is what they revel in, isn't it?*

But there was something different about the school now. The normal hustle and bustle of the school grounds was gone. There wasn't a student in sight.

"Where is everyone?" asked M.

"Semester break," said Merlyn. "I can't believe you've been here this long and still don't know anything about how this school works."

M didn't know if an empty campus would make stopping Ms. Watts easier or harder, but it didn't matter now. "Okay, guys, if you had to hide something this valuable on campus, where would you take it?"

"Around here?" asked Jules. "It could be anywhere."

"Okay, let's be realistic," said M. "We're going to have to split up. Jules, check the Box in the student center. If I had to hide something on campus, I'd hide it in a trap, so maybe it's there. Merlyn, get your hands on a computer. Maybe you can pick up a digital trail, or maybe the meteorite is giving off some radiation that you can track?"

"Where are you going, then?" asked Merlyn.

"West building seven," she said automatically. "Listen, this is real. Be careful, stay safe, and don't trust anyone. If people are here on campus, assume they're out to get us. We lucked out that the Fulbrights stole my necklace, but according to Ms. Watts, there's another rock out there somewhere. So until Wild's meteorite is destroyed, the world is in danger."

The grim thought hung in the air between them. It was time for action. They nodded in agreement and left to conduct their separate searches in the solemn, sunny day.

M kept to the skirt of the tree line to stay away from any prying eyes, but where she was heading would certainly be guarded. Circling behind West building seven, she looked for another way into Dr. Lawless's lair. The windows reflected the swaying tree branches behind her and her nerves kept getting the best of her. With every movement, she thought she could see someone behind her in the woods, but when she turned, nobody was there. Then she saw her entrance, a lone exhaust duct at the back of the building. She darted across the lawn, unhinged the grate quickly, and crawled inside. Thanks to her previous visit to Dr. Lawless's, M remembered that the interior of West building seven was an industrial skeleton filled with giant air ducts . . . perfect for sneaking through.

She made her way through a zigzag of tubes until she reached the third floor. It wasn't easy. Her fingers were frigid in the blasting cold air, but she climbed on. When she finally crawled out of the vent, she found herself directly in front of Dr. Lawless's office. The door was ajar. M listened for sounds of life, but the room was completely quiet. Inching the wood door farther open, M peered inside.

"Ah, Ms. Freeman!" said Fox Lawless himself, sitting at his desk. "I had so hoped we would have another chance to talk. Do come in and make yourself at home."

The once overcrowded bookshelves were empty and swept

clean. The room was barren except for Lawless's desk, his globe, several TV monitors, and one chair where M sat down nervously.

"Spring cleaning?" asked M.

"Something like that." Lawless smiled. He sat still and waited for her to make the next move.

"We can't let you keep the meteorite," M asserted.

"You are full of surprises, Ms. Freeman." He laughed. "Very well, then, you take the meteorite."

He pressed his palm against the globe next to him, and the Northern Hemisphere popped open. Lawless reached in and pulled out the amber-colored rock from Wild's cane. Holding it gently in his hand, he studied it carefully.

"How much is this worth to you, Ms. Freeman?" he asked. "More than your friends?"

Lawless motioned behind M, who turned to the row of TV monitors. On each one were her friends in the midst of their searches.

"Security is waiting in Mr. Eaves's room and keeping a close eye on Ms. Byrd. And I'm watching all of you. When Ms. Watts told me you could solve the mystery of Wild's *umbra mortis*, I didn't believe her at first. But she's not one to be proven wrong. So tell me, what were you hoping to gain from this quest?"

M's stomach twisted in knots at the sight of her friends, who were unaware that the game was over. She hadn't prepared for this kind of standoff. There were so many players, so many people to keep track of, it seemed unfair. But when was being a master criminal fair? Lawless and Ms. Watts had outfoxed her.

"I don't know," said M honestly.

"What did you think we trained you to do at Lawless?" the headmaster continued. "This" — he held the meteorite aloft — "this is destruction. Pure, mad destruction. It would make any other Lawless student's heart ache with anticipation. So why do you want to ruin the fun?"

"A black hole on Earth isn't my idea of a good time," said M. "So do whatever you need to do. Take everything else away from me if you have to. My father's gone. My mother, too. Now you want my only friends. When is it enough?"

"It's never enough, Ms. Freeman," answered Lawless.

He slid the meteorite across the table.

"There," he said. "No great struggle, no great triumph. And so the world continues, not with a bang, but with a whimper."

M caught the odd rock and palmed it in her hands. What was happening? Had he really given up everything to her? Was it a trap?

"Thank you?" she said, confused.

"Leave us, Ms. Freeman," said Lawless. "You do not belong here. Ms. Smith, please see Ms. Freeman out of my office."

M turned to find Zara standing behind her. And behind Zara, the monitors showed her friends struggling and being overcome by the Lawless guards. In the end, she'd given up her only friends for a hunk of space rock.

Putting the stone in her pocket, M followed Zara out of West building seven. Neither girl said anything as they walked through the vacant halls. In the silence, M was overcome with emotions. Her eyes welled with tears as she asked, "Is it really over?"

"It's never over, M," said Zara.

"What happens to my friends?" asked M. "What happens to you?"

"No idea," confessed Zara. "Probably nothing good." She stopped at the front entrance. "M, here's one last lesson. You can't win everything. That's a hard pill to swallow, but it's the truth."

"Were you working with Ms. Watts the whole time?" M questioned.

"Not the whole time," admitted Zara.

"Then why did you turn on me back in London?" asked M.

"Because Ms. Watts would have killed you if I hadn't," said Zara. "I'm still your guardian, you know. We're not all bad people here, M. Most of us don't want to see people get hurt. But we definitely follow a different path. Lawless is all I've got. And you can leave school, but I'm not going to let you ruin it for the rest of us."

Zara smiled sadly and shrugged. The world wasn't black and white. It wasn't good versus evil. It was complicated, dizzying, and draining to try and understand. M could see that now.

"So get on your way," continued Zara as she started to open the door.

But the door unlatched itself and exploded open, knocking Zara and M to the floor. A team of masked Fulbrights blocked the entrance and raced past the girls. Their telecoms were buzzing with activity.

"Upstairs, upstairs," came the calls. "He's not here. Lawless is gone. The records are gone, too. Over."

"Roger that," the masked Fulbright before them replied. "What do we do with these two?"

"Toss Smith. Keep Freeman."

He grabbed Zara and shoved her outside. "Run now," he commanded. Then he turned his attention back to M. "You, come with me." As if she had a choice. They grabbed M's arms and dragged her out of the building as Zara fled the scene. *Live to steal another day,* thought M.

"Where are you taking me?" she demanded, but they did not answer. Instead they marched her through the empty campus. M looked for signs of life, but there was no one around.

Then they entered the moving room and slid sideways until the newly built tarmac revealed itself. They had dragged her back down into the very same runway where she crash-landed the plane months before.

Facing a small army of Fulbrights who stood at attention in front of a jet plane, M was let go by her captives. One Fulbright stepped forward and addressed M directly.

"Ms. Freeman," the distorted voice rang through the mask. "Your friends are safe."

The wall of Fulbrights stepped aside to allow Merlyn and Jules through. They ran to M and they hugged one another tightly.

"Unfortunately," the Fulbright continued, "Watts and Lawless escaped. We have some injuries, but nothing serious. Is it time to complete the mission?"

M shot a confused look to her friends, who mirrored the sentiment back to her.

"Are you, like, asking me?" M asked the Fulbright.

"No," he answered, "I report to her," pointing behind M toward none other than Devon Zoso.

"Good work, team," Devon said with authority. She was dressed in her very own Fulbright suit, her mask dangling behind her like a hood. "Let's prep for liftoff."

"You!" gawked M. "But . . ."

"Little time to explain, M, but all you need to know is that you've done your part," Devon said as she approached M and shoved her hand into M's pocket to retrieve the meteorite.

"It was you!" claimed M. "You were the Fulbright in Hamburg who stole my necklace."

"You mean, this necklace?" asked Devon as she dangled the chain in her other hand. "You got me, M. Way to go, supersleuth."

"Careful," shouted Merlyn, flinching at seeing both elements in the same room. "That's, like, the end of the world in your hands!"

"Hardly." Devon laughed. "I think Ms. Watts grossly overestimated the dangers of some ancient kook's doomsday device. But, just to make sure, let's give it a whirl."

"What?" M, Merlyn, and Jules all shouted at once.

M shot forward and tackled Devon. The Fulbrights quickly grabbed the others, but M and Devon rolled across the tarmac, struggling for control of the necklace. M scratched, clawed, and grabbed for anything she could, but Devon was too strong. With one well-placed kick, Devon knocked the wind from M's chest.

Devon loomed over her and yelled, "You don't get it, do you, M! We're on the same stupid team, dunderhead! Your father was a double agent! You think you're here by chance? This is what he raised you to do! And he couldn't tell anybody. Not Jones. Not your mother. Not even you. And that's why he's dead now! This was a totally classified mission! Think about it. Why would you have special homeschooling? Who learns the stuff you learned? Nobody!"

The world immediately stopped spinning for M. She was frozen, thinking of every aspect of Devon's awful accusation.

"You're lying," said Merlyn. "She's lying, M. She's playing mind games."

"I'm telling you the truth because you need to hear it. You're the weapon, M. You've always been the weapon against the Lawless School. You're the good guy. You're the sheep in wolf's clothing, just like your father!"

And there it was, the truth. It was M's father's voice reaching out from beyond the grave through Devon.

"No, Merlyn," said M slowly. "Devon is telling the truth."

"Finally, she listens! Now all of you get on the plane," directed Devon. "We're going to reunite you and your dear old mom, M, but first I get to finish what you started."

With no play left, M stood up and walked straight on to the plane without pause. Merlyn and Jules shrugged and followed her. Once on board, everyone took a seat and kept to themselves.

It started with a soundless vacuum, an airy sensation of floating, falling backward, as a light wind swept through the cabin of the plane. Strands of M's hair lifted and tugged gently against her scalp as a breeze from nowhere traced her face.

Devon boarded the plane, knocked three times on the pilot's door, and the plane thrust forward at an alarming rate, pushing everyone back into their seats. The walls of the mountain swept past the windows faster and faster until they blasted through the waterfall and into the sky.

The plane pulled right at an extreme angle, giving M a view of the campus below. It was her first time seeing the Lawless School from an aerial view. It was beautiful. It was perfectly placed in the mountain range, a jewel in the heart of a treacherous journey through steep mountains, unbridled jungles, and nests of clouds. Now those same clouds surrounding them were being pulled down from the sky toward the ground. The plane suddenly shook with an unnatural intensity. M could see the wings waving violently, threatening to tear in half midair. And then the hole erupted underneath them.

Dark, deep, and deadly, the *umbra mortis* swallowed the school. The student center bent over and tumbled into the black hole's center like water down the drain. West building seven twisted like a wet rag, ripping and dripping into the bottomless blackness. The trees at the edge of the forest tipped, snapped, and flung themselves into the darkness, all without any sound. There was nothing but silent destruction. How could anyone escape this? She looked for her dorm, for the Masters' building, for the guards, for Zara, for Ms. Watts, for Dr. Lawless, for any sign of life, but there was nothing except the slow, steady pull of the black hole.

And then it stopped, as quickly as it began. The plane steadied. The clouds sat motionless in the sky again and the trees, though still angling toward the hole, held firmly in place.

"I told you," said Devon, from the row behind M. "Grossly overestimated."

Ignoring everything, M stared blankly out of the window. Somewhere down there, she thought she had found her purpose, her calling, but she was wrong. It wasn't down there in the wallowing mess. It was up here on this plane. She carried it in her heart. She carried it in her DNA. It would follow her wherever she went. And the black hole below, M knew that wasn't an ending. It was only the beginning.

Lost in thought, M hardly noticed the yellow gas drift into the cabin. She breathed deeply, thankful to feel something familiar again.

ACKNOWLEDGMENTS

As far as I am concerned, *Lawless* would not have been possible if it weren't for a long list of others who helped craft this story into what you currently hold in your hands. First, I have to thank my Scholastic family for taking a chance on me. Thank you at every level for every step along the way. To David Levithan and Nicholas Eliopulos, whose editorial eyes and ideas are worth more than diamonds . . . you should have them insured! To Josh Adams, my agent and courageous confidant who gracefully puts up with all of the quaking crazy that hides behind my shiny veneer. To Ken Geist and the Cartwheel team (past, present, and future), I couldn't ask for a stronger collection of friends to spend my days with. To Phil and Jake, the masterminds behind the criminally awesome look of the book. To my early, unofficial editors, Jody, Siobhan, and Greg, who pushed me to finish and believed in my vision even when I didn't. To the genius of Danielle Pafunda, Noah Eli Gordon, Blake Nelson, and Paul Fattaruso; you all inspire me in ways that escape definition. To my friends Tom, Nate, Geoff, Jayson, Will, Sol, Dave, Adam Fuchs, and David Zacharis, thanks for never laughing at me when I kept talking about "the book I'm writing" and thanks for being there through the wild times and the weird times. Also, to two past friends who have shaped my life in mysterious, unimaginable ways, Viva Foley and Gerhardt (Jerry) Fuchs . . . you are missed and always with us

Thank you to Greg and Janet, who let me finish *Lawless* in their basement over Thanksgiving. To Damon, who always has a story. To my family spread throughout the country. To my parents, Thom and Linda, who have given me a lifetime supply of unending love and support, thank you for teaching me which way is up. To my brother, Matt, who brings happiness wherever he goes. And finally, to my personal den of thieves: Wren and Dez, thank you for being exactly who you are. And to my wife, Adrienne, thank you for being the blue to my gray, and for teaching me that together we are home.

ABOUT THE AUTHOR

Jeffrey Salane grew up in Columbia, South Carolina, but moved north to study in Massachusetts and New York City. After spending many years playing in several bands, he now works as an editor and author. The suspect was last seen in Brooklyn, New York, where he lives with his wife and kids. He has not been convicted of any crime . . . yet.

The author can prove his innocence at www.jeffreysalane.com.